Anne's Gift

By Heather Kingston

Kingston, Heather, author
Anne's Gift/HL Kingston

Issued in print and electronic formats.
ISBN 978-1-7772945-1-9 [pbk.] ISBN 978-1-7772945-2-6 [Kindle]

Cover design by John Kingston/JFKingston Photography

Published by:
Heat Publishing
Calgary, Alberta, Canada

For Mary who walks with me in spirit and
Michele who walks with me on earth.

Foreword by Susan Doherty - Author of A Secret Music and The Ghost Garden

Anne's Gift is a near-perfect snapshot of the 1970s complete with the music icons, the slang, the wardrobe, teen magazines, the footwear, and the accompanying angst of being a teenager in that era. The meticulous recounting could only be written by someone who lived and breathed those days. Heather Kingston tells the story with such authenticity it's as though she has taken my hand and walked me next door instead of back fifty years. The narrative recounting is a crossover between young adult fiction and contemporary adult fiction and will especially resonate for the baby boomers who will be taken down memory lane in this well-researched coming of age. Like Heather I too stumbled through my high school years in the 1970s.

The layers beneath are what makes the narrative truly compelling. Kathy's blind and naïve navigation of the mental illness around her underscores the real difference between the 70s and now. Mental illness still carries the weight of stigma, but fifty years ago it was as underground as a subway car. Our heroine Kathy manages and does find her way through those struggles to new beginnings. Her life emerges not defined by the mental illness around her, but as a desperate need to live her own life.

Susan Doherty

PART ONE

ONE

The morning radio show invades my sleep. Some jingle about breakfast cereal is filtering into the bedroom, reminding me to wake up. It's the first day of the last year in high school. Jumping out of bed is easy.

I put on my glasses and in the two steps it takes to get to the mirror, I see it. I hardly ever get a zit, but overnight one has appeared on my chin, staring back at me. I look down at my little table, cluttered with cosmetics and hair styling tools. What treatment should I use? Bonnie Bell toner to pop it and soak it, or Cover Girl foundation? What would Cheryl Tiegs do? Both win the '*get rid of the zit'* crisis.

I'm positive; I'll have no pockmark.

Positivity is my theme for grade twelve. I'll shine with enthusiasm, be on student council, care about others, and above all, be the 'cool' girl. If I'm worthy, I'll have a shot at Valedictorian. I have a plan.

"Kathy, get up and out here... breakfast's ready," Mom yells over the radio's weather forecast.

"Okay!" I throw on my robe.

The kitchen resembles a box of junk, all shook up and left where everything fell. Newspapers, dishes stacked, ceramic containers filled with who knows what. I wedge myself in tightly, between the fridge and table, trying not to knock off any fridge magnets from our family holiday camping collection. I manage to flip off 'Hello From Hope B.C.' and a bear waving, 'Sweet to See You in Field B.C.' Sitting down, I fish them off the brown swirled linoleum, and then slap them back up on the scratched metal door. It's seven-thirty on the teapot-shaped clock, hanging amongst the other jumble. The marked-up calendar has a big, red exclamation mark on today's date, the first day of school, September 4th, 1978, in Mom's hand. The recipes along with other newsy articles, cut from the newspaper, are all tacked up there, making it impossible to see the wall.

Dad's place at the table is empty; he's long gone to read water meters for the city of Victoria. The TV area beside the kitchen is dimly lit - the curtains are still drawn. The overstuffed chair and mismatched, worn-out couch have flattened, threadbare cushions to keep them company.

"Mom, you could use my curling iron," I offer, looking up at her hair, all done in rollers.

"That's fine... this set keeps my hair in check," she pats the mass of cylinders. Her hair looks like a giant, brown block when it's, so-called styled. I used to think she liked a 1960's look, but this 'do' has no decade to claim its rigid features.

Somehow, Alan got the brown hair of both parents; I ended up with red hair and freckles. Alan and I barely look like twins, he, with his hair, pale blue eyes and skin that tans a deep brown in the summer; then there's me, with green eyes, and skin that burns all the time.

Alan's *stunning* us with a dull, black t-shirt; he's the man with no fashion, not seeming to care about it. Even his hair is combed flat with no style. "Wow Alan, way to dress up for the first day of school."

He doesn't even look up. "It's school... no big deal," he says, his mouth full of sugar-laden oatmeal.

I'm excited to see friends I haven't seen all summer, check out the fashions, and find out if any boys got cute in the past two months. "I have a ride to school Alan... I'm not walking with you."

"Cool," he says looking blankly at the calendar, wolfing down his last bite.

I'm wearing my new Cullotier jeans, the coolest look this year. Nice high waistline, big flared legs, paired with my whitest, white t-shirt, and four-inch heels. My sideways silhouette looks positively thin! I spin the curling iron through my shoulder length hair. A wood bead, hippie choker, finishes the look. I'm ready to go.

"You're wearing that?" Mom's looking at me like I've shown up in a space alien costume. "For Christ sakes Kathy... those pants are too tight across your hips. Have you *seen* your hips lately? Why don't you buy clothes that suit you better? They're probably cutting the circulation off to your brain... no wonder you can't get decent marks like your brother. Go change into something else!"

"I don't have time. Anne's mom is picking me up," I stammer as she clears our dirty dishes into the sink.

"I'm doing you a favour Kathy. Fine... go to school looking like a stuffed sausage."

Am I fat? Should I weigh myself again? Why are my hips so big? Should I hide them somehow? My hands go instinctively over the bumps that make up my hips. They don't feel huge. Maybe the jeans aren't the best choice. It's too late. I can't change clothes now.

*

I stomp, in heels, down the driveway to the street, looking through tears, up the hill where I'll see them when they drive down. Longmore Lake, across the road, is clogged with Canada Geese, gliding, squawking.

Smarten up Kathy. Next time I'll wear these jeans with control top pantyhose. They'll suck everything in better.

Brushing away tears, a huge breath in, calming myself... I need to go over my plan on how to present myself as mature and confident. It goes like this:

I usually listen to progressive rock, although I dig the Stones and Led Zeppelin. King Crimson's on my turntable, but Emerson, Lake, and Palmer is a favourite. I don't listen to AM radio. I listen to KZAK 104.5FM out of Seattle. Our local Victoria stations have nothing on the Seattle stations, which, in my opinion, are ten times better. I like going to Victoria to do all my shopping. The stores are much better than out here in Longmore, this little hick village in the back of beyond.

With my sense of music, fashion, and confident personality, I'm sure this is going to be the best year ever.

*

Anne's mom pulls up in their tiny white car. If she put a windup key on the back, it'd look like a clown car. Maybe she'll drop us off a block or two from the school. "Hi Anne, thanks for the ride, Mrs. Smith."

Anne is wearing a beautiful outfit. Green wool slacks, a matching vest and beige satin blouse. Obviously expensive. "Anne, you look *superb-ular*! Where'd you get the clothes?" *Where'd she get the money? Her parents don't seem like they have any, and she barely babysat this summer.*

"Mom took me to Irene's Boutique. I had to beg, but she bought this for me." Far-out! Anne's mom bought her something brand new and is driving us to school. My mom wouldn't. I have to buy my clothes, and I can walk the half hour to school in whatever weather. Compared to my mom, Anne's mom is way better. She even knows to drop us off two blocks before the school gate.

"Nice jeans Kathy. Very sexy. The Greek Gods are going to love you," referring to the hunkiest guys in school. Anne gives me the 'Kathy and Anne shoulder bump' as we walk to the building. We came up with this slight shoulder graze a few years ago when we were propping each other up after some letdown I can't even remember. It's become our best friends forever move.

"Thanks!" *To hell with Mom.*

*

It looks like most of the four hundred students are already here.

Sandra spots us. Why does she dress like that? Her large breasts are crammed in a tight black, lace-up t-shirt. Her cleavage is bursting; the laces look as if they are about to give out.

"Hey, how was the rest of your summer after I last saw you? It's been two whole weeks!" Anne asks Sandra.

"Fine. I worked at Dairy Queen a few nights. Brad's been around a lot, so sorry I haven't called." Do I hear resentment? Why's she still with that guy? He's the cliché of Longmore clichés. The 'Longmore Mullet' black hair that is too short in the front, too long in the back. The 'Longmore Dinner Jacket' that classy, of classy red, and black checked lumberjack shirt he wears all the time says 'looser stoner dick' all over. She *should* be with one of the hunky guys at school.

*

There they are.

I spot them coming toward us. The Greek Gods, taller than everyone, walking like they own the hall. Derek, Arch, and Rod. Gorgeous feathered hair cut to the shoulders. Good looking, in a mature way: dressed in the hippest stonewashed Levis jeans, and Black Sheep shirts.

"Hi, guys! Hey, are any of you trying out for student council?" I make my voice as balanced as I can, but the girly twitter shows up. *Darn.* I smile my biggest smile, to look engaged, and very interested in each of them. The May edition, *Sixteen* magazine, recommended, in 'Tips for Landing A Boyfriend,' to only ask questions about them, never bringing yourself up in conversation.

None of the Greek Gods look at me. I may as well win the Academy Award for being the most invisible girl in high school. What did I expect? It wasn't likely any of them would look at me. I have small boobs, giant hips, and a fresh zit that makes my face look ugly. Tamping down the churn in the pit of my stomach, I force a smile and look around the crowded corridor.

"Hi Sandra," purrs Arch. She answers him with a curt hello, glaring past him. Not rebuffed, he continues, "How are you? You're looking good." He takes a step closer, attempting the arm-above-the-head-lean-on-the-wall-move. He fails when she ducks away, walking toward me, leaving him in a mid-arm thrust. He watches her butt as her hips sway, a low wolf whistle creeps out of his lips. Sandra either doesn't hear or ignores it.

Anne is tilting her head, smiling, but not looking directly at any of the Greek Gods. The hallway's packed with students moving in groups. The banks of lockers aren't yet occupied; their doors stand open like gaping mouths. I feel I'm watching a slow-motion movie unfold in front of me. The crowd slightly clears. Rod makes his way over to Anne. He smiles his way cool smile and then backs Anne into the lockers. "Are you going to put me in a locker?" she asks, calm as can be.

"Maybe one day I will." he returns, a bit breathless. The bell rings for us to join the assembly.

Anne, Sandra and I put our heads together as soon as we're out of the Greek Gods range. "Wow Anne, I think Rod digs you!" I'm half stunned, half thrilled for her. He's one of the cutest guys in grade twelve, and he likes Anne!

"No and no."

"Why not? He must think your 100-watt smile is worth taking a closer look at!" I say.

"I'm pretty sure I'm not his type." She says with finality; we find places to sit in the gymnasium.

*

There are the usual welcome back greetings from our truly unfortunate looking Principal, Mr. Hill. He looks like a rat, with his thin face, bulgy eyes, and buck teeth. He squeaks on, but I perk up when he comes to the student council election news. We can put in our nominations, and then after two weeks of campaigning, the voters will decide the winners. Anne said she'd nominate me for vice president. I'm pretty sure Lois Jackman is running for president. I'm not going up against the top athlete and smartest person in the school. I can show off my maturity by being involved as VP.

Over the day, we find our lockers and classes. We use a new way of filling in information on an awkward piece of thin cardboard, rectangular, with a corner missing, and random holes punched into it. We write our names, homeroom class number, and current grade, but apparently a machine, a computer, reads information from the hole punches to get the remaining details. It seems cumbersome.

By last class, my feet are incredibly sore from the four-inch heels. I thought they were a cool idea this morning. I read, 'How can one look mature?' in the July, *Sixteen* magazine. 'Wearing high heels gives you a look of refinement and maturity,' my favourite magazine assured me. I'm not sure how I'll walk home in them.

*

After school, we three girls meet up and head toward home. The sun's warm; the breeze cools us as we walk up the hill. School buses clatter past us, spewing diesel fumes. Alan and his gang of friends are a bit ahead of us, loping along. They're keeping to themselves, which is perfect. I have to get to the most crucial part of the day's events. "Anne, did Rod see you between classes?"

"He said 'hi' and took off. I'm sure it's nothing." She couldn't be more off-handed.

"Are you kidding me? He's the cutest guy. *He likes you*!" I also throw in, "is this the best day ever?" My smile should be a wince – these heels are killing me.

"He's way too cool for me. Sandra, what are you doing tonight?"

Fine. I'll drop it for now. We make a plan to get together after dinner. It's easy for Anne and I to walk to each others house, but Sandra needs a drive over.

"I'll check if I can come or not. Brad wants to see me tonight." The disappointment in her voice does not endear me to dink wad.

We reach the top of the hill. A loud, familiar car screams up beside us. Brad's 1970 Camaro is freshly painted. "Honey, nice blue paint job," gushes Sandra above Black Sabbath blaring away on his stereo.

"Astro Blue. Get in the car you tasty piece." He's leering at her with bloodshot stoner eyes. Mechanic filth smudges his ugly pockmarks and... gross, his nails are filled with black dirt.

Sandra smirks and then heads to the passenger side. "Nice childbearing hips Kathy," he snorts and spits a disgusting gob not two feet from Anne and I.

"Not with you in a million lifetimes," I say, way more confidently than I feel.

"Who loves you, Sandra Dee?" He turns and plants his spittle covered lips on her perfect cheek. He puts the car in gear, peeling out.

"Dick ass," I say. "She should break up with him. Did you hear what he called her?

"Asshole. What a pig. He has to go, but not sure how... yet."

"Tell her she's going out with an asshole and she should break up with him?"

"That'd work except it looks like she's into him. Let's talk to her at school tomorrow if we can."

*

We walk down Dunrod, past the dirty old tire shop, called Tire Shop.

"I'm fat... my hips are huge." I grab the offending bumps and look at them, the right, then left. "These jeans are all wrong."

"No, they're not. You look sexy. I told you that this morning."

"My mom doesn't like them either."

"Don't listen to her! What do moms know about fashion? Maybe polyester double knit stretchy pants, but that's about it."

I give her the K&A shoulder bump, try to smile, "Thanks, best friend forever."

We stop at Costin Lane, right across from the junkyard full of scrap heaps and derelict cars all piled up like a tower of Longmore pride. Jim's Junkyard sign "We Stack and Scrap It" creaks in the breeze. "Maybe we can hang out with the gang," she sounds hopeful. Alan's friends are all right. Anne loves goofing around with them. We always have fun together as a group. "Call you later."

I repeat to myself the rest of the way home, 'I have to stop listening to mean people.'

*

I'm relieved to get to my back gate that's holding in all the overgrown grass, weeds and dead flowers. Crows squawk from the Bing Cherry trees that mark the end of the property. All I want to do is get out of my shoes. What was I thinking? There has to be a way I can change to walking shoes without anyone seeing me. Sophistication has to last all the way home.

"How was your day?" Mom asks when I walk in the door. I'm in pain right now... I don't want to talk.

"Fine." I pull off the instruments of torture. That feels better!

"What did you do?" She lays a large knife down on the counter and looks up from a chicken carcass lying on the chopping board.

"I don't know," massaging toes back to life. The radio's playing a Simon and Garfunkel tune, I start humming along.

"Well, do your homework before you go out tonight." There she goes, dictating my free time instead of minding her own business.

"Mom it's the first day. There's no homework yet. What're you doing?"

"Separating this to make three meals. And take those damned ugly jeans off." Mom stabs the knife into the chicken, with unsettling vigour. Time to get out of her way – a mood might be coming. She scares me sometimes with what she calls, '*the monopause.*' It's one big, single, chaotic pile of never knowing when the other boot's going to drop. She's fine, and then she isn't fine. I never know when she's going to flip out on me. It isn't like she hits me, but she's horrible sometimes. I feel a giant knot in my belly, as I wait for the gush of angry, which eventually ends up spilling on me, at any given moment. Maybe I'm super sensitive to her moods, or maybe she's really a bitch.

"Right. I'm going to my room," I take three steps from the kitchen to escape.

*

My bedroom. My sanctuary. I stare at Snoopy, sitting beside my bed. There was very little under the tree the year I was in grade two, but Snoopy has always been my favourite of all time present. I lie on the bed and quietly sob. Snoopy, with his big black eyes and smiling mouth, all worn out, stares at me silently.

The walls are covered with the story of my life. I stare at cute little posters of trolls, colourful fairy ladies that spark my imagination, and David Cassidy – the world's cutest guy. A poster of the lyrics to 'Smoke on the Water' sits at eye level. I roll over, tuck the torn purple quilt around me, and think about the day.

I tested out mature, active listening skills. I smiled, looked enchanted when spoken to. The Greek Gods didn't even talk to me. Brad made fun of me. I crawl out of bed to look at myself in the mirror. I turn sideways to see how far my stomach sticks out. My hips are big, that ugly belly bulges out, and those breasts are tiny.

I make space on the floor; go into child's pose to stretch, and then waddle through 'downward facing dog,' to 'upward facing dog.' Yoga can make my hips smaller, stomach flatter. Thank goodness Ms. Phips taught us yoga in gym class last year. It's better than basketball, baseball, soccer, you name them, I don't like team sports. Yoga, I dig. I'll check the *Sixteen* magazines for how to increase bust size. I need to stay positive. I'm going to have a great last year of school.

There's a knock at my door. I confirm loudly, "IN," Alan walks in and sits down.

"Kathy, the United States wants to test nuclear weapons in Canada," his eyes dart at everything, and nothing on the walls.

"What? What are you talking about?" I hiss. No one's reporting this. His face is wooden, his eyes hoops of darkness.

"I think the world will end," he anxiously mutters and leaves.

My brother is weird.

TWO

"Get up!" Mom yells through my door. I pass through the kitchen to the bathroom. I stare at the white, plastic weigh scale on the floor. The black swooping hand ready to dictate my self-worth, depending on which number it lands on. I take a breath out and get on the silent tyrant.

I'm not okay. Today's number is 116 lbs. I was 115, but I need to be closer to a weight I can live with. Maybe I can get to 110. I slump back to my bedroom. No wonder I feel fat.

I squash into control top pantyhose, put on my brown tweed dress pants, cream peasant blouse and brown French velvet vest Mom made for me. The fat looks sucked in. Now, the makeup. Avon 'Robin's Egg Blue' eye shadow is even more rad when I add matching blue mascara. It's another day to try to be my best to impress.

"Now what's this look? Hippie librarian? Why don't you put your hair in a bun for at least half the look?"

"Mom! It's the latest fashion." I want to scream at her to stop bugging me about what I wear, but no, not Kathy the peacekeeper in this family. "I don't think I'm wearing anything weird."

"Well, I'm just trying to help you... go ahead, show up to school looking like you couldn't make up your mind what to wear, so you threw on anything."

I'll never get anywhere if I keep talking about what she feels is wrong with my look. She'll go off the tracks if I don't shut up now. I don't feel like getting grounded for 'back talking.'

I sit down in front of two eggs, prepared with nothing on them, and nothing else. "You have to eat more," Mom snaps, her eyes flash. I take a piece of toast, from the pile in the middle of the table, and make an effort to add jam on top. "That's better... you're going to starve otherwise."

Jeez... she thinks I'm fat in my jeans and then she wants me to eat more. I don't want to get fatter. I nibble at the eggs and play with the toast. Mom turns to pour another coffee: I conceal the toast in my napkin, sliding it under my leg. Dad's always at work by now, so I have one less pair of eyes to see what I'm doing. Alan never notices what I do with my food. He stuffs his face and stays skinny as a rail. Not me. I look at food, and it ends up landing everywhere except my boobs.

Sixteen magazine, August, I believe, said coffee's a stimulant and can cut your appetite. "Mom... you know how I'll be graduating in June? I was thinking that I'd like to start drinking coffee... all my friends are."

"No! It's bad for young people and too expensive for me to be handing it out to you," her mouth forms a straight line of anger. *Fine.* I'll ask another time.

"I'm walking today... I should get going," my hand encloses the toast filled napkin which I spirit away from the table, into my room, and into the garbage. Today I put on the platform sandals to look slimmer, and more comfortable than yesterday's heels.

*

Alan and I walk companionably up the hill, to school. He's not saying anything. "You've been quieter lately... sleep okay?" I ask.

"Yep." He puts his head down and picks up the pace. I hurry to keep up.

At Longmore Lake Store we wave to Mr. Nelson who's both waving back and unlocking the doors. Ronny and Steve stride up. We carry on down Gold to Dunrod, dodging potholes and puddles.

Steve's Afro is in full puffball comb out. The black mass makes him look way taller than all of us. "What happened to your cheek?" I ask looking at his large white bandage.

"Rugby practice," he says, "Brutal game... love it."

"Maybe it'll match your scarred skate blade lip," I say.

“What sports *don’t* you play?” Alan pipes up from his quiet state.

“I like to play all of them.”

“I’ll wail on my axe... safer.” Ronny grabs the guitar strap, swinging his acoustic guitar from its back straddled position to the front. “This year I’ll be grooving on Randy Bachman. Did you see him scream down the chords on that BTO special last week? Off the scales! He learned jazz to get better, so I’m joining the jazz group this year.” He even looks like Randy Bachman, with the sandy brown wiry hair, bangs and sideburns–so not in fashion. But what would he know about fashion when playing guitar is all he cares about?

“Look,” says Steve, giving his head a flick, sending his ‘fro all over the place, “old man Payton has another car up on blocks.” The three wrecks, up on cement blocks, are like Longmore’s best attempt at lawn ornaments. “What does he do with them?” We walk by the three piles baffled.

The Drinkle’s big, black dog Brutus, roars out of the yard, only stopping when the chain reaches its full length, grabbing him by the throat, halting the high-pitched barking. Steve, spotting a ball, effortlessly leans down, scoops it up and, with the confidence of an athlete having done it a thousand times before, overhand throws toward the back of the yard. Brutus runs, chasing the ball, we walk on.

“I’m going to quit school,” says Alan in a flat monotone.

“*No way*. That’s stupid. You’re almost done. Why would you even want to quit?” I hear my voice travel up.

“I’m not learning anything,” he says.

“Don’t quit... that’s retarded,” says Steve.

"Never mind... it's not official," he says as we walk into school. We separate for the day.

There's no way I'm letting my twin quit school. We've been through all the grades together. He's the smart one. I need his help to pass grade twelve.

*

I run toward the bathroom, comb my hair, put 'Candy Floss' lip gloss on, and get to class. Our French teacher walks into the room, with a huge bag. I like Madame Claire. "Today we're going to have a lesson on how to order in a coffee shop. I have coffee and milk to make Café Au Lait. You'll take turns being the worker and the guest. Split up into groups of two."

What a fun class, pairing with Chloe, a super sweetie, who's all 'ballerina.' Her hair is in the traditional, high bun, showing off the full length of her graceful posture.

In her childlike voice, she talks about ballet, working at Chan's, and the future. "I'm getting out of here. Longmore isn't the place to study ballet and acting. I'm moving to Victoria or Vancouver." She has a plan past high school–not many of us do.

"I think I'll go to college and become a social worker," is all I can dream up right now. I have no plans for my future.

We have real coffee with milk; it's tasty. Mom will have to let me drink it, now that I've tried it in school.

Although we don't have much time to get from class to class, there's always a moment to catch the action in the hallways. The drama kids say hi, we joke around.

I see Rod and Anne having a quick chat! Grade ten girls are walking like baby giraffes, in heels too high, lurching along the hallway. Sometimes school isn't boring.

*

At lunch, Anne and I launch into our plan for Sandra. "Sandra, can I ask you something about Brad?" She shrugs, so I continue. He called you a 'tasty piece.' Did you get mad at him for being crude?" The lunch hall's noisy, we move closer to each other.

"Oh that. He's not very smooth," she giggles nervously, "but he doesn't mean it as crude... that's his way. He hangs around the mechanic and racecar crowd too much. Don't worry. I'm going to change him." Her face looks set in a fake smile.

"Do you think he's changeable?" Anne reaches across and touches Sandra's hand.

"Change... how?" I say.

"He loves me. He'll change for me. You know, sweeter, kinder, nicer. I know he will. I love him." Nodding like she means what she says.

"Cool," I say. Anne takes back her hand.

If Sandra loves him, what's there to say about crap head Brad? Maybe she's right; she can change him.

*

When I arrive home, tired, feet aching, Mom is banging around the kitchen slamming cupboard doors, opening and closing drawers forcefully, loudly. Dad must be reading the paper in the living room. Alan's likely downstairs in his bedroom.

"Hi," I say quietly, "What's for dinner?"

"Food!" Mom slams a wooden spoon down onto the worn kitchen counter.

I *hate* the tension. Did Mom and Dad argue, or is he drinking, which cranks her temper up? Sure Dad drinks, but he mostly bores us to death talking about his, not so amazing, meter reading career. Sometimes he slurs his words, making no sense, and then the meal gets awful when Mom tells him to 'be quiet for god sake,' next, him telling her to 'stop pestering me.' She's in a rage about something. I'm afraid I'm going to find out.

*

At dinnertime, with a knot in my belly, I sit down to a shredded chicken and peas macaroni meal.

"Alan you can't quit school," says Dad, his face reddening, hands flat on the table. Sober, he's poised and his tone sharp.

"You need a grade twelve minimum before going out into the world," Mom yells, her face contorted into a stern grip of ugly.

"You two don't know anything. I'm going to live off the land. I have a book on how to build a log cabin and be self-sufficient. I can do it, and I don't need money or grade twelve," he shouts, half out of his chair, a forkful of chicken ready to drop onto the floor.

"How dare you speak to me that way!" Dad takes his food laden plate ready to throw it but stops himself. "You *will* complete high school. Your mother and I won't sign the form to release you." He scoops up congealed pasta, shoving it into his enraged mouth.

I stare at my plate. I wish I could disappear into my bedroom, but some terror keeps me rooted to this chair. I try to eat without throwing up. I hate dinner time. I never know if it'll be peaceful, or a screaming match. "Mom, may I be excused?" I whisper.

"NO. There's dessert. You don't eat enough... you'll damn well sit there until we're all finished." Knowing there's nothing more to say I grip a spoon, grind my thumb into its edge, wishing the tension would go away, and then possibly we could be a happy family tonight.

After a small bowl of canned fruit cocktail, I'm relieved to be excused. My after grad plan is to move out of this nuthouse.

*

Anne drops by after dinner. The coast is clear – the parents have disappeared into the living room to watch TV.

"Rod was driving by and gave me a ride the rest of the way home from school!" She looks like sunshine after my stormy dinner.

"Super cool... he has a car!"

“I gave him my phone number... he said he'd call me. I guess I am his type! A Greek God on this,” She gets up and waves her hand down the front of her slim, trim body. The intro to Alice Cooper, 'I'm Eighteen' sends her fingers tapping across the bed frame, hips bopping back and forth to the tune, her jet black, poker straight hair, cut in a bob, sways in time. We dance to Alice for a bit, air punching when the eighteen part comes up.

“Right on Anne! What do you think so far?” We huddle closer on the bed; I turn up the radio volume to drown out our voices.

“Superb-ulous! Can’t wait to get more of him! Cool, far-out... did I mention super hunky? What about you? Any boys you like so far this year?” There’s the big question.

“No boys like me. I don’t see how I’ll ever get a guy to like me special. Day two and I’ve impressed nobody.”

“Maybe turn it down a few notches. Play it cooler. Less smiley faced and obvious.” Ouch.

Anne looks at my droopy face reacting to the sting and goes for recovery, “Sorry, that came out wrong. I don’t think guys’ get how fun and nice you are. They might not ‘*get*’ you until they get to know you better.”

“That’s what’s wrong with me? I’m over the top fun and flirty?” I feel hurt by her comment but take it without denial. I can be too forward. Dad, who *could* be wise, told me to let the boys come to me – ‘Don’t chase the boys. They don’t like it.’ “Okay, I can try toning myself down.” Don’t boys want a girls attention?

“Who’s the crush this year? Come on,” grinning, teasing, starting to drum on my knees. “Who do you like?”

“No one yet,” I mutter, shrugging my shoulders. “I’m looking... you’ll know when I see him!” The one I really like is older and super cool. I don’t even tell Anne I’m hoping to get his attention one day. Glen lives up the street from me, and when I see him, my heart goes bang bang, I feel shaky... full of butterflies – he’s a ten.

*

At bedtime I play Led Zeppelin, ‘Dazed and Confused’ since I that’s the way I feel about my weird brother, angry parents, the idea of Anne and Rod together, and me being left out because I bet my secret crush won’t *‘get’* me.

THREE

I wake up anxious. Today's the Student Council election. I've had two weeks to write my speech. It's going to get everyone thinking about how I'll be the better choice... I have to get up in front of everyone. I'm pretty decent in drama class – I'll have to look *fab*, act confident, and be genuine. I can do this! I didn't read it to anyone because I want it to be a surprise. It'll be well received – I'm positive!

Anne, Sandra and I decided yesterday it's 'wear a dress day' today.

The three of us look like *Sixteen* magazine models. Sandra has suede boots, a tan dress with a deep-cut neckline and a velvet choker. Anne's wearing a belted dress in pastel blue with raglan sleeves. Snazzy! My mint green, jersey dress, which mom didn't complain about, gives me the confidence – I *will* win!

People say it's hard for three to be friends because one will be left out, or jealous, but we all feel close to each other and are best friends. Anne and I have lived in Longmore all our lives. Sandra moved into the area in grade eight and right away seemed as if she was a forever friend. I love my friends, so what else would I need? Anne's been my best friend since kindergarten. In that class photo, we're sitting next to each other. I have the face full of freckles, and Anne has a face full of teeth. Her smile makes me smile, it's so wide it draws me into her happiness.

Sandra has all the looks: thick wavy brunette hair, perfect skin, pretty face and a curvy, wow body. I see guys talking to her chest instead of her face. No one looks at my chest! She's a bit shy, sticking close to Brad when he's with her. He seems to own her, control her, and she goes along with it. No way for me. I want a boy to be a friend and have fun together. Not that that'll ever happen.

*

We assemble in the gym for the speeches. Lois gives her speech. It's fantastic. She gets some laughs, making compelling points. Her opponent, Bill, a sports jock and always on the 'honour roll,' stumbles through his speech, with so many "umm" and "ahh" mutterings, it's hard to stay with him. He looks desperate to get off the stage. He would've been a respectable presidential choice but fails to get his message across.

I'm up next. I feel sweat dripping in my armpits. The papers in my hand are shaking along with my whole body. Big breath Kathy. You can do this. I put the notes on the podium and look up at the audience.

"Good morning everyone!" I hurl my voice forward. "It's terrific to see all of you today. I promise if I'm voted in as vice president, I'll instigate some important new programs. First, I think garbage pick up at lunchtime would make our school look freshened up. I'll assign the lucky groups to make our school the finest ever. A clean school is a happy school! Next, I'd take the junk food out the vending machines. These food choices aren't healthy, and a healthy school is a happy school! Finally – here comes the finest idea – I think our library could use the students help, so I'm proposing a raffle to raise money for new encyclopedias. A smart school is a happy school!" I finish the speech with a flourish of notes brandishing the air above my head. There's polite applause. I'm not funny like Lois, but I feel earnest and genuine.

My opponent gets up next. Here's the class clown, with not a cute crumb on his sorry beanpole body. He runs up to the stage, his skinny limbs looking disjointed, as he flails them around – an uncoordinated goof trying to get a laugh.

Everyone laughs. “Whew,” Clayton starts, “This year, my promise to you is a free day every month where you don’t even have to come to school if you don’t want.” The applause is deafening. “Next up is a school field trip to the Emerald Gardens swimming pool where they just added a slide!” Now the school is raucously cheering. “The last but not least I’ll promote smoking on school grounds. You won’t have to cross the road anymore.” The students go totally tubular. They’re on their feet clapping and screaming at Clayton’s close.

What the heck? He couldn’t possibly get the school authorities to agree on all those ridiculous promises. He’s lying to get votes. How could the students believe him? It seems trying to win an election involves lying and deceiving.

The rest of the day is nerve wracking with students voting, and then the vote counting.

At the end of last class, they announce the winners over the intercom. I find out, of course, I lost to Clayton by a landslide. I got ten votes to his one hundred eighty-three. I was honest and made practical suggestions. I suppose that’s not what the students are looking for in a vice president.

I slink out of class and hide in the girl's washroom until the end of day bell goes. Stupid me. I should have read the speech to Anne and Sandra. I sit on the toilet seat and press my eyes shut to stop tears from coming out. People come in.

“Kathy completely bombed... how did she even get ten votes?” Great, It’s Bridgette, the bitch. I stay where I am, staring at ‘Kari Loves Hank’ scratched into the stall door.

"What a joke!" She's with Coral the hag. The end of day bell goes, but how can I leave with bully girls 'Hag and the Bitch' out there?

"Let's go for a smoke," Bridgette's voice sounds like a nasal disease.

"Nah, let's light up here, no teacher's going to come in."

Laughing.

I hear the match spark up and then smell cigarette smoke. I want to disappear. My stomach's cramping. Staying in this stall hiding isn't going to work. What am I going to do when I leave, walk through the student filled halls or show up for school tomorrow?

I flush the unused toilet, open the stall door and ignore them. After washing my hands, I flick the water in their direction. Head up, looking straight forward, like I did when kids called me fatty, I carry on out the door, down the hallway and outside. I hear snickers and imagine their stares.

*

"One of my worst days ever," I say to Anne and Sandra, as we walk home, high heels dangle glumly off my fingers. I stare at my sensibly shod feet, safe in Mary Jane, no heel, slip on shoes.

"You did an okay speech, but no one wants to pick up garbage, or do a raffle," Anne grinding the truth into me as we walk home. Why doesn't she punch me in the gut? I'm sure it'll feel the same.

"Clayton *lied.* He can't do all the things he promised," my heart's crackling. "How was I supposed to compete with a lying liar? I wasn't that crazy, was I? At least I told the truth."

"Why didn't you let us hear your speech before you gave it? We could've helped set you up with a better list of promises. People like junk food, even if you don't," Sandra breaks off her rant to push hair away from her face.

"OKAY! Leave me alone."

"Kathy... I'm sorry you lost," says Sandra, "I know you tried to get everyone excited about the school year. Don't let them get you down. Come on... who loves you?"

"You do," I say. Sandra nods and gives me a big hug. She hangs on for so long I start laughing as I try to detach myself from the ferocity of her protective arms.

"See you tomorrow," says Sandra finally letting me go.

Anne gives me a solid K&A shoulder bump, "*Cecile playmate, come out and play with me*," she quietly sings as we walk.

"*And bring your sisters three, climb up the apple tree*," I join in the song we've known since grade one.

"*Slide down the branches into the piles of leaves, and we'll be jolly friends forever more,*" both of us sing, out of tune, our 'cheer each other up' song.

"Thanks, Anne," I show her my fake cheered up face as she waves goodbye.

*

I straggle home. The old, run down, moss and ivy-covered houses lean in on me. Cars drive by, ignoring the sideshow of hillbilly scenery. Brutus isn't out, but cars on blocks are.

I see him. He's walking toward me. Glen's wearing his suit jacket and blue jeans, his long, thick, layered strawberry blond hair swaying in the breeze. No one's around to embarrass me. I catch my breath, straighten up, and try to stop shaking. *Terrific.* The day I don't walk home in high heels, is the day he comes along the street. I hope he still likes me, even though I'm wearing children's type shoes.

"Hey Kathy, nice threads," he looks at my dress, up and down. His blue eyes sparkle under soft, blonde eyebrows. His creamy, fair skin stretches over high cheekbones. Angled jaw lines make him look carved by Michelangelo. I'd never noticed before how his lower lip is slightly larger than his upper – not pouty though and oh... he has a tiny brown dot of a mole on the right, below his nose. I wonder what it would be like to kiss him there. I snap down to my feet.

"Thanks, Glen. What are you up to?"

"Dropping off a couple of resumes... I'm still looking for work. Not much out there for an eighteen-year-old with a high school diploma. Hey... you look sad," something I already know. He could tell me anything, and I'd be right there, with my best smile – but not too smiley... or flirty – complimenting his views. "Would a piece of gum cheer you up?" Looking down from his six-foot-plus height, his steamy eyes connect with mine.

"Cool," I reply faintly, taking the offered gum from his hand, trying unsuccessfully to touch him.

"Is Alan home tonight? I might boogie over and listen to some tunes." His smile reveals a pointy tooth sticking out slightly beyond the others, like a soldier out of a perfect white line up. *I'd kiss him there too while we're making out all naked and hot.*

"He stays home a lot... he should be there. You should come over any time you want." As if he'd come over at my request. I feel sweat beading on my forehead.

I mean it though. Despite my grouchy mother's apparent dislike for the world, she and Dad are incredibly tolerant of us having friends over to listen to music, play board games and watch TV. It helps Alan's bedroom takes up the basement, so we don't bother the parents by hanging around upstairs.

"Cool," he ducks down and looks into my glasses. "Gotta go... see ya."

I'm trying not to chew gum like a cow. He turns to go.

"Hey, do you hang around with Sandra Blackwell? He asks.

"Sure. She's one of my best friends." I stop chewing.

"You know her older sister committed suicide?"

"What! *No*! That can't be true. How would you know if that happened or not? I've known Sandra for years – she said Karen went away to live with her aunt!"

"I knew Karen. She dated a friend. Don't tell anyone I told you," says Glen looking into my fallen face. "I know... it's screwed up. I don't know why or how. I only know she was fresh out of high school. Hardly anyone knows about it."

"Not even me. Did it happen and then they moved to Longmore?" I ask.

“I’m pretty sure that’s how it went down.”

“Well, I’ll keep the secret. Maybe see you tonight... if I’m home.” January, *Sixteen* magazine, said not to look too eager when proposing a meetup. ‘Be casual, or one may appear desperate.’

“Righteous,” he smiles again, and I turn, so he can’t see my desperate face.

What a freaking bombshell. Why hasn’t Sandra told us? Why would her sister do that? Wasn’t there any other way? Couldn’t she get help for whatever it was that got her down so badly?

*

“I lost the election, no big deal” I grab a small apple and go straight to my room. Talking to Mom right now is out of the question. I stare at Snoopy, take the gum out of my mouth, methodically eat the apple, around and around. A band of pressure tightens my stomach. Breath comes out in stutters. No one at school voted for me. So much for my big grade twelve plan. Now I find out Sandra has a secret she won’t tell me. Can I blame her? Why would she talk about her sister killing herself? Maybe I’ll be able to get it out of her eventually.

Glen. Was I okay around him? Not stupid? I rerun the conversation like a movie in my head. It’s all mixed up with everything else from today.

I know what I need to do. Being with Alan will hopefully put me in a good mood. We’ll dig his latest album and hang.

“Rough day?” Alan asks as I settle on the empty bashed-up couch.

"Not superb-ulous at all."

"No Student Council for you and no quitting school for me." I relax a bit. He's all stretched out on the couch.

"Not quitting... good... that was a dumb idea." He doesn't respond. I pick up Rick Wakeman, *Journey to the Center of the Earth,* put on side one. We pretend we're playing the organ and synthesizers while listening to the narrator tell Jules Verne's science fiction story.

I'll talk to Anne about Glen's secret. I could use a K&A shoulder bump real soon.

Alan's in the music groove, and I drift away, with Glen on the happier side of my brain.

FOUR

"Why are you telling me this now? Class starts in five minutes!" Anne says.

"It's been burning me up. Should we ask Sandra about Karen?" I'm conscious of the stares I'm getting, hearing the odd whisper and giggles, but I have them all on ignore.

"No way! Glen told you to keep it a secret, didn't he? We have to. She doesn't want anyone to know... we should keep our mouths shut."

"Lips zipped. I wonder if she's hurting inside though."

"She seems happy to me."

"Me too... she's okay."

"What about Glen? Is he on your list of boys you like?"

"Bye." Pounding in my brain, *'Glen didn't come over last night... he doesn't like me.'*

"Hey, I have news too!" Anne's voice trails away.

*

In Drama, Chloe tells me about her job at Chan's Chinese Restaurant.

"I need a job. I don't get enough babysitting jobs to make real money."

"Do you want me to see if I can get you a job there? Jan and I can help train you.

Not much happens until the bar closes... then all the drinkers come over for food," The teacher raises his hand for quiet, looking directly at us.

"Cool. Ask... let me know." I murmur, envisioning my wardrobe getting bigger and money to move out after grad.

*

I find Anne and Sandra at lunch. I get stupid hungry; I can't concentrate if the teacher drones on too much. I look out the window if I can't pay attention. Maybe there's a job where I could look out a window. My stomach's usually gurgling by ten o'clock, but I don't want to gain weight. I make my lunch – Mom can't see what I bring every day, which is usually six crackers with cheese.

We're seated in a corner, away from noisy students, who yak over bologna slices, tucked into Wonder Bread, and warm, bruised apples, waiting to be thrown away.

"I have news," says Anne, her face looking as if she's eating blissful love for lunch. "Rod asked me out for a drive last night, and then he asked me if we could go out steady!"

"Super cool Anne," I grab her on the shoulders and rock her in her seat. She's beaming.

"We should double date!" Sandra looks all smiles as she unwittingly shunts me over to the 'Kathy doesn't have a boyfriend' sideline.

The cracker dries in my mouth like dust. I choke a bit and grab water. I'll be left out. I'm not even close to having a boyfriend. I still can't tell them about my feelings for Glen. They'd laugh at me for having an unrealistic, never-going-to-happen, relationship dream. They'll go on dates and I'll be alone.

"Mom's picking me up after school... do you want a ride?" Anne offers.

"Great, I can keep my heels on now." I keep the shrill cry of unhappiness to myself.

*

Anne's Mom shows up after school, we three pile into the clown car and drive off, with the beginning of 'a talk,' compliments of Anne's Mom.

"Anne, just because you have a boyfriend, you can't abandon your girlfriends. They're important and will last longer than any boyfriend." She speaks in gentle tones. "Boys are like sitcoms... there's a new one every half hour." Hilarious! What would she know about boyfriends? She's a mom.

“Mom, we’ve been a couple for less than a day. I don’t think I’m going to change my life,” says Anne dropping her voice low, looking down at her lap. “I’m not shutting anyone out.”

“Thanks, Mrs. Smith. I don’t want to be left out,” my mood lightens shoulders relax. I was picturing myself deserted, stuck at home while my best friends go out on dates. “I’ll get a boyfriend too. I can feel one coming!”

*

I walk in the door of our house with a soft step in case Mom’s on the warpath about some injustice served up to her on her miserable platter.

She is sitting in the old overstuffed chair, reading a book, not doing anything important. I can charm her about the coffee. “Mom I have news,” she looks up, “Anne has a boyfriend.”

“Why a boyfriend? They’re a pack of trouble,” grumbles Mom. Silence falls between us; our old wall clock noisily ticks the time by seconds.

Although Mom never said it out loud to us, I know she was pregnant when she married Dad. They got married in June 1960, and then Alan and I were born in December. I never did the calculation until last year when a light bulb went on in my head. I’ve never brought it up. “There are other things than boys,” she blathers, putting down her book, ‘*Feminism in British Columbia.*’

I do think of things other than boys. Fashion is crucial. Staying thin is on top of the list. I *try* to pass all my school subjects. “Mom, I’ll be graduating in June and will be going out into the world... I’d like to start drinking coffee.”

"Go ahead, drink coffee, but you have to buy your own." She actually agrees to the coffee? Wow. I caught her on a good day. I need to get that job at Chan's so I can afford to buy it!

"Thanks... the other news is that I may get a chance to work at Chan's Chinese Restaurant with Chloe. She's going to ask if I can come in on Friday. Even if it's one or two nights a week, I can make more money than babysitting."

"It's about time you started looking for work. Alan should get off his duff too. Grad's around the corner." I get up before more is said.

*

In my room, I smile at Snoopy and start yoga stretches. Why would a boyfriend be important to me?

I spent my elementary school years chubby, getting teased, bullied and laughed at. I got called 'whale' and 'fatso.' Mom said to say, 'sticks and stones will break my bones, but words will never hurt me.' I said that but didn't believe it. Then, one day, right before Halloween, I was walking home from school and John Beck, a big older boy was hiding in the bush waiting. He jumped out and threw rocks at me. One hit me on the back as I was trying to run away. I fell; he climbed on top of me, spit in my face, and called me a fat pig. I was ten years old. After, I kept to the other side of the road, and walked with Alan, to be safe. My knees shook as we went by the bushes. Not long afterward, John Beck was messing around with fireworks, and one blew up in his face, severely injuring him. I never saw him again.

I managed to keep all this from Mom and Dad. I never told them about any of it, as if in doing so, I'd disappoint them somehow. I felt ashamed I couldn't stick up for myself.

They always saw me as a happy little girl. I remember, around the time of John Beck, The Avon lady was over for coffee. I could hear Mom and Mrs. Bailey through my bedroom door. "Isn't Kathy the most cheerful little girl?" Said Mrs. Bailey. "She's always happy!" All the while I'm crying my eyes out into Snoopy's belly over the latest round of teasing I got for the day.

I had had enough when I was fourteen. I wanted boys to like me, and to wear better clothes, instead of gross choices from the 'chubby section' of the Sears catalogue. I craved fitting in, being cool, expanding my horizons and well, getting a boyfriend.

I ate carefully, tried to be healthy about it, and chose small portions at meals. There was no candy like in the past, or junk food cheats like chips. An exercise routine really helped me get in shape.

The weight came off: I took in my clothes regularly, practicing my sewing skills. The compliments came in. I was thrilled, Mr. Rizzani, my grade six teacher, saw me when I was in grade nine and was completely shocked. I'd made a complete change in appearance.

"Kathy! I barely recognize you looking all stylish... so grown up!" I remember him saying.

No one teased me about being fat. I started wearing clothes from the regular womens wear section. My happiness and confidence soared. I was Kathy, the new girl.

I lost the weight when I was fourteen and fifteen. Now I'm seventeen and never been kissed.

FIVE

"Burt, I don't know how we're going to pay these," says Mom sitting at the kitchen table in front of two piles of bills, Dad across from her. "We can work on these, while this pile's going to have to wait," her hand on the big pile for what will get paid second.

I make a sandwich to eat before my first shift at Chan's. I'd rather be out of the house, but I need one of them to drive me. I eat at the counter, trying to be invisible.

"Adele, what do you expect me to do? Get another job? I'm already working full-time!"

"You could stop spending money on vodka instead of food!" Mom's staring him down like a cornered rat.

"I need relaxation after work! That's unfair."

"Huh, you talk about unfair... I'll remind you of unfair!" Oh no, her face turns to stone, her soulless, dark eyes jab Dad.

"Don't even bother me about your awful life. You get to stay home all day while I'm out in all kinds of weather, making a living for this family." His hands are on the table, shifting his weight, preparing to get up. He hesitates as if he doesn't quite have his balance.

"I can get a damn job if *that's* what you bloody well want," says Mom from some dark place inside.

"No wife of mine is going to work. I'm the provider... I can provide!" He slams his hand down on the table, shaking the sugar bowl, and walks into the living room.

*

I concentrate on putting my hair in a bun away from my face, neat and tidy. I carefully put on black pants, a white shirt, and Mary Jane shoes, which I think will be comfortable. *Ignore them. Ignore the parents.* I need to focus on my new job.

"I need a drive to Chan's," I say to the kitchen, TV room and living room.

"I'll take you," says Dad lurching off the couch.

"You're not driving anywhere... you've been drinking!" Mom grabs the car keys.

"I'm fine Adele... give me the keys," I can tell Dad's been drinking – it's the only time he'll stand up to her. "Give me the keys," he snatches them from her hand.

"Go get killed then."

"Mom, please... that's awful. I'm sure Dad's fine."

"Let's go," Dad says walking out, leaving me running behind him.

The short drive is punctuated by changing gears as wipers swish the rain from the cracked windshield.

"Dad, look out there's a dog!" He barely misses a huge, grey dog crossing the road. I hope I make it there. I'd put on my seat belt except it's broken.

We manage to arrive in the little village center with its two churches and a string of hodgepodge prize-winning dumps of various businesses. At least the Southwind Hotel was built in this century and looks like it will last a few more years before it gets rain stained, moss covered and falling over in the damp. Even if we had sidewalks and hanging baskets like Victoria the place would look a bit better.

"There you go, Kathy... good luck," he pulls into the car park, banging the curb.

I shake and whisper, "I have this job... I'll never ask you for money,"

I hear and feel a sigh in his voice I don't understand, "This isn't about you."

"Bye." I get out of the firestorm into fresh fear.

*

"You okay? You're as pale as can be" Chloe asks as she shows me where to hang my coat.

"I'm nervous. This is my first job," being honest. I can get away with having my face a ghostly shade from Dad's drunk driving scare.

"You'll be great!" She shows me around the kitchen, introducing me to the staff. They're all Chinese and two don't speak English. I meet Mr. Chan, the owner, he shakes my hand, hands me a menu and then goes back to chopping carrots. The menu is long, with all sorts of food I've never heard of. Chow Mien and Black Bean Chicken are two dishes Mom would never cook! There are hamburgers too for those who don't like Chinese food. I start learning the menu, but there's work to do.

Chloe, Jan her older sister, and I set the tables where pictures of Oriental ladies holding fans against painted faces dot the walls. We set each place with a glass, napkin, fork, knife and chopsticks on a paper placemat printed with a red horse and the line, 'Year of the Horse,' in swirling letters. "How do these work?" I hold one chopstick up in each hand.

"We'll show you how." Chloe clacks the sticks together, showing off her skills. I try them out and drop them on the floor.

When every task is done, we sit down. At seven o'clock, a grey-haired couple comes shuffling in. I follow behind Chloe. She takes the order – sweet and sour pork, with rice. We deliver the little piece of order paper to the kitchen where the cook duly notes it and then starts preparing the dishes.

Mom made sweet and sour pork once with raisins, brown sugar and vinegar. It was disgusting. When I see this dish come onto the heated pass through, it's bright red, with lovely chunks of canned pineapple and crispy mounds of deep fried pork. It looks delicious. I wonder how many calories are in a portion.

I pick it up and almost drop the scalding hot plate. Chloe shows me how to use a paper napkin, folded in my hand, to stop burning my skin. I manage to get the food to the table and let them eat.

No one else is in the restaurant, so it's time to fold napkins for something to do. We fold a plain, flat white napkin, into a cute crown. Jan and Chloe talk about moving away to become famous actresses in Hollywood. A cousin living there told them a movie called 'Fame' is going to be filmed, and they'll need ballet dancers who act. Maybe my friend, from little Longmore, will become famous!

We fold napkins most of the evening, and I try to understand the menu. At eleven o'clock the Southwind Bar, across the street, closes; the people pour in. All of a sudden, we're inundated with a boisterous crowd.

I take a large table with three couples. I'm standing in front of typical Longmore. The men are sporting unkempt hair, dressed in black and red-checkered lumberjack shirts and sloppy oversized jeans. The women are getting their money's worth with those brassy, tight poodle perms– they'll never loosen up. They're all lugging around fifty or sixty extra pounds of fat, all sitting around their floral print, polyester-clad middles.

I want to get their order, but they ask me how long I've worked here and where did I get my freckles. I don't know what to do. I don't want to seem impolite, so I stay and chat until they finally order. All the while, Chloe and Jan are whirling around the floor, taking orders. There are couples, old guys and young groups. Jan and Chloe seem to be able to take an order very quickly and move on. I'll have to learn this technique. I take one other table of two young lovers holding hands, staring at each other. I jog them out of their trance to get the order. I hand in the order and then spill pop all over the counter; grabbing a cloth, I wipe up the mess.

"Don't worry about that right now... get your drinks out," Chloe says as she whizzes past me. I take the drinks out two at a time because I don't know how to hold a tray yet.

"Hey freckles, you're doing a great job," my table of Longmore drunks cheer me, slurring their compliments.

When the order is ready for my big table, I can barely hold the heavy plates. I deliver the food with a dirty napkin tucked between my hand and the plates. I put the food down, mixing up who's getting what dish.

The lover's stare at me, willing their food to be delivered, and when they finally get it, I apologize for the wait, due to it being so busy. I turn from them and go straight to the washroom. I took two tables to Chloe and Jan's fifteen. I pat water on my hot, sweaty face and then dry it off with a paper towel. It's so confusing, so fast-paced. Am I ever going to get the hang of it? I wish I could hide in here for the rest of the night, but of course, I can't let Chloe down. After loose hair gets pushed into place, I head back to the rowdy customers.

People clear out, leaving behind a colossal mess to clean up. I made two dollars in tips! Maybe I'm not so bad after all. We clean up and get ready to leave.

"You'll have to learn how to take more tables," declares Jan in her best put on Chinese accent. I laugh my big Kathy laugh and agree. We get a ride home from Mr. Chan. It's 1:00am... I'm beat.

SIX

I'm hoping Glen will come over tonight to hang with us, but he hasn't shown up. Ronny is playing a song I'm not familiar with. He's concentrating hard, his fingers flying over the strings. Alan, Steve, Mack and I play Rummoli. Alan scoops a pile of pennies off the Jack of Diamonds spot.

"Where's Anne tonight?" Mack looks at me while he rips bits of paper into an ashtray.

"Out with Rod. They may come over," I say, removing the lighter off the table, so Mack can't light up his campfire.

"She's rad!" Mack grabs the lighter from my hand and tries to light the paper; I snatch the lighter back.

"Woah, down boy. She's taken," says Steve laying down a Queen of Spades with a bandaged hand, his latest rugby injury.

"She's still the coolest," Mack playfully punches Steve in the forehead.

He's smitten! I wouldn't date him. Something happened to him. He has a burn on his hand that looks like stove burner rings. I asked him about it – he said his dad did it to him. How could a dad be that mean? Maybe he's lying. Mack lives in a foster home we call 'Fosters' and doesn't go to school, even though he's hasn't graduated yet.

*

After kick out time I lie in bed and fiddle with the radio dial trying to find a good song. Tomorrow I go back to Chan's! I'll try harder this time to be polite, but not chatty to the customers. I've been learning the menu all week. With my first pay cheque, I'm going to buy a 'Yes' album, and the next pay, I'll go to Victoria to buy a new purse, and then I'll start saving to move out.

*

I wake up in the morning, used to the routine of me getting ready, Mom screaming, and Alan solemnly spreading peanut butter right to the edges of the toast, and then gobbling it down. I'm drinking my very own milky coffee I bought with tip money.

"Kathy, have you heard about the imminent testing?" Alan whispers to me, his mouth twitching.

"Alan, shut up about nuclear testing," I urge, putting my finger to my lips, my eyes straining, willing him to shut up. "Nothing's happening. People will think you're weird."

"What are you two talking about?" Mom pierces our twin bubble.

"Nothing!" We both say. I close my eyes for a second. He wanted to quit school, and now he's yammering about the end of the world. I swear he's getting stranger as the school year goes on.

The phone jangles to life. "Who'd call this early?" I grab the receiver. "Hello, Kathy speaking."

"This is Mr. Chan from restaurant. We don't hire you. Too slow. Need person with experience. Sorry." The phone goes dead.

"That was Mr. Chan. I can't work at the restaurant because I have no experience waitressing." The job I wanted, the chance I got, is gone. I'll never get out of here. I'll never have enough money. Each thought sinks me further into the chair of defeat I've folded myself into.

"That's a shame Kathy," Mom places her arm across my back. "You can get another job," stepping back, seeing tears, she grabs me a tissue, then four, from the box on the fridge.

"Where? There's nowhere to work around here! NO FAIR," I remove my glasses, fix mascara running down my freckles.

"I'll drive you two today... get up."

I guess it takes an emotional crisis to get Mom to be nice to me. I can't believe she feels sorry for me and has offered to drive us to school! I don't get her at all. Should I become a drama queen? Maybe, we'd get along.

"Okay, Mom." How can I cry now? I put on my coat, as does Alan, and we leave.

*

In the hallways, I find Chloe. "I got fired this morning by Mr. Chan," I spit out.

"I thought Mr. Chan was fine having Jan and I train you. You were learning fast," her eyes drop to the floor while she adjusts a rogue tendril of hair. "I'm really sorry."

"It's not your fault Chloe... I'll be okay," not feeling one bit okay. I head off, catching Anne and Sandra by the gym doors. "I was told by Mr. Chan I can't work at the restaurant. I need experience... he doesn't want me to get it at his greasy spoon," I say unfairly.

"Total bummer Kathy. He didn't even..." The bell clangs loudly in our ears. "I'm finishing Science in the library at lunch, but, hey, Rod and I are going to Longmore Lake beach after school... come," Anne puts her hand on my stooped shoulder.

"Sorry Kathy," Sandra reaches for the other shoulder propping me up mentally and physically. "I'll put in a good word for you at Dairy Queen," she hands me a scotch mint rifled out of her purse.

"Thanks. You two are fab," popping the mint, feeling its refreshing sweetness in my mouth. Lucky, I saw them. They have a way of calming me down.

*

I got 65% on the Science quiz. That's okay considering I don't like Chemistry. I love Arts and Design. I enjoyed making the leather gloves and got 95% on that project. They turned out beautifully when I added the trim of scrap rabbit fur I found in my junk drawer. It took me hours to hand stitch the gloves with tiny even stitches. Now, I have to keep up the excellent work, with my next project, a quilted jacket. I have the cream satin pieces all cut out. Now I have to sew the pattern of the dragon for the quilted part. I'll do the sewing part in my room and then the stuffing, plus hand stitching when the gang's over.

I manage to get through the day by visiting friends. Slowly, I ignore the earlier disappointment But deep down, I feel defeated.

*

After dumping off homework, I head over to the lake entrance across the street. We all manage to live in our rundown, tiny house, but the best part is living across from Longmore Lake's public beach access. The gravel lane barely fits one car, and the steep ditch on the side looks dangerous. The beach is gravel, not sand, and every spring we have to rake out the weeds. A mysterious underground spring feeds the small lake, so the water is wonderfully clean.

I think of how fantastic every summer is, swimming and hanging around the grooviest place in the village area. I jump in the lake sometime during June, and jump out at the end of August. The parents did something right choosing this place.

"Hi," I cheer. Anne and Rod are sharing a cigarette. Rod offers one, "No thanks... it's not my bag."

“I heard you only worked one night at Chan’s and then he let you go.” Rod looks at me frowning. “That’s shitty,” he stabs the smoke into the lone cement picnic table we’re all sitting at.

“How am I supposed to get job experience if no one gives me a job and takes a chance on me?” I wipe escaping tears away with the back of my hand. “There are no jobs in Longmore. It’s a hole.”

“Kathy, I know how you feel. I was lucky getting on at the gas station... you’re going to get lucky too. McDonald’s is opening up in a couple of months right next to the gas station. They’ll need to hire a lot of people... I bet you’ll get a job there.”

“If I get extra babysitting, I’ll think of you first Kathy,” Anne shuffles next to me, giving a K&A bump.

“Thanks,” I say, eyes burning. MacDonald’s opening could be my next chance to work although I’ll keep looking around in case something else comes along.

We share plans for the weekend even though I’m not into their plan to see a rugby game. We say we’ll see each other soon. Rod peels out of the lane smiling and waving at me as the skidding tires draw up loose gravel.

*

Tonight’s meal is another version of ground beef. This time it shows up as Shepherds Pie with a delicious hard crust of browned potato. No ketchup though – not allowed – too expensive. I take a small portion, mushing it around fast, so it looks like more on the plate. I have a topic in mind for dinner conversation. I quickly jump on it before they notice how little I’m eating.

"I've been thinking about what I could do when I get out of school," placing my fork down.

"What's that? Get a job... I presume," Dad looks up from his food, and then down, maybe assuming the discussion's over.

"Some people are going to university or college. Maybe I should go too... except I don't know what I want to take yet."

"Why would you waste your time and money on useless education? People don't need university or college. You go get a job... that's what you do. Forget about putting in four years of school you can't afford," says Dad.

"Maybe I could get a loan?" I've no idea if there's such a thing as a loan to go to school. I wasn't sure how I'd afford school.

"Oh! Now you're going into debt to go to school for no reason," Mom joins in, shaking her head, looking at me like I've suggested a trip to Mars instead of an education. "Do you know how many taxi drivers and waitresses have degrees? God damn useless."

"Neither of you want to help me get a better education?" I stare down at the cracked plate, a yellow daisy obscured by the Shepherd's Pie goo. A morsel slid off the plate onto the scratched, melamine table. I scoop it back up. I look at Alan for some support, but he's in 'quiet, keep the food shoveling in his mouth mode.' I've lost my appetite over daring to suggest I better myself.

"Well... never mind, you have bad marks. I don't know what you're doing in school Kathy, but it's like you don't have a brain in that head of yours. Why can't you be more like Alan... at least he has good marks," says Mom parading her fork in front of Alans face. "Kathy, I don't think you are smart enough to go to college." Now she thinks I'm fat *and* stupid... *what a bitch*! I don't even know what to say to her, so nothing comes out but a quiet huff and a couple of tears.

"*You* don't need more education. Get a job and learn something while you're getting paid. That's what I did... I'm fine reading meters for the city," Dad's voice twisting up a notch. "Are you too good for us now?"

"No! I'm exploring options! I was wondering is all... don't worry about me. I'll get a job, get a place to live, be grown up and independent," I say quickly to hopefully end the conversation.

"That's more like it," says Mom. "We're not supporting you past high school... you'd better bloody well get used to the idea."

Alan pipes up and he's dead serious, "grade twelve is good enough for me since you won't let me quit. Those teachers in university know *nothing*. *I* know more than them!"

The tension breaks; we all start laughing at his absurd notion. Sometimes he makes these nutty declarations – we can't help but see him as funny. Once he said he knew more than Plato. As if he knows more than a smart Greek dude.

"You don't understand me," he grumps, moving his chair back abruptly.

"I guess not. Shut your mouth and eat your cookie, "says Dad, looking up at the ceiling.

"Fine," taking a chocolate cookie Mom has offered for dessert. At least there's no yelling tonight.

I excuse myself to do homework. I have to study for a test on British history. Why bother? I'm not doing anything with grade twelve except getting the diploma. I may as well glide through and not even try. I'll never go to Britain because I'll get a crap job and never have the money.

*

Tonight, I get to have Sandra and Anne over for a sleepover. We're going to watch *Saturday Night Live* downstairs, with the gang. Then they go home and us girls will pile into my room and talk the night away.

I promise Mom and Dad I'll keep everyone as quiet as possible. They seem happy about having everyone over. Mom always says, "at least we know where you two are." She doesn't seem to trust us, but at least it's cool having friends over.

Steve, Ronny, Mack, Alan, Anne, Sandra and I are squished on the couches. Rod is coming over after work, and Brad's hanging with his racecar friends. We listen to *Pink Floyd, Dark Side of The Moon and Led Zeppelin, Physical Graffiti.* Rod shows up, just in time for SNL. We're all set to watch the season opener. I feel we're a solidified, unbreakable unit of friends tonight. Somehow, Alan's friends and my friends have become *our* friends all together in this gang.

We're getting as comfortable as we can. Anne and Mack are play fighting. Rod is shaking his head at their antics. He doesn't seem jealous of Anne paying attention to Mack. Sandra is quietly talking to Alan, in hushed tones, about some unknown topic. The last of the newscast, before SNL, is reporting the USSR has performed a nuclear test. I hope Alan doesn't go weird on us.

Glen walks in. Glen's here! My pulse is on fire. "I heard you're all watching SNL tonight so I thought I should boogie over." The words come out as if he's slow dancing them across his tongue, into the room.

He sits on the armrest next to me. My shoulder's touching his side. He drapes his arm across the back of the couch, so casual, so nonchalant. He's practically putting his arm around me. If I lean back, I could make it real, but I can't. We're seriously crammed together; I have to sit forward a bit. I've never been this close to him, and I feel the warmth of his body against mine. He's delicious, and I'm wanting. My eyes go to the Rolling Stones, red lips poster instead of gawping at him.

The first sketch begins. The 'Wild and Crazy Guys,' are picking up chicks. Steve Martin is hilarious! Everyone's laughing hysterically as the show moves to Rosannarosannadana. We take a break during commercials. I go upstairs to find Mom and Dad also watching SNL. "You two like this show?" News to me!

"We thought we'd see what it's all about," says Dad. Now they won't kick our friends out early!

The Rolling Stones are up next. We're all silent. They start with "Respectable" and Mick, during a massive guitar riff, walks over to Ron Wood, looking like he's going to kiss him. Mick sticks out his tongue and slides it across Ron's mouth – we're all groaning, cheering, laughing. Ron looks like this's just another normal night. We're all dying except Alan who's serious, not saying a word. He looks at me with a knowing nod and then looks away from the TV. Oh please don't say anything about nuclear testing tonight. He'll ruin the night. Luckily our spell isn't broken; the show keeps us laughing for the duration. When the Stones do "Satisfaction," I have satisfaction as we groove along, bobbing our bodies to and fro. I sway against Glen, and he's swaying with me. His heat makes me light-headed with longing. Right now, at this very moment, I love my friends... I love my life.

As everyone stands up to leave, I sneak a look at Glen, who never left the armrest all night. He looks at me and says goodnight. I want him. I want his lips and his body against mine. His scent of spice lingers. There's no one else who makes me wet.

*

Anne, Sandra and I move off to my bedroom, where we all cram onto the blanket covered floor.

Anne whispers, "I have an idea for fun," her eyes bright.

"What?" Says Sandra who's been silent, staring at her hands. What's her problem?

"Let's rank the guys. We put who they remind us of, and funny things they say." Anne, who has always been interested in Alan's friends, looks poised to start this mad evaluation.

"Sure," thinking to myself – should I reveal how I feel about Glen? "You two go ahead," picking lint off my blanket, trying to decide.

Anne starts with a title.

The Ranking, by Sandra and Anne

- Alan is Einstein and thinks trees talk. He's thoughtful and serious about the world.

Mr. Weirdly Funny

- Ronny is the guitar playing, music nut. Will he ever put that guitar down or is it attached to his body?

Mr. Music

- Steve is a super athlete who says 'it's beige - not corduroy.' That statement gave us gut-splitting laughs last year when he said that! Will he survive his many injuries? How'd he get to his towering height so fast?

Mr. Super Tall Guy Sweetie

- Mack is a pyromaniac. Likes to put paper bits into an ashtray and light them on fire. He loves play fighting, especially with Anne.

Mr. Crazy Dude

- Brad is sweet on Sandra. He's our mechanic and maybe one day racecar driver if he can get the money to own one!

Mr. Macho Man

- Rod is super hunky, Greek God and star rugby player. Best part... his girlfriend is Anne!

Mr. Hunky

– I have nothing to offer about Glen in case my obsession is revealed. Anne and Sandra see him as kind and smart. We don't know much about him.

Mr. Super Cool Mystery Man

Anne folds the paper and gives it to me. It was a gas after all.

"Sandra, what did Alan say to you before the show? You looked a bit stunned," I have to ask, even though I'm scared of the answer.

"He told me the USSR is a dangerous menace, and not to talk out loud about anything in the news regarding 'them.' He looked serious... worried, but you know your brother, he's a bit weird." Is she holding back her opinion?

"I think he's freaking out because it's the last year of school, and he doesn't know what to do after it's over," I lie to my closest friends. There's something else bugging him, but I don't know what.

A tap on our door makes my stomach tighten... am I in trouble? "Girls," says Dad, "small house... voices travelling. Settle down now. Good night."

Okay, parents aren't angry.

"Your parents are so cool," says Anne while Sandra's head bobs assent.

I could, in a low whisper, tell all about my parents, how nuts they are, and how crazy it is to live in this house, with a drunkard dad, a mood-shifting, mean mom and an oddball brother, but I don't. I say nothing to my closest friends needing the secrecy to last, and the shame hidden from view.

SEVEN

All my life, I’ve lived across from Longmore Lake. I’ve looked over the road, past the gravel drive to the shoreline, watching the seasons come and go from its reflection. The walk to school has always taken me past Longmore Lake store where, as a little kid, I’d spend my ten cents allowance on penny candy. Now I spend most of my two-dollar allowance on a *Sixteen* magazine every month.

The leaves from the Garry Oak trees are falling fast. My feet drag me through it all to another day at school. I'm full of turmoil but I don't know exactly where it's coming from. I worry about Alan being weird but don't know what to do with him. So I do nothing. Even today he wouldn't wait for me and took off. He's moving away from the closeness we've always had. At least Anne has been true to her word and hasn't abandoned me. Her and Rod aren't all 'lovey-dovey' when they're hanging out with the gang.

Glen is always on my mind; but when I see him it's with the gang, and I can't seem to catch any special attention. He's sweet and talks to me. The 'us' I fantasize about is just that, a fantasy. My time for love will never come. I must be ugly and hopeless for a boy to not even care one bit about me.

I stay out of trouble but the parents don't trust me much. I wonder how they'll react when I say I'm going to the Halloween bonfire.

I like some of school, but mostly I blank out or talk to friends in class. It all seems meaningless. My plan for being the reinvented, mature woman, full of positivity, is sliding into a pit. I try to keep up a sunny disposition because I don't want anyone to know what's going on inside. I'm like a ball of elastic bands, tightly wound and being thrown against an invisible wall. Nothing is going the way I'd hoped, and I'm starting to wonder why I bother putting one foot in front of another.

The first report card this year seems to address some of the chaos. Science, Social Studies and dummy Math I'm holding steady at my usual 65% average. Creative Writing, English, Arts and Design, French and Drama classes boost the percentage to 75%. I wish I could do better across the board–but wishing isn't doing–and I'm sure not doing except talking in class instead of working.

*

After a morning of dull classes, Anne, Sandra and I meet for lunch at the bottom of the stairs where we can sit in peace. We discovered this available nook only this week... a place where no one bothers us.

"Rod likes to make out... a lot," Anne says as if stating a fact, and then continues eating a celery stick without adding anything else. I must have known inside me that they'd be fooling around... something I'd like to do with Glen.

"Brad's always on me." Sandra says, dragging the 'always' out like I drag my feet across dead leaves. "I feel like I'm being mauled instead of loved." I wonder if making out isn't all it's cracked up to be. "We can't even hang out together without it ending up in a huge make out session." She starts picking nothing from under her fingernails.

"I think I need to go on the birth control pill," whispers Anne.

"Is it that serious? Do you think you want to go all the way? What base are you up to?" Sandra asks.

"No home run yet, but it could happen, and I don't want to end up like Janet." Janet was the lamest little greasy-haired, mouse of a girl, who thought she was hiding her pregnancy by wearing a giant pink coat. No one had a clue who the father was. She kept her head down, and everyone talked viciously behind her back. Eventually, she left the school at the end of last year to have the baby and never came back.

"I'm already on the pill. Brad and I went all the way this summer." Sandra fesses up, tipping her head back, lightly bonking it on the wall behind her.

"What was it like?" My only reference is romantic movies on television. There are always candles, soft music and fireworks.

"It's okay. You'll find out when it happens to you," she waves her hand nowhere. Not exactly a ringing endorsement for the act of making love.

"I need to get a boyfriend first," I remind. "How did you get the pill?" I rearrange myself closer, if you went locally, someone may see you and snitch to your parents.

"Victoria has a free clinic for anyone, and your parents don't have to know you're going. The clinic doesn't ask for your parent's information... they were cool."

Sandra's way ahead of Anne and me on the 'I'm a modern woman of the '70's' front.'

"Wow, Sandra... what's with the holding out? Isn't this essential girlfriend sharing?"

"Wasn't into anyone knowing..." she pauses, looks down, returning to fingernail grooming, shifting her back against the wall.

“No big deal,” I move away from possibly hurting her feelings. “Anne, do you think you’ll go to the clinic?”

“Yes... Sandra, will you come with me?” says Anne looking past me to Sandra, who nods yes while packing up her lunch.

I’m ten blocks away. I’m the lonely puppy in the children’s book. I’m a thousand light years behind my friends. The bell rings. I trail along behind them, feeling my posture slumping, stringy hair droops over my glasses. I follow the fractured linoleum floor, through obscured sight, to class.

*

“Alan,” I start, we happen to be walking home together, alone, “Am I repulsive to boys?”

“You’re loud and immature.” He looks at me like, *‘Duh, isn’t it obvious?’* My eyes widen: mouth opens, in fly catching mode – his head’s shaking back and forth. It’s like being slapped across the face.

“What exactly is it about Anne that boys like?” Continuing a demeaning critique, “she isn’t super pretty,” I stamp dried leaves into crushed remains.

"She doesn't act like a little teeny bopper like you. She's nice... not dorky." He has to throw it all at me in a traumatic pile. I try to be funny, but somehow I must be perceived as the opposite. Like the time I was walking around with a tall pampas grass stalk in my back pocket pretending to be a radio, trying to get a laugh. I didn't think I was goofy in an immature way. Or the other time I was screaming Elton John's 'Your Song' across the lake from the public beach area so that I could hear my echo back. That was last year. Can't people forget about the old me and start fresh with the new me? I'm wondering if Glen thinks of me this way. If true, I don't have a chance with him.

"Fine." Now I know. We continue home in silence. I'll re-read the *Sixteen* magazines to glean more useful tips on how to be appealing to guys. My friends are moving on, leaving me out of the, 'I'm Having Sex with My Boyfriend Club.' I have to remind myself of Anne's mom telling her to keep her girlfriends. I hope Sandra and Anne don't abandon me.

*

Mom looks up from the newspaper when I pull in. "How was your day," and "fine" get exchanged. I go to my room, do yoga stretches and then open my homework... *Sixteen* magazines. French quiz can wait.

There's a lot of information regarding how I should act, think, dress and apply makeup. I look at the models enviously, wondering how they get skinny and gorgeous. If I do everything in the magazine, will I become one of these beauties? There's an avalanche of pressure to carve out pieces of myself and replace them, with what I'm reading. My stomach rumbles, reporting a pang of hunger the apple doesn't fill. I ignore it, put 'Stairway to Heaven' on the little turntable, lie down and let Led Zeppelin carry me away for a while.

EIGHT

“It’s a Halloween bonfire... what’s the big deal?” I’m pissed off at the parents considering if I should be allowed to go tonight. “Alan can go, so why do you think I can’t?”

“Because you’re a girl,” says Mom, “girls can get into trouble at these things.” I know what she means, and I know she’s vague because she couldn’t possibly tell me in plain language what she wants to say. Dad is standing there letting Mom do all the talking.

"You're afraid I'll get pregnant?" I uncover the truth, more to myself than to them. I mirror her arms, tightly crossed in front, creating a battering ram. "Don't worry Mom and Dad, your daughter is so ugly, stupid and revolting that, not only will I not get pregnant, I'll never have a boyfriend to attempt the pregnant making event. No one will ever have sex with me because I'm a dog!" Alan looks like he's turned into a slack-jawed, simpleton. Mom's face turns cold as snow. They all look at me as if I've gone mad. Maybe I have. "You hate me!" The kettle starts to whistle, blistering the air with hot steam.

"Adele, Kathy stop it," Dad yells, taking the kettle off the burner, slamming it down on the trivet. "Alan if you go to the bonfire with Kathy, then I think that's fine... as long as you're home by 10:30. Kathy, you're a beautiful girl... stop worrying about a boyfriend."

I stomp to my bedroom, out of the war zone, safely behind enemy lines. I can't believe I had to agree to have Alan babysit me like a wayward child. I hate my parents because they hate me, and don't want me to have any fun.

Dinner is excruciating. I can't smile. I can't talk. I don't know how I'll eat macaroni and cheese without the stupid canned peas choking me. The parents have decided to ignore me and discuss the latest current events from the five o'clock news. Something about how taxes are going up seems more interesting than me. I eat in silence and fury. I can't wait to get out of here for the night.

*

People here call it ‘a Scotch mist.’ Suspended droplets of rain cling to our faces, swirl around, creating a suitably spooky atmosphere for the bonfire. My mood’s improving with each step away from the house.

I honour the deal I made with the parents to go with Alan. This lasts the entire fifteen-minute walk.

“I’m going to take off. Are you cool with meeting up later?” I ask.

“Cool. There’s Ronny... see you on the flipside.” He takes off, leaving me to wander.

There are gypsies and pirates eating treats and drinking hot chocolate as they trail behind their parents. Plenty of adults are dressed as monsters, witches and skeletons. The grounds are overflowing with people laughing and chattering.

“Hey, Kathy!” Godspell Greg drags me toward the other drama kids. They’re all practicing ‘Godspell’ songs for the yearly drama production.

“Come on Kathy, join in!” says Judy.

“I can’t sing... you know that. If I could, I’d be in the play!” I give them my best ‘we beseech thee, hear us.” Judy plugs her ears.

The fireworks begin, drowning out the chorus. For crappy Longmore, the show isn’t too bad. Screamers and shooting stars fill the air. Everyone’s cheering at the display. When it’s over, I drift off through the smoke and mist, looking for Anne.

There's Glen! I tap his shoulder; he turns around with Lynda Ball hanging off the opposite shoulder. I feel the blood drain from my face. *Her? He likes her?* She's a twit! Her loony giggle drove me crazy last year and now she's graduated, apparently into the arms of Glen.

'Hi Lynda," I mutter through a clenched jaw. Her garish makeup and too long, red painted nails look trashy. She's ugly... I hate her. "Hi, Glen... see ya." I turn away and get the hell away from them. There goes my last hope for Glen. He's taken. No go. Glad I never told Anne and Sandra about my crush on him. It's come to nothing. I saved myself from getting laughed at for having a stupid crush on a guy way cooler than me. The thought of seeing Glen, *my Glen,* with Lynda hanging all over him is making my stomach grind into a twisted mass of gloom.

I need to move to Victoria, away from Longmore, away from Glen.

Jeez... I'm supposed to meet Anne, Rod, Sandra and Brad, but where are they? I wish I had a Star Trek device to call them. I need Anne to cheer me up...

I see them in the distance. They look incredibly happy. Anne and Rod hugging, laughing, kissing. Brad and Sandra necking up a storm surrounded by five hundred bonfire attendees. I'm not going over there to be the odd one out.

"Kathy, Kathy," Mack steps in front of me. He's weaving around like a drunk because that's what he is. He stinks like something Dad would drink. "Mack. Do you want to sit down?" I ask.

“I’m in love with Anne... I love her.” His words are all shuffled around, but I can understand the mumbling.

“Mack, everyone loves Anne. She’s the best person ever, but she’s with Rod... they’re a serious couple. Let it go.” I say.

“No.” Tears start cascading down his face. I’m out of my league here. His big strapping frame is leaning on me. The snot is running, and he’s weeping into my rain jacket. I put my arms around him giving him a pat. I knew he liked Anne but not so much that he’s a drunken, blubbering mess about it?

“Alan,” I call. He sees my flapping arm and jogs over. “We have to get Mack out of here.” Alan takes one look at Mack, grabs his back, and we guide him out of the crowd.

“He can’t go to Foster’s like this. Let’s take him home first and sober him up. Where’d he get the booze?” says Alan.

“Who knows.” It’s really ugly trying to get Mack to move along. He is stopping, staring back to where Anne and Rod were. He’s still crying and stumbling.

“Hey!” Glen is behind us. “Let me help you.” He grabs the side I’m on, taking over. Once Glen has a hold of Mack, the walk is easier. We try getting him into the house quietly to avoid the parents, but Mack falls over at the door. A huge crash brings Mom and Dad over.

“Get him in the house,” says Mom. We sit him down at the table. “What happened?”

“He’s drunk,” says Alan

“We can see that! You two better not be drinking!” Dad says.

“No!” we both say. They seem to be satisfied we’re telling the truth. The dagger eyes are off.

“Should we make strong coffee... like in the movies?” I ask.

“Go ahead, make some toast. See that he drinks and eats. Pour him a large glass of water... it helps to push the booze through,” says Dad like he knows what he’s talking about because I’m sure he does.

“Don’t disappoint us by drinking,” says Mom. “This is what happens. People turn into complete fools.”

I’m not sure if she’s talking about Mack or Dad but at least she hasn’t blown a gasket. “Thanks for being cool about Mack,” I say.

“At least we know where you are,” clips Mom.

“You two are good to help Mack,” says Dad nodding.

We get Mack in better shape over the next hour. Alan, Glen and I sit at the kitchen table reviewing the evening.

“You’re dating Lynda?” Alan asks.

“No! She’s my cousin... she’s an idiot.” Glen looks at me when he says it.

I’m reeling in the realm of possibility. Bubblehead isn’t with Glen! They aren’t a couple and I can keep my fantasy alive! “Thanks for helping with Mack,” I say smiling.

“Righteous, Kathy... no skin off,” He’s still looking at me! My heart’s beating steady. I don’t feel like a twittering teenybopper. Tonight, my focus is on helping Mack, being there, as a friend when he needs one.

We all walk Mack home, getting him to his door quietly so he won’t get caught and kicked out. “Thanks, guys,” Mack says, disappearing inside.

“Goodnight Glen,” I say as he and Alan grip hands together.

“Goodnight Florence Nightingale!” Damn, he’s so gorgeous.

Alan and I walk the short distance home. “Do you think he got the booze from the Russians?” I joke.

“Not funny. You don’t understand how serious they are about invading Canada,” Alan turns to me, his eyes penetrating.

“Sorry... never mind... goodnight.” If the Russians bombed us now, I’d die happy.

NINE

I don't mention Mack's bonfire confessions. "We walked home together, Alan, Mack, Glen and I."

"The fireworks were okay," Sandra says. Anne shrugs.

"I had fun with the drama crowd," I say.

"Are you abandoning us Kathy?" kids Anne.

"Not a chance... you're stuck with me!"

Rod comes over, checks the clock overhead, and starts our ad hoc meeting. "So, I hear we're doing a play for the Christmas Pageant."

Anne, Rod, Sandra and I decide on a skit based on "Twas the Night Before Christmas," by Clement C Moore. Rod will be the dad, Sandra the mom, Anne is the excited child, and I'll narrate.

“I can get the neighbours' dog to be the reindeer. We can rig up a sleigh for Truro to pull across the stage.” Anne says.

“You’d better be a well-behaved daughter, or I’ll spank you,” Rod says putting his arms around Anne, giving her a squeeze.

“As long as I can spank you back,” she gives him a big kiss on the cheek.

“Okay, you two... I have to go. We’ll figure out a plan to work on this... we have just over a month.”

During Social Studies I start writing the play. The French Revolution is dullsville. Now I have something to keep me busy. Tomorrow is Christmas shopping day, so I make my list in Science class. Light refraction is boring.

*

“Kathy, you can’t go into the city until you finish your homework,” says Mom in a louder than usual screech.

“I did it last night and this morning... bye,” I say as I see Sandra and Brad pull up in his car. Anne’s in the back seat; I hop in beside her. “Christmas shopping let’s go” I sing out. “I’m getting Alan an Emerson Lake and Palmer album... if I can afford it. They cost around $6.00, so I may not be able to do it. Mom wants a homemade gift.” Anne and I will work on this together since her Mom asked for the same thing. We’re going to decoupage flowers onto wood plaques. “Dad wants a shaving brush, which is a boring present, but easy to get and not over budget.”

Brad's loud Black Sabbath music blares for the half hour drive in. We pull into the Hudson's Bay parking lot and decide to split up. Sandra and Brad want to head off; we plan to meet at Denny's at four o'clock.

Victoria is decorated for the Christmas season, unlike Longmore where all of us poor people are. There are candy canes and Santa, Christmas trees with colourful shining balls and angels everywhere on rooftops. It's lightly raining: it doesn't look like the Christmas TV specials, where everything's covered in snow, all festive and lovely. It hardly ever snows here and even less of a possibility on Christmas day. It's always a disappointment.

Our first stop is the record store. I manage to find an ELP Alan doesn't have on sale for $4.50. That's nine hours of babysitting just for his present, but at least I get to listen to it too! We find the crafting store easily. It's like a golden treasure for me. There are plenty of crafts I could see myself making. Too bad craft and art are for hobbies. That's what Mom and Dad tell me. What can I do? I keep dreaming of the next project. I can do creative work in my spare time. We find the wood ovals, varnish and flowers. We'll work at home, in my bedroom, and then hide them in the closet while each layer of varnish dries.

At last it stops raining as we wander along, finding the other gifts. We stop to look at the mechanical dolls in the store windows. They're skating, singing and visiting the jolly Santa.

"What the hells your problem?" Is that Brad? Anne and I look at each other, walking toward the yelling.

"Nothing," I hear Sandra's low reply.

We turn the corner, there they are. Brad's muscled bulk is standing over Sandra sitting on a bench. He has a twisted look on his face, jaw set at a rigid angle, teeth gritted... his booming voice is frightening.

"Bitchface, what are you looking at?" he snarls as Sandra looks between him and us. "Fuck off... find your own way home," He stomps off down the street.

"Sandra," I say. She's crying into her hands. We can't get her to look up. People are staring at us. A man, with a concerned expression, stops and hands a pile of tissue over, then walks on. Sandra takes the tissue and tries to stop wailing. We sit on either side of her, wrapping our arms around her heaving body.

"What happened?" Anne lets go to face our tearful, alabaster mess of a friend.

"He doesn't understand my period cramps and thinks I'm making it up. He thinks I'm in pain to ruin his day," she looks at the sidewalk, her hands protectively press her middle. Holding her breath, gritting her teeth, she breathes slowly outward, "I took some Midol."

"What a jerk," Anne says. Sandra starts crying again. "My dad might be able to pick us up." She digs out ten cents, eyeing the pay phone. I can't hear the conversation, but there's nodding. Walking back, thumb in the air, she confirms "he'll meet us at Denny's in an hour."

*

The restaurant smells like hot, freshly griddled pancakes. We take a booth, in the corner, away from onlookers. Sandra's face is still streaked with tears.

She's pretty, even in her state of misery. She's even beautiful. I consider Sandra as she appears on the outside, and the fragile being she is on the inside. Her burnished, brown hair is a thick, long magnificent length. It frames her milky white, flawless China doll complexion. I look at her almond-shaped eyes, peculiarly captivating because green flecks mix in with the brown. She has a perfect figure... thin, tall, flat stomach and big boobs. She even carries herself as if she reigns with confidence. But inside, she's like a wounded bird. Sandra seems a together person, but now she's lost.

"Sandra, what the hell's up Brad's ass? Doesn't he care about how you're feeling?" Anne takes her hand.

"I think he's having a bad day, like me."

"But he's not nice to you! It's pretty hard to listen to him talk crap. You deserve to be treated way better. I care about you..." I say, my voice faltering.

"I care too! Don't let him treat you like that," says Anne gripping Sandra's hand in a firm lock.

I place my hand over theirs. "What are you going to do?" I ask.

"I know it looked bad. He loves me, cares about me and I love him. I bet tomorrow he'll say sorry and give me flowers," says Sandra lifting her hand away reaching for the hot chocolate that has arrived. We all take a sip of the sweet drink, letting it warm us up.

"Flowers would be cool," is all I can say. The look of adoration for this creep is making my head spin.

"Sandra, we know you love Brad. He loves you. I hope you work it out and move on," Anne is almost inaudible.

Sandra digs a makeup case out of her purse, snaps open a gold-coloured compact and peers into the mirrored lid. We watch her wipe up her woe with a few wand strokes of mascara and a fresh layer of pink lipstick. She firmly snaps the compact case closed, shoving everything into her purse. "I'm fine... let's see what you bought!"

Anne and I exchange a slight shake of our heads. I put my bags on the table. We show each other what we bought and discuss how festive the city looks at Christmas. We all agree to have the happiest Christmas ever.

Anne's father walks in, and we wave him down. He's the most stoic, peaceful dad I've ever met. He corrals us up, without asking pointed questions, and we head back to Longmore.

*

I run from the car, thank Mr. Smith again for the ride, blow into the house laughing, "Hi everyone," relieved to be home.

"You're late," Mom is at the table, with a cheque book and some bills. She looks up, and I swear she's going to throw that pen at me. I forgot to look at the time and phone home to let Mom know what happened.

"I can explain... you're not going to believe it," plunking myself down on a kitchen chair, dropping the shopping bags on the floor.

"You know we aren't late in this house. I don't see how your explanation will change breaking the rules around here. Go to your room. You're grounded for the rest of the weekend." I almost laugh, picturing her head unhinging and spinning around.

She can't mean it. "Brad took off on us... we had to call Mr. Smith to pick us up," speaking double fast, trying to get all the facts out, "Sandra was crying... a real mess... it wasn't my fault."

"Go-to-your-room," her voice drops to a new low, breaking up each word into jagged pieces of broken glass scraping across rough granite.

"For what? Why are you so *angry?* What have I done? I *told* you what happened! This is bogus crap! Do you hate me or something?" I pick up my purse wanting to hurl it at her. *I hate her*. "I said I'm sorry for being late. Call Mr. Smith... he'll tell you what happened."

"Go." She points to my door. She looks at me like she's staring at a pile of vomit. I never know which Mom is inside the house when I walk in the door. Today she's the '*Monopausal Nightmare*.' I'm twenty minutes late, I realize, when I look at the clock. She wrecks my weekend, doesn't believe me, and this is for a whole twenty minutes of tardiness. I shut the bedroom door without banging–that could get me another weekend of grounding. Crashed onto the bed my burning eyes travel to cobwebs floating in the ceiling corners. I'm stuck in this craphole of a house with a mother who makes my life hell. Do stupid fat girls deserve this? Maybe we do and I should join, 'My Mother is a Nagging Bitch and It's My Fault for Being a Fat and Stupid Daughter' club. I'd be president.

I put on Moody Blues, 'Nights in White Satin' and sing along, never reaching the end. Alan comes in; I whisper to him what happened.

“Sandra’s a whore,” he rasps, turning tail out of the room like a frightened animal. Where'd that come from? What’s wrong with him? Alan isn’t unkind like that. He’s always liked Sandra. I’ve never heard him utter one nasty word about her. Why did he say such a horrible thing?

Moody Blues are still playing. I crush my head against the pillow, close my eyes and crawl into a ball, sinking into their musical brilliance. I try to forget the world.

TEN

After another mind-numbing day at school, I'm met by Mom who's sitting at the kitchen table with the Sears Catalogue open to the fabric page.

"Sit down Kathy, let's pick out some fabric... I'll make you something for your birthday," she's all smiles.

"Okay," I sit tentatively, not trusting her to stay in a good mood for any more than one minute. I check the second hand on the teapot clock.

"Do you like this velveteen... how about French velvet? I know! I'll make you a skirt to match your vest! Kathy, wouldn't that be wonderful?" Her voice sounds shrill, like our car trying to get out of first gear.

"Sure." Here it is... the equivalent of an apology from a person who can't muster up a sorry for the way she treated me. She must have talked to Mr. Smith and found out I was telling the truth. "That would be gorgeous Mom," pulling the words out robotically. Dragging the fight up again won't get me anywhere. "Can you afford it?"

"Oh, silly you... don't worry about the cost." She circles the item number. "I'll phone the order in right now, so I can have it made by your birthday. Go off now... get that homework done!" An unknown tune emits from pursed lips, her head rocks back and forth in contented time.

Does she forget the yelling, arguing and how she was mean to me? Now she's trying to make it up to me in faked breathy tones saying she's going to make me something to wear? I think her head has detached and spun in the other direction.

Sandra told me today Brad apologized and gave her bouquet of flowers. She says they've made up and are stronger than ever. Shoot me now world... put me out of my misery.

*

"She's here," I hear Mom after she picks up the phone. "Kathy, it's Theareh Vos on the phone."

Babysitting Ben for Theareh and Dan! I grab the phone, "Hi Theareh!" When they moved in next door, it took me a few tries to pronounce 'Thee-rah' correctly.

"Hi Kathy," sounding hurried, "I have a proposition for you... I need help getting all my craft items ready for a big Christmas sale next week. Can you help me assemble everything, and then help me at the booths for the next two weeks? I'll pay you."

"That's hip Theareh... I'd love to help out!" Wow, a real job that isn't babysitting. "When do you need me?"

"Right away if possible... I'm way behind. Whenever you can start... soon maybe?"

"The only other commitment I have is the school Christmas concert. We're fine tuning the act for the performance on December 8th." I look at the calendar tacked up by the phone. It's already December 2nd. "I can come tonight for two hours though." We plan for me to come at six o'clock. I explain to Mom what I'm about to do.

She looks up from furiously scrubbing a frying pan, clasps her hands, and declares, "Hallelujah, a job."

*

Having Ben run into my arms at the Vos's door is such a buzz. His three-year-old imagination sets up fun play. We build forts and fight off bad guys!

I step into the cedar finished interior. The wood stove fills the small house with a campfire fragrance that hangs in the air like summer memories. I wipe my shoes on the doormat but keep them on. The floor is old wood planking that snags socks. I hang my coat on the iron hook crafted by Dan. The cozy house is covered in Macramé hangings of every imaginable sort.

Theareh and I sit at a large table she's set up in the living room. It wasn't here the last time I was over. It's covered in incense sticks, moss in a woven basket, candles and bath salts. "What are we doing?"

"Well, I want to put together a Zen Pampering Kit," Theareh says, waving an arm at the heap.

I give her a blank look and laugh, "Is this a cool hippie thing? I've never heard of Zen before."

She laughs, "It's a Buddhist method of relaxation and meditation." I don't know what Buddhist is, but Chloe had talked about meditation, so at least I have some understanding. "Let's get started." We sit down, Dan scoops up Ben, says hello, and wanders off.

"Take the incense in bunches of three, wrap them with ribbon, then take the bath salt... put a scoop in these little bags... tie them with a tidy bow. Add a matching candle, and then put it all on the moss, in the wicker basket. We'll place a card on top and cellophane wrap them later. I've created an in-home relaxation experience, which hopefully, people think is a unique Christmas present."

"This is neat stuff, Theareh." I still feel funny calling her and Dan by their first names, but they're hip, and want me to be casual with them.

We settle down to start. Theareh asks me about school and the concert. I can't help but bubble over about how it's going. "The concert's going to be excellent. People are singing, dancing and I narrate 'Twas the Night Before Christmas.'"

"Any cute guys?" She asks like we're girlfriends. I laugh nervously, getting red behind the freckles.

"Yes cute guys, but none that like me... I'm repulsive to boys."

Her face crinkles up into a questioning ball. "Why would you say that?"

"Because boys want pretty girls, with big boobs."

"Kathy, you're a gorgeous young woman! If they want big boob girls, then those boys aren't for you... they're the immature ones. Boys are complicated, but the right one will come along... he'll like you, for you."

"It's never going to happen. Look at me... I'm turning eighteen next week, and no boy likes me or even seems to like me. I'm doomed."

"You're *only* eighteen. You have loads of time. Think of what kind of boy you'd like to have as a boyfriend... he's going to show up."

"Is that a Zen thing too?" We're both laughing as she explains it's a method of focusing your energy to create what you want in your life. "Well how'd you and Dan meet?" boldly asking her such a personal question.

"We met in California, protesting the Vietnam War... a war we shouldn't have been in. Thousands of men died horrible deaths or came back with terrible injuries. There was a fear of Communism taking over the world. For Dan and I, it was hippie protesting, free love and a lot of weed. Dan was going to get drafted into the war, so we moved to Canada. Now we both have Social Work degrees and can't move back.

"Dad called you 'draft dodgers.' Mom and Dad think you're a rad couple." They were the first foreigners I'd ever met when they moved in next door, last year.

I look at Theareh, with her long, stringy hair, parted down the middle and nothing else done with it. I think her unshaven legs and armpits are ugly, but Dan and her are cool with hair all over the place. Dan loves her, even though she doesn't look pretty, or dress nicely unless they both dig sack-style clothing. Maybe there's a 'Dan' out there for me one day. I hope his name is Glen. We talk a little more about the war protest, the hippie movement and then we finish for the night. I'm treated like an adult, by adults, and I enjoy the feeling. She even said they smoked weed. I thought only the potheads in high schools did. Maybe other people smoke weed, and I don't know about it. All I know is that no one I know has the five dollars to get a nickel bag of the stuff.

*

There's time left in the evening to see who's visiting Alan. He hasn't been weird since his horrible insult about Sandra. I grab my quilting project and join the guys downstairs.

Ronny and Steve are on their way out, but Glen is splayed out on the couch tapping his feet to Jethro Tull.

"Hey Kathy, the working woman," Glen folds himself up to make room for me. "I'm still looking for work. It'll be easier after December 9th to find a job."

"Why?" I settle in beside him. I'd rather be squished up against him, but there's an arms length between us.

"Full disclosure, I'm born on the same day as you two, a year earlier. Alan and I put that one together tonight."

Same day! We're both Sagittarian – the best! It's our destiny to be together. Glen and I! Me and Glen! "Jeez, come over on our birthday for cake... mom makes a deadly chocolate one for us."

"Will there be a present too?" He looks right through my glasses into my lust.

I'd love to give you a body-to-body present. "Maybe... what do you like?"

"Surprise me." His eyes leave me for a second, and then they're back.

"Deal. How's the job hunt going?" I say as I start stitching.

"The parents are bagging on me big time to get work. The Ugly Bugs can use me on gigs in licensed joints. They're getting out there more... ripping metal rock. My lame fake ID doesn't always work... it'll be righteous to be legit."

Great, He'll have a hundred girls after him. *Kathy, you have no chance*. I pick up some quilt batting, and Alan puts on Pink Floyd.

"Alan, did you read in the last '*Music,*' that Pink Floyd had to help music technology producers –EMI– create the synthesizer VC53 to make the sounds they wanted for Dark Side of the Moon?" Says Glen, being all musician techno buff. Only Alan and Glen would care about synthesizers.

"No shit?" Alan kicks back, and we all let the synthesizers take over the room.

ELEVEN

My life is piling up, and I'm having a blast! I speed off to school, looking hip, and way faster on the makeup part. On goes the mascara and eye shadow. Lately, no zits to cover up; so a bit of lip gloss to finish and it's go time. School's better because of the Christmas concert. I know someone in the play in every class, so we discuss how it's evolving.

The dress rehearsal is stellar... tomorrow we do it for real. I buzz through the rest of school, doing all my work in class, so for once, no homework.

*

“Mom, I’ll be back at nine!” I race over to and give Ben a giant hug. We play for awhile as Theareh gets the table ready. The *Baker Street* album is on the turntable. It’s different from other music I listen to. I think the song, ‘Right Down the Line’ is going to stick with me all night.

We settle in, start assembling, and Theareh recalls her day to me. “I went to a women’s liberation conference today.”

“Mom’s a ‘women’s libber,’ she says women are treated unfairly. Women don’t get paid as much as men. Women should have equal rights... she can get on a tirade about it while she’s folding clothes or making dinner. She doesn’t even work... what does she care?”

Theareh’s doubled over in her chair, “what’s so funny?” I ask.

“Kathy, you’re so honest. That’s how you see your mother? She looks after you, feeds you, cleans your clothes and does all the other little things you don’t see,” Theareh straightens up, composing herself.

“It isn’t a job... she doesn’t get paid!”

“I get why you may think that... paid work is considered work and a job. Your perspective’s enlightening. Trust me though, what she does as a homemaker is a full-time job... no doubt about it.”

I never thought about how Mom does all she does and doesn’t get paid. She doesn’t even get a thank you.

“What do you want to do after you graduate?”

“No clue. Mom and Dad want me to get a job and move out. When I know, you’ll know... I promise.”

She nods, offering no opinions, or judgments. I walk home with my mind full of questions. What am I doing? Where am I going? How will my life turn out?

*

The Christmas pageant is incredible. We did it for the school during the day and now at night for the parents. I see Mom and Dad in the crowd and wave to them when I start the narration. Anne is the textbook excited child that won't go to bed, and Rod's stern dad is a hit. Sandra nails the mom. The biggest laugh is when Truro walks halfway across the stage and then starts doing donuts in the middle of the journey. People go hysterical! The unexpected event stops my narration until the laughter finally dies down and then Truro manages to walk across to get his doggie treat.

Chloe dances, 'The Sugar Plum Fairy' from Nutcracker. Everyone is spellbound.

At the end, the entire company sings, 'We Wish You a Merry Christmas.' We're enjoying our second standing ovation. I'm in my glory, thrilled to have the lights and applause. The curtain closes for the last time. Now we get to have a 'deck party' on the stage.

I don't have a care in the world dancing to Blue Oyster Cult, Meatloaf and lots of other rad tunes. Anne, Sandra and I get a ride home with Rod. We sing Christmas carols at the top of our lungs the whole way, killing ourselves laughing.

*

"Kathy, you're going to be late. Theareh's going to be here soon," Mom yells. Sheesh, I wish she'd stop yelling. Maybe I'll get the guts up to ask her to leave me alone, or maybe I'll live with it until I can move out.

Theareh and I drive to the craft show venue, find our table, and set up the beautiful looking baskets under bright lights while Christmas music plays. We'll be responsible for sales, taking cash and keeping the table stocked.

I practice our sales pitch. "Here's a pampering basket to make a person feel relaxed and calm. Run a bath, add the bath salts, light a candle, and an incense stick, turn out the light and relax. The salts are beneficial for your skin... the incense calms the soul."

I evoke the prospect of serenity, using my best drama skills to draw in the crowd. I think it's all hokey stuff, but I can't get over how people believe me. We're talking up the baskets, making sales and restocking. I barely have time to eat.

The sales pitch worked! We sold sixty-five of the seventy baskets we made. Instead of Theareh looking excited, she has a look of strain on her face. "Why aren't you ecstatic?" I ask.

"There's another big sale next week, and I don't have anything prepared. We sold almost everything!"

"I'll keep helping you!"

She puts her palms together as if she's about to pray. "Thank you."

There's a pile of cash to count. She takes $30.00 out, giving it to me. "Thanks... are you sure? This seems like too much money."

“You deserve decent pay for work well done. We gals have to stick together on this one.”

I don’t want to burn my bra, but I’ll go for generous pay in this feminist movement!

*

I walk into the house exhausted, cautious. I almost forgot it’s our birthday. Will home be calm or tense?

Mom has a big chocolate birthday cake ready for Alan and me. Her familiar scribing, ‘Happy Birthday Alan and Kathy’ is across the top of her homemade cake. The ‘Happy Birthday’ banner that has gone up, for every birthday I ever remember, is on the wall in its usual place. It looks all tatty and worn on the sides but it’s a tradition I love. We eat with happiness and I regale everyone with the story of my day. Nobody’s nasty to me, and we all get through cake and singing as if we’re a normal family. Alan’s all smiles with his new, second-hand, reel-to-reel tape recorder

Mom gives me the brown velvet skirt she’d promised. “Thanks, Mom and Dad,” I say looking at the three-quarter-length skirt. I swear the shade of brown is different from my vest but I’ll know when I try it on.

Alan’s anxious to get the reel-to-reel hooked into his system; we all excuse ourselves and move into our own corners. Dad sits in front of *Hockey Night In Canada* and Mom putters in the kitchen. Alan and I aren’t doing anything special – just having people over to hang out. I rearrange hair and makeup and put on the new, birthday present skirt and vest combination.

Uh oh! I'm right. The colour of the vest and the colour of the skirt are both brown- but different shades. Didn't Mom notice the colour difference? The outfit looks mismatched... horrendously homemade gone wrong. It's too late to remake it in the correct brown. The fabric's expensive. I can't complain to Mom about it after she went to the trouble of buying the material and making the skirt. She'd freak out on me if I dare complain about her gift. I'll say I'll wear the outfit for another special occasion and leave it at that.

I pick out a long, cream-coloured crushed-velvet skirt and a nifty patchwork top. I'm looking good. Glen's coming over; it'll be special because we're born on the same day, and we're both Sagittarius, which *obviously*, should mean something to him.

By the time I get downstairs, Ronny, Steve and Mack are there. Anne and Rod show up a little later, and Brad graces us with an appearance, holding onto Sandra.

"Sandra, you look gorgeous," I say admiring her tight pink turtleneck and black pants.

"If I tell her I think she's a fox, it'll go to her pretty little head," says Brad smiling at Sandra like he's made the joke of the evening. Everyone stares; no one speaks.

"Let's sing 'Happy Birthday,'" says Sandra, all light and happy sounding. I give Brad a frown– as if showing my displeasure will make dick wad stop being a dick wad.

I get Avon Strawberries cologne and a wall hanging that says, 'Hang in There Baby' with a cute cat hanging off a branch. I open up some pretty Yardley lemon soaps and feel like a queen for the day. Alan gets records. He puts The Who on the system, cranks the music up, and we sing and dance up a storm in our minuscule little space.

No Glen. We shut down at ten thirty. He hasn't come over. Bummer. He said he'd come over... I saved him some cake! I found a penny from the year of his birth and wanted to give it to him as a present.

We say goodbye to everyone and I change into pyjamas, a tacky, quilted, shiny lilac polyester affair that Mom picked out for me last year. Alan and I are in the kitchen when the door sounds a knock.

"It's kind of late..." Alan makes his way to the door. Oh no! It's Glen and I'm wearing ugly, old lady PJs. Alan parades him in and I have to act like nothing's repulsive about my attire.

"Happy Birthday, Glen. I'm about to hit the hay but I'm glad you came over," I breeze as if everything's cool.

"Sorry about dragging my ass getting here. The Ugly Bugs needed me to set up their equipment." He's looking at my face, not my PJs. I want to run my fingers through his hair. I'd love to give him birthday kisses... all over his body.

We eat cake together, and he likes the penny I've given him. It's a short visit because the rules are clear at home; everyone has to leave by eleven. At my request, Mom takes a photo of us three altogether at the kitchen table. Glen's holding up the penny.

I follow him to the door. He turns, leans down and kisses me on the cheek. “Goodnight birthday girl,” he says and walks off. I press my hand on the kiss as it sears my skin with hope.

TWELVE

I'm happy the school holidays are almost here. We have a few quizzes, but overall not too outrageous. Assembling baskets with Theareh is every night.

"I'm leaving!" Mom doesn't yell some command as I go out the door. Maybe I'm proving myself as trustworthy. Luckily, I don't have chores at home like some of my friends. Mom's at home all day, with nothing better to do, so she does the chores.

"Hi Theareh, Dan... hi Ben!" Ben hands me a pirate hat, we chase around looking for bad guys, and then we settle into our tasks, humming to 'You're So Vain.' The bath salts are her department; I work on incense stick bundling.

"What's it like being a Social Worker?" my considered career.

“Right now I’m working with pregnant, unwed mothers. It’s rewarding and awful all at the same time. These women have an uphill battle.”

“Couldn’t they marry the dad?”

“Many men that get women pregnant refuse to own up they’re the father or they may just take off.”

“That’s crap! Can’t someone make the men responsible? Isn’t there a way to know they’re the dad?” Dan coughs from somewhere in the house.

“No test for that, so no consequences. Usually, the pregnant woman is blamed for getting herself ‘in trouble.’ Right now I have a woman who was fired from her job for getting pregnant. She has no income and no man to help.”

“How can she get fired for being pregnant?” In the background Carly Simon’s voice trails off, leaving the needle scratching the centre of the LP.

“The employer has the right to discriminate against pregnant women.” Theareh gets up, flips the record over and replaces the needle. Carly’s voice fills the room.

“That’s not fair!” I sit up on the chair, elbows on the table.

“How about this. A pregnant woman needs the father of the child’s signature to allow an abortion if that is what she wants. We don’t get to decide on our own, even though the dad may have no interest in the baby’s life, and doesn’t want to marry. If you’re under twenty-one years old, you can’t even have an abortion without the consent of your parents."

“I’m confused... doesn’t birth control work?”

"If you use it. The act of becoming pregnant is such a human impulse... we're here to procreate. It doesn't sound romantic, but couples become overwhelmed by their emotions, have no birth control, throw caution to the wind, and then a baby's on the way."

"I'm never doing that! Tell me more." I'm whipping through basket assembly.

"I have a friend trying to get into university to become a doctor, and she's having a tough time being accepted anywhere because of her gender. She told me it's the same for women trying to get into the law department. And then, even if they get in and get the same education as men, women are paid less than men. The thought isn't that it's equal pay for equal work, but rather the woman makes less money because she has a man to look after her and pay the bills."

"Dad's proud to tell us mom doesn't have to go to work. He says he's the provider and can provide for us all," relaying his words.

"The world has to change Kathy. I know your Dad means well, but different situations come up. We can't paint ourselves with a 1950's perfect family brush... you're part of those brush strokes." She leans down to retrieve more candles from the box on the floor. I huff under my breath.

We're NOT a perfect family. She doesn't know about Mom's moods or Dad's drinking. I don't even know how I'd explain Alan's odd behaviour, not that I'd tell her anything about our family crap. It's too weird. "Could you not tell Mom and Dad about what we talk about?"

“Part of my job is to keep confidences, so no problem.” We pack up the work we’ve done for the night.

I’m never getting pregnant. I won’t be one of those unprepared women. Getting pregnant would be the worst thing imaginable.

THIRTEEN

This ought to be interesting. Sandra's dad's girlfriend has invited us over tonight to drink eggnog and go Christmas carolling.

I have the second craft sale to do. We load up the vehicle and set out for another day pitching Zen. We roll up and see there's a long lineup of women waiting to get in! "This looks promising," Thearah smiles.

Once again, we're run off our feet. The response is phenomenal! People are buying five at a time, naming off who will receive the baskets as they pick them up off the table. 'This's for Amy, and this's for Donna.' It's our last sale thank goodness because we all but sell out. Theareh is planning a spring sale now. I agree to help.

"Thanks a bunch for hiring me... it's been a blast."

"We're a good team!" We finish packing up. She puts $40.00 in my hand and I thank her again. I'll save this money for something important. I don't know what yet, but I know it's a start. I'll see what I get for Christmas before spending my earnings.

Fortunately, Theareh drives me right to Sandra's house. 'And now for something completely different' I announce in my head, like John Cleese in Monty Python's Flying Circus.

*

I knock on the door, Sandra answers. Anne, Rod and Mack are there. "Brad's not coming... he's not much of a caroler," Sandra excuses him.

Brad isn't much of anything, except ass wipe. We're a small group crammed into the galley kitchen where the girlfriend makes a grand entrance.

"Merry Christmas everyone! You can call me Auntie Sue!" She's very upbeat and enthusiastic. I gather she's trying to make a positive impression with Sandra's friends, but Sandra's right...'Auntie Sue' is trying too hard to be cool and friendly. She has fake-looking blonde hair, all teased up in a floozy bouffant. She's trying to cover up her age by using the wrong-coloured beige foundation on wrinkled skin. The eyeliner and mascara are miles too thick. What magazine does she read? '*Look Overdone Monthly*'? We each have eggnog and cheer the season. 'Overdone' sends us out the door, with a promise of more eggnog when we return.

What a trip! We don't sing the carols but yell them as we go door to door. Mack has a Santa hat on, and children are running up to him as he gives little candies out. We holler our way through 'Rudolf the Red Nosed Reindeer,' 'Wish You a Merry Christmas' and a whole pile of songs from a free handout in the newspaper. I thought carolling was dorky, but we split a gut laughing.

*

The rain's beating down hard, waking me up to a dull Sunday. My appearance in the kitchen is greeted with calm. Maybe it'll be a stress-free day at home. I'm tired and have to finish the quilted jacket, due tomorrow. Everyone leaves me alone.

Maybe this is the change? My family will normalize themselves. I pick up the jacket to complete the work. The dragon looks like a dragon, and the raised texture looks well done. I settle in with King Crimson while the rhythm of the rain taps on the roof.

I learned heaps from Theareh. I feel confident in front of people; she's given me a lot to think about regarding life and where to go with it. But I don't know how to organize my thoughts. I feel unrest... what is it? Yes, I could make a list of how I have no boyfriend, my family is weird, school's boring, and I have no idea what I'll do when I graduate, but there's something else. Change is coming. It's in my gut like a volcano about to erupt.

FOURTEEN

It's Christmas Eve... no one's home when I come in the door from delivering Anne's wood plaque present for her Mom. What a fun afternoon at her place! Her mom made shortbread cookies; we decorated them with silver balls and coloured sugar crystals. Anne played some carols on the organ, and we wrapped presents.

There are Christmas specials on TV tonight. We'll watch the 1951 version of 'The Christmas Carol,' and then, 'The Walton's, A Homecoming.' I like saying some of the corny lines. 'John-Boy go milk the cow,' is my favourite.

The car pulls up; everyone comes in the door.

"Get in the house right now!" Mom's voice lashing venom. She pushes Dad in the door, I see what's going on. He stumbles toward his chair in the TV area. He plunks down demanding vodka. "There's no alcohol in this house. You're a drunk." He must have been at the Legion with his war buddies and had too much. "You sit there and don't move." She snarls, her voice hitting the roof. She starts banging pots and pans around to finish cooking dinner.

"I'm not hungry," I say in a weak voice.

"Me neither," whispers Alan who's been staring at the floor.

"We'll eat together as a family. It's Christmas Eve, damn it." Mom isn't thinking straight. She's having a misplaced sense of tradition. There'll be no hiding in our rooms. The Huron Carole plays on the radio, I hum nervously, trying not to think.

We sit down to Christmas Eve dinner of meat pies and reheated beets. The crimson fluid bleeds down my plate, seeping into the pie. Where did our Christmas go? Dad has the power to ruin our family Christmas, and he does. He's the lowest of the low right now with his bobbing, weaving attempts to get food into his mouth. The pie falls from his fork, and he stabs at it like a blind man. He's mumbling about how we're all important to him. So far, there's nothing scary about Dad except Mom's vicious anger. If we can get through the next fifteen minutes, we can all escape.

"I fought in the war by God... it was hell... I was bombed on in London," he slurs. "I want more vodka," banging his water glass down, sending the contents all over the table.

"The war's over... get over it... there's no vodka," Mom spits, jabbing a beet, hurling it into her mouth, shutting the spew for a few seconds.

No one talks when she slams her chair backward, gets up and starts spooning ice cream into bowls. The bowls land in front of us, the contents try to slide out.

Dad's spoon full of ice cream is halfway to his mouth, his chin on his chest; the food drops back into the bowl. He starts to sob, "I was in the war..." I hand him a paper napkin as I get up. Time to go away. Mom can deal with him. Jolly Old St. Nicholas begins... I'd like to slap that radio.

Alan has somehow kept his head down, remaining neutral during dinner. Amazing – when put to the wall of family dysfunction, he isn't part of it this time.

He and I head downstairs, dropping in front of the TV, away from drunken dad and furious mom. We watch the Christmas specials and not say a word about upstairs. Alan's quiet; I look over and see his eyes piercing the screen. Mom doesn't come downstairs all night and I wonder if Alan and I are thinking the same thing. Dad will be okay tomorrow; we can forget about tonight. We whisper Merry Christmas and go to bed under a quiet roof. The sick knot in my stomach has been there for hours and is still there as I try to go to sleep.

Silent night, horrible night.

*

I hop out of bed with guarded optimism. Christmas is here. I'll be the best sister and daughter, with joy and goodwill to all, even Dad. He'll be okay today, and we can ignore yesterday.

Dad's super quiet, I swear he's still drunk. He can't say words without slurring. I don't understand how this's possible.

We raise ourselves up to the occasion and Mom does her best to be cheerful while covering up the elephant in the room. We open gifts, eat fruitcake and shortbread cookies. Mom loves her wood plaque I made, and Dad mumbles out a thank you for the shaving brush. Alan got another turntable!

My big present is a three-quarter length, brown leather coat. It's the first coat in my life that isn't handmade by Mom. I notice the familiar yellow tag from the Salvation Army charity store. I pretend it's not there. When I asked for this coat, as a possible gift, I'd never have hoped to get one even if it is second hand. "Thanks, Mom and Dad," I choke out, "it's *supreemo*," admiring, putting it on seeing it's in perfect condition.

We finish opening gifts. Dad remains quiet, but not contrite. He's going through the motions of not being a total idiot. Alan has already disappeared with the turntable, and the album I bought him.

I have the parents on ignore. I'll be civil to them and speak to them when I absolutely have to. This will be my protest. They probably won't even notice.

I beg off to my room to work on the necklace beading kit that Alan gave me. I hate my life. I tried hard to make Christmas special this year, and Dad barfed over everything. The tension between Mom and Dad is unbelievable. It's like a silent war out there. Mom's snapping at Dad, and him hardly saying a word. My protest of not talking is working. They know what happened is awful. When this gets done, I'm going to ream Dad out for wrecking our Christmas. I don't even care if Dad tries to throw a plate at me – I'm telling him off.

FIFTEEN

It's Boxing Day, all is quiet in the house.

"I'm going to the store to pick up some groceries," Mom barks through my closed bedroom door. I hear the keys clink as she picks them up and walks out the door.

Nice, I can tell Dad off when no one's around. In my mind I've gone over how I'm going to wipe him clean with my wrath-driven speech. I stalk off to the living room, gathering steam, to where he's lying on the couch reading a book.

This is between him and me.

"Dad," I start in on him, arms crossed in front of me, "you wrecked Christmas." Arms uncross, flailing upwards. "How could you be blotto drunk around us? You acted like crap... I'm majorly pissed off at you," I lean into his face with my whole body... I feel like spitting.

Quiet.

The sunlight's streaming through the blinds, a shadow of bars crosses his face. The radiator hisses to life, hot water flows through the ancient iron vessel. "Sit down Kathy," dad's hand gestures toward the little stool, covered with mom's first crocheting attempt. I drag it over, fire in my eyes, heat in my heart, teeth clenched. *This ought to be rich.*

"You ask me how I could be drunk around you," he exhales and takes a moment, "I build up pressure and let it go. I have a drink with the boys, and it leads to another. I start to feel the pressure release, and I keep drinking. That night we were toasting another friend from the war who died recently," his voice depleting into nothing. I see defeat in his face, eyes lowered, a slight slump changes him into a sad man.

"That's no excuse to be a jerk around us." No stopping me now.

"Kathy, I'm trying to explain myself. I'm not looking for you to understand, but I do want you to hear what I'd like to tell you." At the window, a bird lands on a branch and cocks it's head at me. *Go ahead Dad.*

"The war was horrible. I have scars you can't see... they're inside me. We came back from that disaster and got on with living. No one talked about what happened. I'll give you a glimpse. I saw a room full of dead people sitting up like they were asleep... they'd been gassed to death. I've been bombed on in Plymouth. I hid in a building under a pool table thinking my life was about to end. The man next to me was crying and praying... the noise was deafening." He pauses, shutting his eyes tightly. I sit, trying to fathom the dread he must've felt. His eyes open and he looks at me.

“Yes, I lived through it, happily married your mother and raised you two, after a long time being a bachelor. I sometimes drink to forget what happened, but having a family has been the strongest, healthiest part of my life.” He shuffles his book from hand to hand, staring at the wall and then back to me, “You’ve made me happy... I let you down, and I’m sorry.”

Dad’s face is grey. I reach over and take his worn hand in mine, breaching the divide.

This is between him and me.

A cloud crosses the sun – the bars disappear. My eyes well up with tears. “I didn’t know... you keep it all inside you,” halting, whispering.

“It’s what us war veterans do Kathy. We came home, shut up, and got on with life.” He squeezed my hand tightly. “I don’t expect you to understand, or accept my apology, but I’m being honest and hoping I cleared the air. I’ve talked to your mother... she’ll be okay.”

“It’s okay Dad. Thanks for telling me.” I brush tears off my cheeks.

“You’re growing into a wonderful gal. It took pluck to face your dad like this,” he smiles, and I do as well. Now I feel a bit ashamed of myself for acting like a fiend.

“Thanks, Dad.” The back door bangs open and Alan lumbers in, breaking our moment. I lean over and kiss Dad on the forehead. He winks at me, I smile.

Alan peers in the doorway. “Want to play Monopoly?”

“Sure, you set it up... I’ll be right there.”

*

Anne wants me to come over. She has news to share, and I'm happy to get out of the house.

"Rod's dad is getting another military posting within the year... Rod's expected to move with them." The unlit cigarette she's tapping on her little bedside table is going to explode all over the place.

"He'll be graduated, why would he go?"

"They want him to live at home while he goes to college... to save money," Anne squishing her hands together, pushing them along her jeans.

"Would you move to wherever they go?" I can't imagine them not together.

"I guess it depends where. I didn't know how *much* I love him until he brought up leaving... I don't know what to do." Anne pretends to light the cigarette, dragging in the non-existent smoke.

"It's a year away, maybe everything will work itself out. Who knows what'll happen by next year." Now's the time. "So, I got something... umm, you know who I really, really, really like?"

Anne perks straight up, leaning in close. "Ronny?"

"Ronny? What... no way... jeez, he's like a brother." regrouping, "It's Glen." Okay, I finally said it.

"GLEN?" Her mangled cigarette droops out of her open mouth. "Way to shoot for the top! Has he made a move on you yet?"

"He kissed me on the cheek," involuntarily, my hand touches the sacred spot.

"Far-out... I think you're in!"

"Well... the chance of him wanting an underage, grade twelve me is pretty much a no go. I'll never get him... still, I can be gaga over him."

"If I have anything to do with it you *are* going to bag Glen right in his heart. He's not going to know what hit him. He already knows you, he just has to step further into your clutches."

I let out a big Kathy laugh, "What a schemer Anne! Hey, don't tell anyone, okay?" A K&A bump confirms the secret.

*

There's no work with Theareh and no babysitting until New Year's Eve. Christmas break's boring for the gang, but then Ronny shows up at our door. He asks Alan, Anne and I to come outside. In our driveway, is the coolest car I've ever seen. "What is it?" Alan asks.

"Mom got it for Christmas from Dad. It's a Karmann Ghia," Ronny's patting it with both hands. We check out the mandarin orange sports car, looking at its oversized hood and trunk. The interior's tiny, allowing four people to squash into. "Get in... let's go for a cruise!"

We jam ourselves in. The car's roof is removed, so it feels a little less like a shoebox. Ronny steps on the gas, and we're off like a shot. The car goes incredibly fast. We're spinning along back roads I never go on. The corners are tight, and we're driving way over the speed limit. It's a thrill ride, we're all laughing, excited.

We pull back into our driveway; it's by far the most fun I've had on Christmas break. Alan is laughing, happier than I've seen him in a long time.

Mom's a real downer when we get in. "What are you doing in a death trap car like that? They are little coffins for stupid people to drive."

She's such a drag.

SIXTEEN

Back to school today and I totally messed up. I don't like Social Studies, but I also don't want to fail the subject. We had an assignment to finish over the holidays, and I completely forgot about it.

"Kathy, I know you can do better, so I'll give you a chance to bring up your mark from an F," He hands me a piece of paper with the outline idea. "Do an oral presentation on the luxuries of the Palace of Versailles. Explain the architecture, furnishings and how it was all afforded." He shakes his head, "don't mess this up."

"I'm determined to get an A. I mucked this one up... I promise you I won't let you down."

*

I'm at it until four o'clock. Hopefully, I'll get a top mark. Yawning, I hoist the books into my bag and leave the library.

On the familiar path down Dunrod, there's no one else on the road. The whooshing of the giant fir trees sounds louder today. The wind's fierce, the sky's darkening fast. I walk fast, shivering, getting ahead of the storm before it sends in the rain. I look up at the blackening sky, and then down at the little houses along the way. Everything's dead on the branches, looking brown and menacing. Jim's Junkyard sign is squealing furiously, the metal on metal sounds like the introduction to a horror movie. I hurry my pace once again.

As I turn, walking onto Gold Street to go down the hill for home, I see the traffic's all backed up. People are sitting in their cars patiently waiting for the unknown hold up to clear. No cars are coming the other way either.

I don't care; I'm almost home. I'll be in the door shortly and hopefully no drama. I continue down the hill and see a crowd of people in front of our house, standing on the street. Mack is walking toward me. I see he's crying and says simply, "It's Anne." and continues. I step closer and have no understanding of what's in front of me.

There's a grain hauling truck turned over on the road. The grain has exploded everywhere in a sea of beige. Rod's car is on the road, all busted up. The roof has been torn off, and it's an almost unrecognizable, twisted, broken piece of metal. There are people everywhere, standing, crying. Mrs. Smith is sitting on the ground staring at the car. There's a man I've never seen before lying in the fetal position. Shaking all over, his head is buried in his arms. Alan, Mom and Dad are standing, staring at the mangled car. Mrs. Leon, our neighbour, a nurse, is saying, through tears, "It's not good. It's not good."

I go over to the car. The wind bellows through the thick stand of fir near our house. Over the thunderous rolling, I hear the sound of an ambulance coming. It pulls up, as I do, alongside Rod's car.

My mind is disordered; I look in the car and feel my face tighten... I can't grasp this. It seems like part of the grain truck is twisted into the car. Rod's pushed under the dashboard; his head is where Anne's feet should be. A shiny metal pipe has shot through the length of the car, parting their bodies, like an arm trying to keep them apart. Anne is sitting in the passenger seat. She's upright, her eyes closed, looking unharmed, except for the minuscule dribble of dark blood coming out of her mouth, spilling out the right corner. She's wearing the outfit her Mom bought her for the first day of school. The green wool is clean, the blouse isn't wrinkled. The vest has slightly shifted from its perfect fit. Anne's hair is in place. There's no other blood I can see.

The Paramedics are there, with a stretcher sliding in close to Anne. I stare at the workers gently checking her over, assessing injuries. They don't speak to Anne, each other, or me. I watch them raise her up and out, ever so carefully, as if she's an angel lifted on high. I can't help but see that Anne's body is jiggling like Jello with a total slackness that startles my brain into wondering if that's normal after an accident, or is it a bad sign? Anne is whisked into the waiting ambulance. Mrs. Smith climbs in with the medics, and they're gone.

A second ambulance and fire engine drive up, a stretcher is ready for Rod. The firefighters get out of their vehicle, carrying what looks like a giant clamp with enormous pincers on its tips. They descend into the wreckage, start up the apparatus and start prying metal away from Rod. He hasn't moved, and he doesn't move. He's still wedged up under the perverse tangle of car parts. It's taking forever to get at him. He looks unresponsive to the help at hand. I watch, knowing they're doing their best, and then I feel an arm around me. It's Alan. "Let's stand back a bit," he gently leads me away. I see people milling around, I spot Glen in the distance. We walk over to Steve and Ronny, where they've been sitting outside our house for who knows how long.

"Anne and Rod will be okay," says Steve shaking like he's freezing cold.

"Sure," Ronny sighs, and tears seep out of the corners of his eyes. I've never seen him cry... my arm goes around him. We sit in silence, only broken when Steve audibly sniffs and shudders.

We wait like sentinels for Rod to be lifted out. It takes too long, or is it two minutes? The emergency vehicles make a swift retreat, all the lights and sirens full tilt. We're still sitting when the rain starts. Mom comes over to us, "Come inside," she asks in a calm tone, belying the taut, shocked look on her face. She shuffles us to the door, inside the warm house where, on the counter, Mom has left apples: some peeled, some sliced, all turning brown – all abandoned.

The room's quiet; the kettle starts to sing its familiar tune. Alan, Steve, Ronny and I stare at the boiled water swirling into the teapot. We keep watching, not knowing where else to look. Everyone gets tea and resettles, saying nothing, staring endlessly at the brown, cracked teapot.

*

The phone jars us out of our distraught silence. Mom grabs it on the first ring, "Hello, yes, oh, oh, okay. Thank you for calling." Mom puts the phone receiver down on the cradle and turns to us. "Anne and Rod have both been pronounced dead. Rod at the scene, Anne in the ambulance." Mom, the tough person, never showing her sensitive side, bursts into tears. Dad's up quickly, they're hugging and weeping. I've never seen my parent's cry, and never publicly embrace. They hang onto each other as if they may float away untethered by grief. We're looking and not looking at their display of tearful anguish.

"Someone needs to get Mack," I whisper, stunned by the news. "He needs to be here with us and understand what's happened." Realizing Sandra needs to come over, I call her.

I plod through the dial pad, she picks up. Numbly, I manage to say, "you have to come over right now. Anne and Rod have been in an accident." I can't tell her the full truth over the phone.

"I'll be right over..." Her voice is shaky like she's figured out the news already.

"I'll go get Mack," Ronny heads out the door. Mom has broken away from Dad, regained her composure, quietly sniffling.

We retreat to Alan's room to wait. Wait for what?

Ronny, Mack and Glen come in the door. I've never seen teenage boys this messed up. They're crying and not trying to hide it. Sandra and Brad come in, I tell them Anne and Rod were killed in a car crash in front of the house. I get those words out of my mouth. They seem false and unattached to my lips as if I'm reciting something authored from a lousy movie script. Sandra sobs into Brad's shoulder... he pales. We don't speak. Alan puts on 'Stairway to Heaven.' We listen to the loud, pulsing guitar riffs and the wailing voice of Robert Plant as if for the first time in our eighteen years.

"Where are they?" Mack wonders aloud.

"In heaven, of course." Sandra sounds like Robert Plant's last line.

The music's turned off. "They have to be in heaven. Where else would they be?" I say to calm myself while tears flow.

"Are they together?" Alan asks, looking around the room.

“Yes. Rod and Anne are Catholic... they’re in Catholic heaven together,” sounding as bright and hopeful as I possibly can. I need to believe they’re somewhere else, somewhere safe and happy, together in love.

“Will they be okay?” Alan’s voice splits into pieces.

“They’ll be okay,” Glen pipes up. “Heaven is for kind, loving people like Rod and Anne. They’re in a sheltered, warm paradise.”

His words save us from complete, unhinged sorrow. We all shift in our chairs and sit upright. Anne and Rod are in heaven. They’re together, in love for eternity. We’re all pressed together on the couches, physically bonded in tears.

“Our friends are gone,” I say, shaking my head in disbelief.

“Remember Rod got his wheels stuck in the ditch at the lake...” says Steve.

“And she came here and called her dad to get them out...” says Ronny.

Steve looks up from the floor, “bet they never made out there again!”

“And shit, they were so competitive playing games...” says Sandra.

“Monopoly... the battle was on,” I say.

“But they...” Brad says.

“Loved each other...” I say.

“I wish I had that,” says Mack, staring at the wall, his eyes film over with tears.

"They were tons of fun at the Christmas concert rehearsals. They brought Truro, the little mutt dog we had to pull the sleigh, and he starts humping Rod's leg... he shakes him off and then Truro humps the drama teachers leg!" I get a few chuckles.

"One time they showed up at rehearsal with matching green sweaters... ."

"Trippy... ." says Mack

"Dweebs..." says Steve with a smile.

"One of his rugby friends dared them," I say.

"I'm not fucking doing that..." Brad mutters to Sandra. Everyone starts laughing hysterically like we're unhinged from reality.

"Are we going to be okay?" asks Alan.

"Let's see what happens tomorrow," says Glen looking straight at me.

We stand up, hug each other and file out of the basement. Everyone says goodbye. Glen lingers.

"Would you walk me home, so that we can turn around, and I can walk you home?" He's speaking that close to my face; I can feel his warm, sweet breath on my cheek.

"Yes." I follow him up the stairs, grab a coat, and put on shoes. We carry on wordlessly, up the street, to his house. I usually fill the air with chatter because I don't like silence, but I feel, right now, I can't say a word. We arrive at his house and then turn around. At my door, he brings his hand up, tilts it slightly and brushes his fingertips across my face making my skin tingle. "Goodnight Kathy."

Home is quiet. I go into the living room where Mom and Dad are sitting, whispering. "How are you, Kathy?" Dad asks, sighing.

"Anne and Rod are in heaven. It's safe and warm. They're in love for eternity." My response is like a blanket of protection wrapping around my loss. My closest, dearest friend and her boyfriend are gone. I can endure thinking they're somewhere else, together and happy. "Goodnight," they look relieved as I part for the protection of my bedroom. I go over to Snoopy, lift him off the shelf, and hold him tightly in my arms, the way I used to when I was a sad little girl.

How did it happen? Both dead.

I can't... it's not... you can't be gone. The tears flow.

PART TWO

SEVENTEEN

“Do you two want a drive?” yawns Mom, her eyes still red and swollen.

“We’re all walking to school together,” Alan grabs his lunch, “bye.” He seems to be fine. There’ve been no oddball statements like it was the Russians that drove the grain truck or some other weird outburst to worry about. Maybe he’s handling this and won’t be a mess.

The grain is still spread all over the accident area. The truck and car have been taken away. Vehicle pieces are strewn alongside the road. Unbelievable the accident was last night. Time has been suspended like my belief *any* of this has happened.

Ronny and Steve are at Longmore Lake Store. We’re quieter than usual as we walk along, in a line, taking up most of the space across the potholed road.

"Anne loved banana splits almost as much as she loved Rod!" I break the silence.

"Anne loved collecting matchbooks," Ronny shakes his head back and forth, half smiling.

"Rod was the best rugby player," adds Alan. We tell stories like this all the way to school. The reminiscing keeps us walking. I think Anne and Rod could be listening to us from heaven.

*

School is a tomb. Everybody walks by me in a zombie shuffle. People stare at me, but no one comes close except Sandra. We hug and whisper to each other, "they're in heaven, in love and safe." I think everyone knows what's happened by the way the teachers and students look at us with sad eyes.

I gather my books for first class. My blue science notebook isn't in my locker. Oh no. No. *No!* I lent it to Anne to copy notes. She has it. My chest tightens; I try to catch my breath, realizing it's probably in Rod's car. This isn't real... it's not happening... yesterday Anne was alive and I lent her my science book. My heart's thumping out of my chest.

I sit at my assigned table with Sharon and Marylyn – both I've known all my school years. They look at me, with strained faces, saying how sorry they are. I bow my head in silence, barely holding it together. Miss Woods, starts talking and writing on the board while I quietly doodle on a scrap piece of paper.

I'm concentrating on filling in the doodled circle with neat, evenly penned lines. "Where's your notebook, Kathy? What are you doing? Pay attention!" Miss Woods yaps, looming over my doodles.

"It's in, I... I... I," is all that can come out. Free falling, tumbling, dizzy I start to heave. The wind's been knocked out of me. My lungs don't work. I'm desperate for breath.

"Go, Kathy... go... get away from her," Sharon's helping me up and across the room to the door. My classmates glare at the teacher. "Bitch," I hear someone hiss.

"Go to the guidance counselling office... Mr. Hobbs and Mrs. Muir will help you," says Sharon quietly. I lift my head in assent, surfacing for air. Stars are popping out of my eyes, swirling around in front of me.

*

Running – the halls darken around me. I hear the squeal of car tires unable to stop in time. Anne's horrified face, unearthly screams coming out of her, as metal rips metal, shredding, scraping, spinning. Spinning through hallway doors without breath again as my chest tightens. Glass shattering: howling winds crashing through trees: smashing through the destroyed car. Staggering downstairs, a heavy weight bearing down, spiralling through blackness and nothingness. Anne is dead.

*

With shrunken breaths, I open the counselling office door. I see Sandra's blotchy, distorted face. I'm crying and screaming in pain. Don't console me; I'm beyond it all. Anne's gone, and I can't laugh with her again. A flood of hate and anger wells up in me as I cling onto Sandra. How cruel to take our friend from us. The one always full of fun, who never did a wrong turn in her life. Inconceivable rage is pouring out of me, and I allow the agony to fill me up and overflow. I see the counsellors through my haze, their tissue box on offer; I take handfuls and, futilely, try to wipe the grief away.

I'm consumed with an ache that's soaking every limb. My body is in pain as if it's been broken. *My heart physically hurts.*

When I finally move my head off Sandra's wet shoulder, I see I'm surrounded by misery. Anne's friends and other students have come. Some people found out this morning and are still in shock. Others are voicing anger and sadness... tears are everywhere.

I hear the bell ring for class change – none of us move. No one speaks for a long time.

"Kathy," Mr. Hobbs unsuccessfully holding back tears, "Rod and Anne were, are your friends," he fumbles for wording, "You and Sandra knew, know them better than any of us. Could you share a story about them?"

I blow my nose into a fresh tissue. Maybe I can try it. Anne and I had lots of fun times together. Sandra has stopped crying and is looking around the room. Barely audible, she hints, "Kathy can you tell the story about us in the raft, on Longmore Lake, this past summer?" I understand where she's going. The stories and memories shared last night were cathartic. If not for memories, we have nothing. I'll try.

"We all piled into the rubber raft and decided to paddle across the lake. We weren't paying attention to the weather, which was changing fast. The wind decided to pitch up when we were halfway across. The waves were big enough to come over the edge of the raft, and it was filling up with water. We were bailing out the boat with a sandwich bag, a coffee cup and a hat. Bailing like crazy... not able to paddle. None of us noticed Mr. Maclean, the Fire Chief, who lives on the lake, came alongside us in his quiet little electric motor boat. Well... I guess we were all screaming! We were all relieved to get out of the raft. We laughed it off, thanking him for saving us. We walked the raft home on our heads. We looked like idiots... a raft with legs." A few smiles form at the thought of us traipsing down the road, looking wacky.

"Rod and Anne would be lovey-dovey cute together. They'd trade little notes to each other when passing in the hallway," Sandra added to the crack of light in the room. "I have one. Anne shoved it in my purse before the teacher saw it. I'll read it out."

Dearest Anne,

You are the nut in the peach,

The bench under the tree,

And the one taking up all the space in my heart.

Love you, Rod

"Aww!" everyone's drying their eyes.

"He wouldn't win a poetry award!" says Sandra smiling.

"Tell us more stories." And we do – all day long. People come and go. A sandwich appears in my hand, and someone brought water. Where's Rod's gang of friends? Maybe they're with the rugby coach or the gym.

The counsellors stay quiet and in listening mode. Why? I don't know. They don't seem like they're doing their jobs. I've never been to this office and never needed to meet with either of them. Mrs. Muir is definitely hippie material, like Theareh. Mr. Hobbs's hair looks like a rusty scrubbing pad, with a matching, caterpillar mustache sticking out from under a bulbous nose. *THEY'RE DOING NOTHING.* Sandra and I are doing all the talking while they sit stunned, holding tissue boxes. There's no helpful guidance – there is no help.

The end of day bell rings, and I can't believe I've been here all day. My body still hurts, but I'm not crying right now. I'm comforted by happy memories Sandra and I have been sharing.

I'm going home, where despite all that happens under its roof, is the only place I want to be.

EIGHTEEN

Mom makes hamburgers, and we're allowed all the ketchup we want. We sit around the dinner table with me telling stories about Anne and Rod. It worked at school, and it seems to be working at home. No one comes over tonight, so we all watch TV together. First Jeopardy, then The Muppet Show and a Monty Python rerun. No one snaps or gets out of hand. It's the first time in a long time I'm with my family and don't feel like my stomach is in a knot.

*

Mom doesn't scream at me to come for breakfast, and I show up on time, ready for the day. Alan and I take off to meet everyone for the walk to school.

Why didn't we see it yesterday? Jim's Junkyard has two new additions. The grain hauling truck is stored here and is visible from the road. Worse is Rods car, the wreck they were entombed in, now is sitting right there for the entire world to see. It's a hideous, mangled wreck. "Does anyone know exactly what happened?" I ask.

"I think Rod and Anne were crossing Gold Street from the public beach to your place and tried to beat the oncoming truck. That's what I overheard Mom say," explains Ronny, throwing a rock at the wreck. "There's a police investigation about it. People are blaming the truck driver for speeding."

"Was he the man curled up on the side of the road, with his hands over his face?" I think so but...

"Yah, that was him. I wonder if he *was* speeding?" Steve's question is too much to soak in; we turn away. Lots of people speed on Gold Street. In the past residents have tried to get the speed limit lowered to no avail. It's depressing to think it might take death to change a speed limit.

At school, everyone's still walking around like zombies. No one dares bother me in morning classes, and it seems I've been given a wide berth. The teachers have grasped our entire school's in mourning, regardless if the students knew Anne and Rod or not. At lunch, the Greek Gods come over to talk to Sandra and me.

I'm stunned to see they've been crying. Even the most gorgeous, together, bigger than life guys have been taken down.

"How are you two coping?" I say to Arch and Derek, looking into their bleary eyes.

Shrugs from both.

"They're together in paradise... they're not alone. They're in love and happy," recites Sandra hesitantly, as if she's now trying to desperately convince herself of this unknown.

"I get it, but don't you miss them and know you can't hang out together anymore?" Derek's lower lip trembles. I did what would've been impossible at the beginning of the school year – I give each of them a hug, and the gesture is returned. Their muscular bodies are around me, embracing, shaking. Never in my universe, until this day, this lunch hour, under these painful circumstances, would I have ever thought I'd be hugging a Greek God.

Mr. Hobbs and Mrs. Muir come over and ask us to the counselling office. The four of us dumbly trail behind them, swallowed up in our own thoughts. When we're comfortably seated in Mrs. Muir's office, she comes to the point. "Anne and Rod's families have contacted the school. They want to set up condolence books to be signed by the school population, and a fund is to be set up for a memorial in the school. Could you four help out?" We all nod.

"Sandra and Kathy, could you go over to the Smiths after school and pick up the books? You can start the signing on Monday at lunch. The donations for the memorial will be informal... the gifted money brought to the office," Mr. Hobbs avoids eye contact by shuffling papers on his desk.

"I have a recent photograph of them... what if I make copies for those who'd like a memory photo?" I'd thought about this last night but wasn't sure how to fit it in. Everyone nods.

"There's one more thing the families have requested," Mr. Hobbs's looks up; his bulbous nose twitches back and forth. "Could you pick out the pallbearers, Derek and Arch for Rod, Kathy and Sandra for Anne?"

Who else knows their friends better than us? I'll rise to this responsibility. I have a purpose in all of this, and resolve quietly, to myself, to not fall apart and to keep my head on straight. I won't let the families and school down. Do the others get strength this way? I won't ask, in case all the tears start again.

*

"Kathy Johnson and Sandra Blackwell, please come down to the office," I startle out of dummy math class trance, hearing the intercom.

I meet Sandra, and we go in. The secretary waves us over. "Kathy, your mom's going to pick you two up after school to go over to the Smiths... don't walk, she'll meet you in front of the gymnasium." Mom never picks me up; she must want to go together, even though she can go anytime she wants.

We find out what's going on soon enough when the end-of-day bell rings; we see Mom in the beat up, slime green, Datsun 520. "Don't sit on the baking!" The back seat is half full of baked goods: loaves, squares, pies and cookies.

"Is this what people do for a death in a family? They bake a pile of food?" What do I know about death? Nothing, that's what.

"People want to do *something* for the family..." Mom pulls out into traffic, rattling the car into first gear. "Bringing food is sort of a tradition, I guess," Mom explains, gripping the steering wheel like it's going to escape.

"Why doesn't everyone leave them alone? I can't imagine how awful they must be feeling." I burst out, louder than the inside of the car can handle. Everyone jumps.

"I think it's nice for the Smiths to know people care about them," says Mom. I hold down the banana loaf before it sails off my lap.

*

We pull up seeing other cars in the driveway. Their house is always quiet, but this is almost unbearable. I don't know where to look. The tiny living room's full of adults. An older woman, with a severe, tight gray bun, is reading aloud from a bible. Mr. Smith is slumped over, holding a wet handkerchief. He gets up, shuffles toward us, asks us if we would like coffee, and then drifts to the kitchen to fill three cups. Mrs. Smith is sitting on the living room couch with her hands covering her face. She's moaning softly, "it can't be, it can't be... my baby" A lady I think is her sister, puts her arm around Mrs. Smith's shoulder. Always kind, and now these people have lost their only child.

Everyone's dabbing their eyes listening to bible passages. It's so painful. I want to scream, "They've gone to heaven... they're in love for eternity. Remember Anne's goodness!" This is what's keeping me sane, but in my barely eighteen years on this earth, I can't appoint myself to the position of grief counsellor. I drink the coffee quietly, listen to the bible lady, and keep my mouth shut.

We're given the condolence books when getting up to leave. "We'll take care of them and make sure everyone signs." I also add, "I have a photograph of Anne and Rod... I'll be printing copies for everyone who wants one," the bible reader tries to smile. I can't leave fast enough. It's ten times too sad, and the funeral hasn't even happened. I feel a crawling dread.

*

After another peaceful dinner, the gang comes over to play board games. Alan has Neil Young, *Harvest Moon* playing on tape; his little table is set up with Rummoli. Glen sits right next to me; I'm happier than I think I should be. Maybe he truly likes me.

Steve and Ronny come in, "we scored a half sack!" Steve opens Molson's, Canadian beer for everyone.

"Choice," says Glen taking a long drink. "I'd deliver... except I'm broke."

"No big one," says Ronny clinking bottles with everyone.

The game gets going. We're a bit more normal tonight. Glen teases me, "watch your own money pile you."

"Don't mind if I do," pretending to snatch pennies from him.

"We may as well join up and play as a team," he slides himself against me.

"Works for me money bags," I snitch all his cash, and he puts his arm around my waist. I put my hand on his leg, as I casually take a sip of beer. Alan looks at me and rolls his eyes. Ronny and Steve carry on as if nothing's happening.

We're glued to each other for the rest of the night. Glen's hair brushes against mine as he consults with me on what our next move should be. It's everything to stop myself from kissing him. *Later.*

He's the last person to leave at 'kick out' time. "Can I see you tomorrow?"

"Sure," I try to think. "I'm walking to the photo shop to order prints of an Anne and Rod picture."

"Can I come along?" Steamy blue eyes look at me. Oh jeez, is this is a date?

"Sure, see you at ten?" I manage to get out somehow.

"Okay. I'd better split... tomorrow then." He leans over and kisses the sacred spot on my cheek where he kissed me on the night of our birthdays. He leaves me in a state of swoony, head-spinning love. I float into my closed bedroom door head first, banging hard, and then into my room feeling no pain.

NINETEEN

He came through the door in a rush. My head turns to him, heart beating fast, my eyes set upon his raw beauty. I could give all of myself to him at this moment. He swept me up in his strong arms, exuding power and control over my destiny. This kiss will be the moment my life will change forever. He lifted me up onto the kitchen table and put his lips upon my breast. I will never be the same.

"Kathy, why are you reading that trashy novel?" Mom is standing over the romance novel and me at the kitchen table.

"Huh? No reason. Sandra reads them... she lent it to me," putting it down, hearing my own heart beat loudly.

"Life isn't made up of romance... oh never mind," turning away, returning to whatever she's doing in the kitchen.

Ya Mom, never mind. Leave me alone.

"What are you doing today all dolled up?" Mom is beating something in a bowl.

"It's just nice hair and make-up... hardly dolled up." trying to downplay the sort of date I'm about to go on. But I did curl my hair and went over my make up with a fine tooth comb to put on what I hope he likes. "Glen's coming over. We're walking up to the photo shop to order the Anne and Rod prints." I'm waiting for something negative to dash my hopes for the day. Homework's done: the bedroom's cleaned to at least some kind of decent standard, and it's the middle of the day – how much trouble does she think I could get into?

"Let's see the photo," Mom takes it and looks at the smiling couple, sitting at our kitchen table; Rod's arm around Anne's shoulder. "Why don't you ask the person there to enlarge the photo to remove Anne holding a cigarette. Her parents don't need to see she was smoking."

"Okay. Good catch."

*

The door sounds a knock and Glen bounds in. I smooth my hair and wipe my sweaty palms on the sides of my jeans.

"Hi Mrs. Johnson, what are you making?" Glen looks into the bowl with what looks like chocolate chip cookie dough. *He looks like something I want to eat. I'll start with his neck then, taking my time, move to his lips.*

"Here, go ahead... try it," Mom smiles at Glen. Now what's going on? She's nice? Mom's okay with Glen and I spending time together? Thanks Anne for the heavenly intervention! She must be in on this as I can think of no other explanation.

“Bye Mom,” I say after we both stick our fingers in the delicious batter and start out the door.

We walk up the hill, past Longmore Lake store. I dangle my arm close to his side. *Hold my hand.*

Glen shoves his hands in his pockets, “Okay Kathy, tell me your desert island music choice?” I can answer this one.

“If I was stuck on a desert island, with one album, I choose Elton John, *Yellow Brick Road* because it’s a double album and one of my favourites of his.” *My hand is right there. Last night he was touching me, now he seems uninterested.*

“Decent. I choose Led Zeppelin, *Physical Graffiti.* The songs go deep... I feel every vibe,” the groovy sound of his voice is like every romantic song, doubled.

We talk music all the way to the photo shop, all hands in pockets. The shop owner not only agrees to crop the cigarette out of the photo but also to make fifty copies at no charge. “I’m deeply sorry for your loss. It’d be a pleasure to do this for you and the families.”

*

As we walk back home, Glen reaches for my shoulder with an outstretched arm. *This is it!* He brushes a pine needle off my coat returning his hand to the pocket.

He’s not attracted to me the way I am to him. He’s giving me the sympathy treatment with kisses on the cheek. Nothing’s going to happen between us. He feels sorry for me. Crap. Here come the soggy eyeballs.

“What’s going on in there?” says Mr. Pretending to Care.

"My life's been turned around," plowing forward anyhow. "It's like the photo shop guy. It was so nice for him to help like that. People have been extra nice. I feel like an ocean has parted... I'm walking through the divide unharmed."

"Kathy," he stops me on the side of the road under one of Longmore's majestic, Douglas Fir trees. He releases his hands from pocket captivity and puts them around me. I feel the small of my back being gently held. I wish I could stop with the tears. "You've had your best friend taken from you and seen her either near death, or dead in front of you. It's more than most adults go through in an entire lifetime. Nobody has any idea how it must feel to be you right now." His lips move toward mine.

Tears run down my face. "I don't know how I feel either. The funeral's next week and I have to get through it. Are they going to throw dirt on her coffin like in the movies? I'm afraid of Anne going into the ground forever."

He touches my tears with the cuff of his jacket. "I think that only happens in the movies, but we could ask that it doesn't happen." He releases me, and we walk on.

"Sandra and I have to pick out the pallbearers. Would you be one?" I look hopefully into his face.

"I'd be honoured."

At my door, he fidgets with his coat, puts his hands back into jail and brushes a tender kiss on my forehead. *My forehead?* My lips are right there!

Alan appears mid-kiss, halting any further kissing action. "Bye," I say and go in the house. Alan looks at me, rolls his eyes while shaking his head, saying nothing.

*

I sit on the kitchen floor, in the tiny space between the fridge and the telephone table and try not to knock off 'Paula's Best Apple Crumble' recipe, withering on a tack. Sandra answers. I tell her about my day with Glen.

"OOOOOW! Any necking?" Sandra's voice picks up.

"No! He kissed me on the forehead, but nothing else. What's with that?"

"Were you crying?"

"Ya, ya I was crying."

"Why would he want to kiss you passionately right now? He's probably trying to be a decent guy and not be pushy."

"He'll never kiss me properly. I can't stop crying." I look at the floor and sob into the mouthpiece. "Oh, Sandra... I miss Anne so much."

"Me too... I almost phoned her this morning. What are we going to do without her?" Both of us are crying. I sit twiddling the phone cord around my fingers, not wanting to end the call.

"I thought of something we could do for Anne's family," says Sandra eventually. Let's get all of our photos together, make copies and do a photo album for them."

"Good one. Do you want to come over tomorrow after school to work on it?" We make a date.

TWENTY

“Sometimes I feel like a freight train has run into me.” says Sandra laying down the photos and negatives on my bedroom floor.

“Is Brad being supportive?”

“Brad’s not great at the touchy-feely, sensitive stuff.”

“Does he make you feel worse?” I take a negative, hold it up to the light, and mark the photo I want to be reproduced. Maybe she’ll talk.

“I don’t know. When we first got together, he was like a giant warm blanket protecting me from the other shit in my life. I felt stronger with him there for me.”

“What other shit?”

She slumps over the photos, “I never wanted to talk about it before. I didn’t need to dump my problems onto new friends.” She sorts through our Quebec school trip pile and picks out a few.

“I’m pretty sure we’re over the new friends part. If I can take this... I can take anything.”

“You want to know? She drops the photos onto the carpet. “My mom took off with some asshole, leaving Karen, Dad and I. She left us... really left us. I never see her... I have no mom. Then Karen couldn’t take it and killed herself.”

“Jeez.” I know because Glen told me. “I’m so sorry.”

“Not as sorry as I am... I started creative writing again... it works for me.”

“I love what you write. Anything to share?”

Sandra takes the folded paper from her purse and starts.

Facing Our Lives

What shall we do?

Lament, weep and live in sorrow?

Or remember our friends and live!

Memories are alive and live with us forever.

They are dead, and so we cry.

We can’t bring them back to life - so cry!

After your sorrow has ceased, remember they live in our hearts and in our minds

Reminisce and smile, then laugh and let them live on, close to us all.

"You're going to make me cry again. I'd like to think she's still with us somehow... like if I talked to her she would be able to hear me," I say.

"I wish it too. The viewing's on Thursday. They're going to be in open caskets... we actually see their dead bodies. Creepy."

"I don't know how I'm going to get through that and the double funeral."

"We'll have each other. We have all our pallbearers right?"

"Glen, Mack, Ronny, Steve, Alan and Anne's cousin Chris." I count on my hand.

"They'll be there with us. We can do it... we have to."

*

It's *another* calm dinner. "We got grief counselling in Mr. Humphries class. I don't see how it helps. They're not coming back," says Alan shrugging.

"My grief counselling was two stupefied adults sitting there letting Sandra and I run the show. We got no counselling at the counselling office! Way better to have someone trying to sort out the meaning of it all."

"Not sure of any meaning... they're dead." Alan is doing his lost in the universe, far off voice. Everyone shuffles uncomfortably, eating silently, while chairs creak in time to lifting forks.

"I don't know if I can go to the viewing. It's going to be horrible to see them lying there," I say.

Dad puts down his fork and looks at me thoughtfully, “It’s a peaceful way to say goodbye... you may regret it if you don’t go.”

“Okay... Alan, will you sit with me?”

“Yup,” staring off at nothing.

It’s like I’m drowning in a pool of muddy water and can’t see the edge. I’ll have to clear the pool if I’m to get through the next few days.

*

It’s different in the central hall, during lunch, when people come to sign the condolence books. Lots of people are still sad. Pretty much everyone has signed, but Sandra and I set them up anyways. “How are you doing?” is the number one question we get from everyone.

“I’m okay. Wave to them in heaven!” At least I get smiles and people waving at the ceiling. “Say goodbye... see you when I get there!”

*

Tonight’s the viewing, and as I walk home after school, I don’t look into the junkyard. I should go home a different way, but I’m on autopilot and end up walking the exact same route I’ve walked for years. Glen’s walking up the street!

“Where’re you going?”

“Up to meet you... I wanted to ask you something,” he stops and wipes a raindrop off his cheek.

“Err... okay.” Another raindrop lands on his cheek.

“I’d like to sit with you at the viewing.” He looks down at me, his soft hair blowing back in the rain-speckled breeze. He gives me the once-over; a smile curves onto his lips.

“I’m scared it’s going to be a nightmare... Alan said he’d sit with me too.” I look up at him and get raindrops splotched on my glasses. “We’re going from my house at six.”

He produces a black ‘west coast special – buy them everywhere’ umbrella, puts it up, forcing me to walk close to him. I bang into him a few times. Holding his arm would make this easier, but I don’t. Chicken me.

“How are you doing?” Glen asking me sounds like the first time I’ve ever heard the question.

I’d be better if you put your arms around me like you did the other day and then kiss me for real, on the lips. “I’m doing okay.” I look up at him to show I’m not crying. He puts his arm around my shoulder and keeps it there.

We say, ‘see ya,’ at the door, but no kissing. Maybe Sandra’s right. He’s keeping a respectful distance from me. If I had more guts, I’d lay one on him.

*

Storming in, I come right out with it, “Guess what,” to Mom who’s opening a Swifts can of ham for dinner – fancy! “Glen said he’d sit with me for the viewing. I like him. He’s sweet to me.”

“He dresses funny,” she sniffs, continuing to wind the can open with the little key it comes with.

Really? No, he doesn’t. What does she know? “He dresses in the coolest, most bohemian fashion. He’s super cool Mom.”

“Velvet jackets?” she puts the opened ham aside and grabs a can of sliced pineapple. Yummy! “No one dresses like that. And what’s with all that hair?”

“He looks righteous. He’s got his own look!” I take off giggling.

*

The gang assembles at our house and piles into the parent’s cars. The funeral chapel is in Calling. I see it every time we drive through the village but have never gone in. I’ve never known anyone that died.

Rain is sheeting down as if angels are crying their hearts out for our friends. Mom and Dad visited this afternoon so they leave us to run for the chapel door.

Inside the warmly lit room, I feel a peaceful hush. Wooden pews line both sides. Dominating the front wall is a large wooden Jesus hanging on a cross. Under Him, the area is covered with massive floral arrangements surrounding two open caskets. *Anne, will I be okay to see you?*

Mr. and Mrs. Smith walk up the middle aisle greeting us.

“I had to change her hair... they did it wrong,” Mrs. Smith whispers into my ear. Her voice sounds far away, tiny, distant. “I gave them a photo... they did it wrong. I fixed it”

“Oh Mrs. Smith.” I give her and Mr. Smith a warm hug. He looks blanked out, pale.

Sandra and Brad wave – the gang sits next to them. Alan is good about sitting next to me, and Glen’s on the other side.

A gray-haired man in a dark suit, wire-framed glasses and a serious expression passes out a small sheet of prayers for each of us. "Let us begin." We recite the first prayer, and then he starts talking about God. I feel myself vibrating.

I hate God. Why did they have to die? Why are my friends gone from us? Why didn't the grain truck show up five seconds later? Even two seconds would have saved their lives. The mysteries of God are crap.

"'The sword of Narsil has been reforged into Anduril,' " Alan mutters.

"Alan... you're quoting Tolkien?" I whisper at him. *I can't deal with you right now.*

"'Let the thralls of Mordor flee me,'" his chin juts out defiantly. Before he does anything weirder, I shush him. His chin drops to his chest, lips pinch shut. I grab his hand; he whips it away.

Glen reaches across and places my hand in his. I look up and watch him wipe tears. The prayer paper is crumbled at his feet.

People rise to pay last respects. I walk up to Rod's gleaming wood casket; it's brass details shine in the lights.

This isn't Rod. It looks like a wax figure trying to be him. The body is shrunken, skinny and his face has make-up on it. I close my eyes, "Goodbye. You were the cutest of the Greek Gods. Anne loves you, and I hope you and her are having fun wherever you are." I return to my seat feeling ill, and then wait for everyone to see Anne before going up. I need time. After seeing Rod's misshapen body, I'm not sure I can do it.

"Do you want me to go with you?" Asks Glen.

"I'll go alone... if you'll wait for me," unsteady on my feet, I gather myself up, with no courage to be found, and walk to the beautiful white satin casket.

"Anne..." She's lying there wearing her favourite navy blue, white polka dot dress. She looks asleep... not dead. I take off my heart-shaped brooch, a piece of jewelry, a gift on my fifth birthday from my parents– the age I met Anne in Kindergarten. I pin it on her dress.

Taking her hand, I feel a penetrating cold. "I miss you. You're with Rod, and that's what I can live with. I'm going to be okay... I hope. Thank you for sending Glen to me. You told me if you could help get us together, you'd make it happen." Not a hair's out of place. She's wearing the Avon 'Soft Pink' lipstick I bought for her birthday. "Anne... I wish you didn't die." Unbidden moans escape, travelling over her, consuming, crushing me.

Sandra comes and kneels beside me. Her closeness helps calm me. I manage to settle after a while. Neither one of us speaks.

Arm in arm, we see our friend for the very last time.

*

The day of the funeral has come too soon. Anxiety crawls over my skin in an advancing mass of chills. *Kathy, you have to get through this.* Trying to steady my hand while applying mascara is impossible. It's not worth bothering – I'll be crying too much anyways.

The Smiths requested for Anne's friends not to wear black. I feel a bit odd wearing any other colour, but they don't want us to be dour. There's a navy dress sitting in the closet that hasn't been worn for a while because the length is a bit long and the pleating makes it too hard to hem. It'll be fine. Mom, Dad and Alan have been waiting patiently for me. I guess I'm ready.

*

The Catholic Church has dominated the village for as long as I have memory. The large, white building with its soaring bell tower looks oversized for our small village centre. There are a lot of people here, many I know, and many from Rod's side I don't know. Sandra waves; we sit down two-thirds of the way back from the front. I silently hold her steady hand, commanding myself to quit trembling. She squeezes comfort into my palm. Our families and friends surround us. I can't see them; I can only look at the front. Anne and Rod in closed caskets, flowers everywhere and the god I hate staring down at me.

Father Gerald starts the service.

I'm not used to a Catholic service of any kind. It's unlike our plain United Church across the street, in a building a third the size. This reminds me of the palaces I'm learning about in social studies. There are gold cups and elaborate paintings of Jesus and Mary. Elaborate woodcarvings cover the walls. There's incense burning and bells chiming. The Father is shaking water from something that looks like a giant, silver, baby rattle. What gets me in all the pageantry is when Father Gerald talks about Anne and Rod.

“Here is a couple very much in love. Maybe one day, they both would have been here under different circumstances. Anne in a white dress, Rod in a tuxedo.”

Sandra and I look at each other and burst out laughing, quickly clamping our hands over our mouths. It’s the most absurd idea that, at this age, they would’ve contemplated marriage. We’re barely eighteen! Luckily, everyone around us has too much dignity to turn and scowl.

After the service, we slowly make our way out. The families are at the door to greet people as they leave. I’ve never even met Rod’s parents before this moment. They’d sat with their heads bowed the entire time. Their swollen, red eyes try to focus as I introduce myself. They nod, smile, mouths quivering, perhaps acknowledging they’ve heard of me before, but no other exchange happens. I move along.

Glen was able to borrow his Dad’s wheels to take us to the cemetery. I didn’t even know he had his license. The gang piles in for the short drive.

*

The pallbearers make me proud as they lift and carry Anne’s pure white casket adorned with a massive flower arrangement of red roses. Rod has his rugby teammates carry him. His casket is arranged with white roses. The funeral director helps them place the caskets on the carpet laid railings above the graves. There are more words, and both families are staid throughout. Through my tears, I see my friends crying. My parents hang onto each other. It’s sad, I understand, but there’s a grand significance to the ceremony that makes me feel this is the best way to say goodbye.

I remove roses from both caskets to keep forever. I touch Anne's final resting place, turn away, and can't look back. Glen's by my side, he opens the car door for me, I slide in to sit next to him. We're all going back to our house. It's over.

Mom and Dad offer us a small drink of sweet wine to '*calm the nerves'* as Dad puts it.

"It's been a hell of a day," Dad's eyes turn to the floor. "I got a letter after the war from your Aunt Eleanor. I kept it, and I hope it means something to you too." He pulls a yellowed, bent up envelope out of his pocket. Slowly, carefully he unfolds the thin, fragile looking paper. "Let's see if I can do this..." uneven breathing tapers. "Here's the part I'd like you to hear."

" '*Dear Burt,*

When you are feeling low, be reminded once again of how short life is. Go out and enjoy every day with purpose and friendship. We've lived through terrible days, but I know there are good days ahead. Move forward, with intention. Be kind. And as Mother always told us, 'don't hold grudges, they aren't worth it. You don't know when your last day will be.' "

He folds the paper; we all take a drink for Anne and Rod.

TWENTY-ONE

It's been three days since the funeral: casket roses are drying in the little vase Mom gave me, the navy dress is back in the closet. The latest *Sixteen* magazine is sitting on my bed. Its job is to distract me, which it does, but not the way I expected.

Paging through it, I see how much garbage there is about how one must look and act. The models aren't what women look like in real life. The content is superficial. I'm never buying one of these stupid magazines ever again. I can't believe I got sucked into these empty-headed beliefs. My life isn't happening in a magazine.

*

The halls are bursting with everyone trying to get to class. Here comes the Social Studies teacher right at me. "Kathy, I was thinking, if you don't want to complete your oral presentation, I'd be fine with giving you an 'A.'"

"That's okay Mr. Whittaker, I like public speaking... I don't want a free mark. I'll do the work." He smiles with a sort of an 'aww shucks' feature.

"Hey good looking, are you hanging in there?" Arch eyes me on the way to first class.

"Stop with the flirting bad boy!" We both laugh and carry on. I'll enjoy the attention from him, but my eyes are only on Glen.

"Hey Kathy, you look nice today," says Bridgette. At least she's *trying* to not be a bitch.

Clayton rushes over before final bell. "Kathy, I need your help on a student council project,"

"Me?" I lost to him so resoundingly. "Why would you want me to help?"

"Ya, you... I know you care. Come to the council room at lunch if you're in.

"Sure Clayton. Thanks. I'll be there, but don't make me work too hard!" In the last few steps to class, everyone's smiling at me.

"Sit here Kathy," says Bill. Chloe has left this school to attend a special ballet school, so my French partner isn't here anymore.

"Cool."

*

I pull in the door after school and see Mom and Dad both sitting in the TV area. “Hi. I’m sort of back on student council. They want me to help organize a flyer for our graduation promotions.” I plunk myself down.

“Good!” Mom looks up from ‘Grappling Womens’ Issues in the 1970’s’ book.

Dad places the newspaper on his lap. “Are you feeling back to your old Kathy self yet?”

“Getting there... I think.”

“Look, we wanted to talk to you... the thing is... whatever you want to do after you graduate is fine by us, and we’ll support you whatever way we can.”

“You’re kidding?” *What the hell?*

“No, we’re *not* kidding,” says Dad. “You’re a young lady. You need to explore and find out what makes you tick.” He *seems* sober.

“Find your passion in life,” Mom’s voice sounds weak, “I never did. You go for whatever you want that makes you happy.”

“We’ll figure out how to make it happen,” says Dad.

“Anne dies, and you do a one-eighty? Does your deal include Alan?”

“Of course it’s about Anne. Do you think them dying didn’t hurt us too? They died so young...and of course Alan’s included,” says Mom softly. Crap, is she going to *cry?*

"So, let me get the gist of this. You've changed your minds about me going to college or university?" I watch them shift uncomfortably. "No, wait... maybe a job would still be what you'd prefer for me?"

"What do you think you'd like to do?"

"I have no flipping clue... I don't." *What the hell am I going to do with myself?* "I'll think about it. Okay... thanks guys." They both smile and I'd better take off before it all goes sideways. "I'm going to the Vos's right now, bye."

*

Ben runs to the door and goes for the leap into my arms. "You melt my heart," I say putting a kiss on his pink cheek.

"Sorry we haven't had a chance to have you over until now. Come sit down," says Thearah motioning toward the kitchen table. Ben rests on my knee and starts playing with a pile of blocks. Thearah maneuvers a glass of orange juice around his masterpiece.

"How are you?" Dan sits across from us, moving blocks out of the way.

"Weird actually. Everyone at school is so nice to me... like even the people who never gave me two seconds of their time before are talking to me now. Even weirder, my parents are super cool with me. Instead of treating me like an irritating little kid they're way nicer. It's as if they're treating me like a grown up. What do you think?"

Thearah brushes some of the mop of hair out of her face, "I talked to your mom and dad. They're having a rough time coping with your friend's deaths. They're impressed with the way you've handled yourself. Maybe you're the one that's acted more adult than the adults," Thearah offers, looking directly into me.

"Ya, but why are *other* adults so choked up? They were *my friends,* not theirs! I don't get it!" I hear my harsh tone. "No one was rushing to care about us teenagers before they died." Angry tears are welling.

"Do you think maybe the deaths have hit everyone so hard you're seeing changes in all sorts of people?" Dan softly taps a block on the table in time to a Janis Ian song coming from the living room.

'I guess..." I put two blocks together with a loud snap.

Ben jumps and looks up at me, "Wuv ooo Katee."

"Wuv oo too Ben. You make me smile... see?" *This kid...*

"Is it possible people are reevaluating their own lives and trying to make the best of it now?" Dan asks.

"That'd be cool. Hey... Are you going all Social Worker on me?" My tears sink back.

Everyone laughs except Ben who hands me a block. We all build towers in silence for a minute.

"Okay. I never thought about how it would affect Mom and Dad, or other adults who hardly knew them. But it's mostly Mom and Dad that have blown me away."

"What I know is that they love you and want the best for you," says Dan.

"I get it... I think. Thanks for listening to my rant. See you soon," I kiss Ben goodbye.

*

The Longmore Gazette newspaper is sitting at the door; I grab it and head down to see Alan. Thin Lizzy is blaring from his speakers.

Crapulation... a photo of Rod's flattened tin can of a car is plastered on the front page. I turn down the volume and read aloud, "'Teens Die in Horrific Crash. Young Driver To Blame.' Under the caption I read, "'Two teenagers died following a collision with a loaded grain truck that left this auger rammed thought their small car. The driver, Rod Whitehall, cut across the road, causing the fatal accident.'" Jeez Alan, how could they do this to the families? I wonder how Anne and Rod's mom and dad feel? What a crap reminder for them to have it shoved in their faces. It was Rod's fault... he tried to beat the truck. He made one bad decision, and in that split second it cost them their lives."

Alan grabs the paper out of my hands, "Shithead reporting," he folds up the paper.

"Alan. You never talk about it. You hardly ever talk at all. Are you okay?"

"You wouldn't understand," he goes pale.

"You look scared," I turn down the volume again.

"I'm always scared... you should be too."

"Scared of what?"

"The United States and Russia are coming for us," darkness covers his face.

"I don't believe that. Come on... snap out of it."

"I'll be prepared... I'll save you." He's unreadable.

"Fine. I'm going upstairs." *Not dealing with this!*

"Don't tell the parents," he warns, "I'll let them know when the time is right."

"Oh, don't worry. I won't." As if I'd pop the twin bubble and tell them Alan's acting weird again. Maybe his level of grief is higher than mine, and he needs to find peace. Like other people have told me... time will heal all.

*

Later in the evening there's a knock at my door, "come in."

"Hi," Glen peers around my bedroom door, "is it safe in here?" I think his fake British accent might be even worse than mine.

"Snoopy will attack!" He steps in, and I throw Snoopy at him.

"Can we hang out tonight?"

"Sure. Alan's downstairs."

"I mean us," sounding like Prince Philip with a lisp.

"Sure... I'm walking to the Smith's to visit and pick out a piece of Anne's jewelry. It'll be sad though."

"I'll be there for you and with you," he says switching to another type of bad British accent, bowing down, all arms and legs splayed, in a cartoonish fashion, and then tosses Snoopy back at me.

I *'tee-hee'* like the Queen and get my coat. It finally stopped raining, and I can see a few stars peeking out. We walk up the familiar road, except this walk includes him slipping his hand in mine.

*

"Hi. Come on in," Mrs. Smith whispers. "It's good of you to come over." Her hair looks hastily combed, she adjusts a beige, cable knit sweater, hugging it around her. Mr. Smith still looks pale, unshaven and incredibly sad; his drawn face attempts a smile.

It must be painful to live in this house when your only child isn't coming through the door anymore. There's Anne's navy blue raincoat hung up. We take off our shoes and place them right next to Anne's black leather boots. It's like she could walk in the door.

Sandra arrives; I guess she got dropped off– no Brad. She gives me a smile and a wink when she sees Glen and me together.

Glen introduces himself to both parents. I notice he looks right at them while firmly shaking their hands.

There's some kind of religious chanting coming from the radio. We sit in the dark living room, looking at the flecked green wallpaper and emerald green curtains shrouding the windows. On the coffee table sits a painting of Jesus, his hand raised, waving at me. A recent photo of Anne is placed right beside Jesus. "Our Anne is with the lord now," says Mr. Smith.

"Yes," I say. *NO WAY... she's with Rod, NOT Jesus or God.*

On the table in front of us is Anne's jewelry box. I always got a kick out of the white exterior dotted with painted pink ballet shoes because when opening the lid, a little ballerina springs up dancing to Swan Lake. The Smith's ask us to take something. I pick out her puka shell necklace and Mood ring. Sandra chooses a cross necklace and a beaded bracelet. I'm also given a length of dark blue, polyester twill fabric Anne was going to sew into something. "I'll make something snazzy out of it. I'm thinking a jacket."

We stay for hot chocolate. I promise I'll keep visiting them; they want to find out what's going on in Anne's friend's lives. They're both inscrutable – seeming as if they want to talk to us, but I swear they aren't listening. Both are handling a string of black beads. "What are the necklaces for?" I ask.

"They're Rosary Beads... we use them to pray," says Mr. Smith.

"Oh... cool, I see," They each hold a bead on the string and wordlessly say a prayer and then move to the next bead. *Who dreams this stuff up?*

Sandra's dad arrives to pick her up – we make that our cue to leave. I hug them good-bye. Staying strong for them, I don't cry. "Thank you... this means a lot." holding up Anne's jewelry and fabric.

*

I fiddle with the Mood ring, now on my finger. The night is turning out clear and full of stars. I'm quiet about the visit, and Glen doesn't ask any questions about the Smiths.

“Want to walk down to the beach?” Glen asks, putting his warm hand into mine. The heat on my cold skin gives me shivers.

“Yes,” tucking myself a little closer. The crunch of the gravel under our feet reminds me of Anne and I walking down to the shore. *Anne, I wish you were alive, so I could tell you about tonight, me holding Glen's hand, me feeling him next to me. Are you there? I say you are. I hear your laughter in me, around me...*

We sit on the little cement block down at the shore. I’ve been here a thousand times but tonight is magical. The lake is like glass and the night is awash with the glitter of a million stars shining down. ‘*Anne, you’re my best friend forever,*’ I think as I look up to the sky. I’m blessed with a friend who brought me this man, who in my grief, has cheered me up and brought me hope for going forward in life, whatever that might be. Tonight, I only care about this moment.

I turn to him and with his hand, he cups my chin and leans down. When he places his lips on mine, my glasses don’t clunk on his face, I don’t turn to mush, but instead, I respond quietly to his touch. We fit together. I put my hand in his hair gently combing its thickness. There are sounds off the lake; we break to see the resident pair of white swans quietly glide by.

“Thanks for being there for me.” I trace my finger along his cheekbones.

“No skin off... I’m your bad British servant,” his lips nuzzle my neck, just below my ear.

"No one else could have brought my smile back like you have." I shift away. *I don't want to tell him about how for months, I've pined for him.*

"Come here," he kisses me for a long time. I see stars even though my eyes are shut.

"I need to go home now... curfew." I breathe finally, getting up, feeling slightly dizzy.

His arm slides around my shoulder, and I put my arm around his waist. At the door, he kisses me goodnight on the best night of my life. I glide in the door to a quiet house, go to the living room and say goodnight to the parents, then in my room, I sit in front of the mirror and it doesn't mock me. I look at the Mood ring, a deep blue, the colour of love. My whole body is warm from Glen's touch.

Thank you for being here from wherever you are.

I turn out the light and say goodnight to my topsy-turvy world.

TWENTY-TWO

I head out to Glen's. His little brother, an eighth-grader I've been getting to know, is at the door. "Hi, Jay. How 'bout those Canucks?

"They're going to the Stanley Cup... all the way." Both thumbs go up.

"Cool... I think so too. Glen home?" I ask.

"He's in his room waiting for you, kissy kissy ..." Teresa bounces up with something in her hand. When I first started coming over she was shy, but now we're cool. "Help me do my hair? She holds up tie-dye patterned hair barrettes.

"Ya, Ya! Nice barrettes," I put her long, brown hair in a messy updo. "You'll be the coolest girl in grade six."

"Ya right..." she laughs and takes off.

*

I dig Glen's room. It's full of band posters floor to ceiling. Pink Floyd, *Dark Side of the Moon* is my favourite.

He takes me in his arms, "Hey beautiful." At first, when he'd say this to me, I'd say 'no I'm not,' but now I'm used to him saying nice things to me.

Lying on his single bed, we listen to music and spend our time reveling in each other's smell and touch.

His tongue slips into my mouth. A tingle goes through me. My hand reaches around his back scraping my nails down its length. I press myself against him. I feel my bra unfastened. He makes my breasts feel bigger than they are, the way he teases the nipples, cups them in his palms. "More than a mouthful's a waste," he murmurs heading down. I drag my hand through his heavy mane of hair, loving being turned on by him.

*

The mixed cassette tape clicks off; I turn from Glen to flip it over. It's getting harder and harder to back off from our make-out sessions. Better go to the clinic soon. We lay on the bed, all tangled up in a blanket.

"Glen, why pick me? There are lots of girls around here your age, and out of high school." I understand the crisis that set this in motion, but he's still with me after three whole weeks!

"You don't act fake Kathy," he says right away, "I don't dig chicks that try to be something they're not. You're the true deal, purple pyjamas and all."

"Oh, you remember those tacky PJs, from our birthday. I didn't think you were coming over!"

"Babe, don't blush! That's what clued me into knowing you were cool with me and didn't act like a little twit. I felt like I could trust you, being you... without all the immature shit some girls involve themselves in. You're not like that... now I know you're even more than I thought."

"Now you Miss K, tell me." He flicks on the radio. 'Hotel California' is part way through. '*what a lovely place... .*'

I know he isn't looking for me to boost his ego. We're that comfortable together. I believe we could say anything to each other. I confess.

"Glen, I've been nuts about you for months. I dig your velvet jacket styles and all your looks. You're rock solid gorgeous. I love your perfect face, and your hair always looks far-out. You've always been sweet to me, treated me like a friend, not Alan's sister to feel indifferent about. You ended up liking me... no one has ever been interested in me before. I love you."

Oh no! I said it. Why did I say *those* words? They're for down the road, when we know each other better. Why did I jeopardize this relationship? Too fast is what. He stiffens up, and I sense our first complication hitting me in the gut. I start to speak; he puts his baby finger on my lips. He hikes up his lean body, drapes an arm across me and looks into my eyes, "Dear Miss K, you send me righteous vibes." He whispers into my ear, "I love you too."

I think this is love beyond childish love, like when Ben says, "Wuv oo," to me. This is different than the love I have for my parents, which is full of turmoil. I'm shedding my girl skin and becoming the woman I want to be.

*

“Should we work on the posters?” Glen shifts. I unpin my, now, fully-asleep arm that’s been tucked under him. Those stupid magazines don’t write that that’s going to happen. I shake it while setting up glue, scissors and poster board on the kitchen table. We continue a montage poster for Glen’s friend's band using cut-outs provided from my dim-witted magazines. There’s delight as I cut up and make something better out of them. The ‘Ugly Bugs’ have no money to print posters; we offered to make some.

Glen’s parents walk in the door and see us working away like a couple of innocents. Righteous! Caught in the act of *not* fooling around. Glen’s father, a tall, burly, balding man, leans over our work, “Get a job today buster?”

“Nope.” Glen doesn’t even look up.

“Christ! Get out there tomorrow,” rattling a yellow, nicotine-stained finger. “I’m heading to the den.” He leaves, in his wake an awkward silence. I flip through a magazine.

“Kathy, want to see how my latest vision is coming along?” Glen’s mom jumps in. Julie is a flower power, artsy woman originally from France. She has a slight accent to this day, even though she met and married Glen’s dad and came here, far away from French influence. I follow her petite form, swishing brown curls, to where she’s working on the ensuite bathroom redecoration. It’s floral wallpaper, but she cut the flowers out individually and glued them onto the walls in an entirely new pattern.

“Stellar Julie! So creative... I’d love to do this,” my eyes trail along the flow of bright orange flowers up and over the mirror and then onto the ceiling.

“Would you like to go to art school?”

“My parent’s want me to pick something to do... I think it’s going to be a job, not school.” She’s quiet – her eyebrows raise halfway up her forehead.

“If you have a passion, following it may lead you somewhere rewarding. That’s how I ended up in interior design and owning my own shop. Maybe you could get a job that has something to do with art,” she says. “You’d have to look for work in the city... there isn’t much out here.”

“Thanks. I could look into it... I suppose,” smiling politely. *Right now my passion is your son.*

*

Back in the kitchen, I sit down, grab a supermodel and cut off her head. “How’s the job hunt going?”

“It’s a bugger. Nothing’s going on in this newlywed, nearly dead area. Not many jobs around here,” shaking his head.

“What’ll you do?” I pick up the glue and swoosh it all over the poster board, not wanting to hear the answer.

“Don’t worry Miss K. I look all the time... something will come along. I can start applying in licensed joints now that I’m nineteen.” He picks up a guitar and a model, gluing them down.

“Okay... sounds decent,” with a cheerful slant on ‘decent.’ I don’t want him to work at night because we’d never see each other. He needs to find a job, or his Dad will keep bagging on him. I look at the time, we box up the project, and he walks me home.

*

We round the house; Alan is in the backyard, staring at the fence chanting something in very low tones.

“Alan, dude, what are you singing?” Glen tries to sound like nothing bizarre is going on.

Alan snaps out of his trance not focusing on us. His eyes are casting around the sky. “Nothing. Grim... doomsday,” he mutters. He seemed to be doing better. Now this!

“Jesus Alan... you’re so full of it,” I spit out.

“Don’t take the lords name in vain,” angry, he runs into the house.

“What’s with Alan?” Glen says nervously, a smile plastered on.

“He’s got a thing about war, and I don’t have a clue what the ‘lords name in vain’ is all about,” I say trying to not burst our twin bubble we both protect.

“Seriously? There’s no war... is something wrong? He’s never said anything to me.” We both walk over to the picnic table and gingerly sit down hoping it doesn’t collapse.

“I don’t know when I started noticing him acting differently... maybe last year sometime,” I falter.

“Did you always hang out and get along like you do now?” A supporting arm goes around me.

“Mostly. Jeez, I remember tons of good times like when we were little... like we’d play Hot Wheels for hours then make it into a Star Trek story. In the summer we’d be gone all day swimming and jumping off a dock that used to be at the beach. In between we’d run around those hills playing ‘Cowboys and Indians,” I stab my hand at the set of rolling hills behind our house.

“You were lucky to have someone right there to play with,” We’re both looking at the Bing Cherry tree leafing out.

“I didn’t even think about it... we were always together... the most normal thing in the world.”

“What about more recent?”

“There was a short time, in grade eight, he thought Anne and I were goofy teeny boppers, but then that got better when Sandra started coming around, and all of Alan’s friends wanted to get to know her, so we all started to hang out together in one big gang. Ever since it’s been right-on, until now.

“Do you think he’s okay?”

“I want to think so. He’s always been a bit eccentric... he’s super smart, so the teachers say he’s an ‘intellect.’ To me, he’s just my brother who I’d watch Saturday morning cartoons with, play with and be there. I don’t know... he’s just being weird. It’ll pass.” I feel my face turn red as I try to cover what Glen’s seen. “Just ignore it.”

*

After dinner, I head down to Alan's bedroom. He didn't come up, claiming a painful headache. I tack up a 'Do Not Enter' sign on his door, so none of the gang bothers him. There's no lock on the door by order of the parents. No privacy allowed in this house!

"Alan, I'm worried about you. How are you doing?" I ask quietly.

"Did you see the news? Nuclear bombs." I can barely hear him.

"No Alan, there is nothing nuclear in Longmore or Canada. This is something you somehow made up. Why are you saying this?"

"There's a nuclear threat... might be Russia." He's sweating, and I don't want to bother him anymore. His eyes close and he shuts down on me. I'm wondering if he's had headaches other times when he's been odd. Maybe it's a headache problem or stress. I won't mention it to Mom and Dad. I'm sure it's nothing major. The rest of the evening I sit with him, and he asks to have a Yes album put on at low volume. We sit in silence listening to music. I hear footsteps come and go from the door. No one bothers us.

TWENTY-THREE

The next morning, he seems better, but even quieter than usual on our way to school. I avoid eye contact with him. I want to forget his behaviours and not worry about him. Maybe it's about Rod and Anne, and he's still really sad, which is understandable since he was close to them too.

"Hey, I know I asked you already but how are you doing about the deaths?"

"You wouldn't understand," said like a light switch clicking on and then quickly off. He pulls his baseball cap down lower across his eyes.

The thing is, sorting it out in my mind as I kick a rock down the road – we're twins, and *I* seem to be doing okay, and if *I'm* okay, he should be okay. Our brains can't be that much different if we're twins. I shouldn't worry so much. I'll keep my thoughts to myself and keep our twin protection bubble intact.

Glen and I should include Alan in the poster making to see if he'd like that. We should try to hang out more. Alan and Glen have been such tight friends, and now I've gotten in between that. Never mind... everything will work itself out.

*

It's like pre-accident times as we walk home all in a row along Dunrod. The wrecks in the junkyard are long gone to places unknown. Familiar potholes are there to be dodged.

"I gotta get some wheels going," Steve's afro's bouncing all over the place, "need to impress Judy with the bodacious ta ta's."

"Judy with her ta ta's aren't going anywhere with a tool like you," Ronny swings the ever-present guitar around to protect himself from Steve's quick reflexes. 'Killing Me Softly' intro is our serenade.

"Ass wipe, your git box is your girlfriend!" Steve whips a rock at old man Payton's cars on blocks. Even 'Alan The Quiet' laughs.

"Alan, what's that rolled up paper?" I ask.

He unfurls a six-foot section of newspaper print roll.

"What the hell?" Says Ronny leaning in.

"It's the shadow of a Japanese person vaporized after Hiroshima got nuked." We all stop and look at the human shadowed in gray artists charcoal. "It's going on my ceiling."

"You're one freaky dude Alan." Steve shakes his head.

"Hm," he rolls it back up.

"Why Alan. Why that? Was it an assigned art project?" I ask.

"Free class. I got an 'A.' He tucks it back under his arm.

"An 'A'? Jeez, I worked for hours on my Social Studies presentation and got the same mark. My project's normal... yours is majorly strange," I say.

"I should have taken art if it's that easy," says Ronny.

Alan's weird-o-meter just went up ten points. But then... the teacher did give him a good mark.

*

Glen opens the door and lets me in. The house is so quiet I can hear the fridge motor kick into life.

"GLEN! What happened?" His face is all red and swollen on one side. A blackening bruise is rearing up.

"Come." We go up the stairs and turn right into his bedroom. I sit on the bed beside him. "Courtesy of the old man. No job... I'm getting kicked out soon."

"Crap. You'll get a job..." What a dick head for a father.

"It's not going to be around here. Alberta's got jobs... I'll have to head there."

"Don't say that! Keep trying...let's look at the Classifieds again. Maybe you missed something?" I jump up to grab the newspaper lying on the floor.

"I rechecked it." I sit back down next to him. "He told me to cool it with you... you're a distraction."

"Me?" I knew it was tense between them. But hitting him, and including me in the problem?

"He's being an asshole... Mom will talk to him." He flips a cassette into the player and snaps the start button. "And I haven't gone yet Miss K, so come here. I want to do something to you."

His hands carefully pull the blouse away from my jeans, tracing up my back slowly. Heart, 'Magic Man' is playing. "Glen... you know what this song does to me?"

"That's why I'm playing it," I'm drawn back onto the bed, straddling him as he works to unclasp my bra.

"Magic hands," kissing his forehead: the tip of his nose: the nape of his neck, avoiding the weal. He takes my breasts in his hands. He lingers, touching taut nipples, caressing.

I sit up on him feeling his hardness. Slowly, I undo his shirt buttons, my tongue travels down his chest. Its smoothness is rustled into a sheen of sweat. My blouse and bra go away.

We've gone this far. Should I? I don't want to get pregnant. So far, I've only felt him over clothes. I lay beside him; my fingers play with the snap on his jeans.

"Yes," he whispers, reading my thoughts. I work his snap until it pops and work the zipper. "Yes," he sighs. I touch him for the first time, my hand on his flesh. All clothing disappears. My hand is stroking; he responds like a fire raging... eyes closed, body moving with me. *I want to...*

His hand goes exactly where I love it to be. This time, we are naked. Pressing, caressing, *that circular motion.*

His fingertips are persistent, unyielding. My breath is fast. My back arches toward him. Everything explodes... I'm gasping, tremors hit me... it's a rush I've never felt. Involuntarily, I move on top. I have him in my grip and make a move to put us together. My hips shift over to meet him.

"Oh crap... we can't do this," coming to my senses I let go.

"No!" His face contorts: eyes closed, head rocks back. His hand replaces mine and in two strokes a burst of fluid covers my belly.

"Fuck. That was close... I was having a good time," Glen props up on his shoulder.

"No one in those stupid magazines tells you what to do with all the goop," grabbing my underwear wiping up the sticky mess and then shoving it into my jeans pocket.

"You okay Ms. K?" He grabs me up in a body plastering naked hug.

"I'm okay now... Glen, what happened with your ex Valerie?"

"We did everything but the deed. She was pretty religious and wanted me into all that... not my scene, so I spilt.

"You've never gone all the way?"

"Nah... I date good girls... like you babe. "Did you enjoy the big 'O' that sent you rocking?"

Why am I feeling shame? The heat is on my face. "Sure." *It was me that was ready to take the chance and go all the way... stupid.* I put my clothes on quickly.

"That was hot," Glen shifts against me.

"Best one yet magic man. Let's do it again, but I can't get preggers. I'll go to the clinic."

"Sure babe. I don't want to be a father."

TWENTY-FOUR

I wake up early to get homework and bedroom clean up done. Juggling school, homework, Glen and adding work with Theareh is a lot to deal with, but I'm motivated.

Before Sandra comes over at one o'clock, we have a special nostalgia lunch. Jonny Quest is on at noon like it was every Saturday when we were little. It's a special rerun, and we all hope its the one with the giant eyeball spider. It's scary – we dig scary! All four of us get ready, and Mom has gone to the trouble to make Cheese Dreams the way we used to have them. Open-faced white bread with lashings of Cheez Whiz topped with a tiny, postage stamp sized piece of bacon, and then broiled in the oven to bubbly excellence. We sit with equally nostalgic, lemon flavoured, sugary juice and start the show. It's the one about the giant eyeball spider! Alan, Mom, Dad and I sit glued to the screen and enjoy all of it. I look around the room and wonder if we'll remain calm. Mom and Dad are trying hard to make home life better for us. I wish it didn't take Anne and Rod dying for my parents to be kinder.

*

I'm eager to hear Sandra's latest work and spend time with her. I never saw her as much as I saw Anne because she lives farther away, has a job and a boyfriend. I miss Anne to the point I think I'd go crazy if I opened that door all the way. I try not to dwell on what I can't change... but it's hard.

The door softly taps, and I let her in. We sit in my bedroom; Alan joins us on the floor.

Sandra is starting a short story about our grade twelve year and will include the loss of our friends as the climactic part. I wish I thought of writing about it. She'll take it up to graduation, four months from now. She reads the beginning.

"*Grade Twelve was going to be the happiest high school year. Everyone was on deck for those last perfect few months...*"

It's light-hearted, and she's kind about everyone. She makes it sound like we live in a picture-perfect land and I think it's fun, but not our real life.

Alan's turn and he has one poem to read. He solemnly draws the paper close to his serious face.

'The trees wave

They are the earth mothers, and I listen

There are the rocks holding the earth in place

They stay silent.

The waterfalls roar and I hear a cry.

Nature is in me, and I hear.

The End'

Sandra and I affect normal faces, so we don't discourage him. "Decent Alan... really deep!" I think I sound positive.

Sandra's critique is equally positive, "Great allusions Alan."

Oh oh. I see Alan drifting off into weirdo land. He eyes cast off to the wall and shakes his head. "It's my fault," he's barely there.

"What's your fault Alan?" Says Sandra turning her head so she can see his face.

"I made him do it..." his hands are brushing against the carpet like he's removing a deep stain.

"Who's him, and what did you make him do?" He's doing his oddball stuff in front of Sandra. Crapulous.

"I distracted Rod that day... I waved at them. He was looking at me, not the road... I killed them," his head lowers into his lap.

Sandra and I look at each other. "Alan," she says quietly, "It's not your fault."

"Yes. They told me it was my fault," he sighs, head still buried.

"It's not your fault. I hate to say it out loud, but it was Rod's fault. He was driving and should have looked for traffic." I say.

"Who is 'they'?" Sandra asks.

He pops up, looks around and gets up so quickly the papers scatter around the floor. "I gotta go." He takes off without saying anything else. We're left to stare at each other.

"Alan... he believes it was his fault. There's no way... could you talk to him later and make him get some sense?" asks Sandra, collecting the errant papers.

"I'll talk to him. He's been acting weirder and weirder... I don't know what to do."

"Do your parents see him acting weird?"

"No... he's become quiet around them. We promised each other a long time ago to protect each other. I don't want to tell anyone about it... I'm hoping he snaps out of it."

"He's eccentric," sounding thoughtful as if this idea just popped into her head.

"Eccentric? Maybe that's it... he's being artsy and bizarre! Why didn't I see this? He's not going nuts... he's his own kind of wacky! Everything's going to be fine." A giant weight comes off me.

"Be proud of him. Don't worry... he'll be fine." Sandra sounds sure of herself.

"You're right... everything's cool. How are you and Brad?"

"I feel like we're an old married couple," she says a little too lightly. "We're good. How about Glen?"

"Well, Ms. Worldly Woman, I want to go on the pill. Will you come to the clinic with me sometime soon?"

"I'm not *that* worldly! Of course I'll go with you. When?" We both stare at the 'Longmore's Hardware Center,' calendar on the wall. I'm either with Theareh working on baskets, or selling them, and Sandra's working at DQ. We pick a Saturday that works for both of us.

"I'll tell Brad we're going clothes shopping... he won't want to do that. We'll take the bus in."

Obnoxious honking comes from outside the house, "Brad's here... see you in school," she says, getting up, putting on her raincoat.

"Bye," and there she goes to dick face's car.

I hate to say it, but she isn't Anne. Sandra's a sweetie, but Anne was my best friend and confidant. I miss our talks, hanging out and being funny. Sometimes I sit and whisper to Anne sharing my inner feelings about Glen. I believe she's an angel on my shoulder. I don't want to forget her; she's in my conscience.

*

"Alan, believe me, it's NOT your fault!" The music is loud as usual.

"Not now!" He turns up In-Da-Gadda-Da-Vida.

I turn it down. "Please listen to me... we never talk anymore. You're scaring me... you're acting eccentric or weird... I don't know anymore."

"Worry about yourself... don't worry about me," he mumbles, hugging an Isaac Asimov book to his chest.

"You didn't cause their deaths... please believe me." I feel my arms losing control as they dart around my pleading.

"You don't know... you weren't there." He looks at me accusingly like somehow that afternoon could have played out differently.

"I wasn't," I slump further on the couch, "but you didn't, so stop it with the blame."

“Never mind,” he reaches for the volume control.

My hand gets there first. “Do you want to talk to the school counsellors?” I ask, even though I think they’re useless.

“No way... not even close. I don’t need help... I’m fine. You’re the one with the hang-up.” Up goes the volume, so I leave.

TWENTY-FIVE

“What the HELL is this?” Mom storms into my room.

I’m going to die... she’s holding up the goopy, now crusty, underwear.

“Are you two having sex?” Whispering, vicious, throwing it at me.

“NO!”

“Don’t lie to me Kathy!”

“I’m not... I’m not lying... leave me alone... I’m not doing anything bad.”

“You get pregnant and you’re out of here.” Her whispering isn’t a threat. It’s a plan.

“I’m not doing anything bad...” tears of guilt, and shame, pour out.

“Nothing bad? What the goddam hell do you think you *are* doing? I can guess well enough... opening your legs to the first guy that comes around. You’re a whore... you *look* like one most of the time. You’re not even good enough to be called a slut. You sicken me.” she backs out of the room, her face a contortion of disgust.

I grab my purse and coat and then run out of the house as fast as I can before she can accuse me further. I’m at the payphone outside of Longmore Lake Store not really remembering how I got there. Sandra picks up.

“Mom went ballistic on me... she said I’m a whore... and a slut,” I tell Sandra through my bawling what just happened and where I am now.

“Is she crazy? You’re a goodie-two- shoes!”

“I don’t know what she is, but I can’t go home right now. I’m walking to your house,” I wipe my face off with the sleeve of my coat. Two neighbourhood kids look at me laughing. I turn away.

“It’s a long way, and I can’t pick you up.”

“I don’t care... I’m coming over.” I hang up and start running.

*

My breaths are coming in rage-filled gasps, but when Sandra opens the door, I have nothing left except my truth to share.

"Oh my God... come in, no one's here except the cat." Sandra hugs my sweaty overheated body and then leads me to a brown cloth couch covered in cat hair. *Days of Our Lives* is on TV. I smell cat pee coming from somewhere.

"What's going on with your mom?" I take the glass of water offered.

"She's nice and then she turns into a bitch. No one knows about how she is... don't tell anyone."

"Between us... no worries," says Sandra.

"My mom... well..." I stutter along not sure if I should confide a family secret, but I plow ahead trusting Sandra. "Dad says she had a tough start in life and that's why she has 'blackout anger' as Dad calls it. She had a shit childhood... sick parents and they were 'dirt poor,' but we don't really talk about her crappy past. We just keep her moods and her past swept under the carpet like it can go away if we hide it deep enough. I'm not a hundred percent sure that's it... I'm guessing. Whatever it is, she drives her anger over me like a tank on a mission. And she doesn't treat Alan like this."

"Kathy..." Sandra holds me as I place my head in the crook of her shoulder.

"She was nice after Anne died, but now she's gone back to being mean. It's like being nice is fake, and this is the real her. But this time was different... she was worse." I sit up and wipe salty, sweaty tears away. The chilled water splashes down my parched throat. I place the glass down quietly.

"I'm so sorry," Sandra's voice is calm.

"Mom hates me... *my mom hates me*... I saw it in her eyes. She thinks I'm a whore." I hear myself falling apart, sobbing.

Teddy, the cat, jumps up onto my lap pushing my hand for a pat.

"Mom wishes I died instead of Anne." Saying the truth out loud helps me understand.

"No!" Sandra grabs me by the shoulders and shakes me hard... *Jeez, Anne would never have done that*. "Stop that... No one wants anyone to die like that. Look at me Kathy."

I lift my defeated head from Teddy's glare. "It's true," I mumble.

Her brows knit together; eyes stare into my sadness. "No one wants you dead... look at me!" She shakes me again. "You're having a low... *look at me Kathy*." She brushes stringy sweaty hair from my red puffy face and sets her beautiful eyes two inches from mine. "Your Mom's being a psycho. Do you think Glen loves you for no reason? You are hugely loveable Kathy... I'm so lucky to have you as my best friend. You are loved. I love you... Glen loves you."

"Thanks... okay... I know Glen loves me and you... you love me too. But what am I going to do?"

"This is what... we'll get an apartment together in town, after grad. Let's split from all the bullshit."

"Say good-bye."

"Yah! Friends forever!"

"Friend's forever! I can hang out with Glen without crap parents treating me like crap. I'll get a job, any job to get out of here. Do you think you could do it?" I grab Teddy up into a fuzzy cuddle, feeling a bit better.

“Ah... about the getting away deal... I have news. I may get a grant for U Vic... we can get a place near the school!” Sandra’s hands are clenched with hope.

“No way! You have a shot at a university grant? That’s super cool!”

“Well, I haven’t aced it yet, but it’d get me out of a money pit at least a bit... school’s expensive!” Sandra’s got joy all over her face.

“I’ll keep all my fingers and toes crossed for you! I might look into a grant, but I still don’t exactly know what to do with myself.”

‘You’ll figure it out... maybe Glen and you will work it out together.”

“I’ll believe you Ms. Worldly.” I get up to leave.

“You going to be okay about your mom?”

“Here’s something... she was pregnant at the altar, so who’s she calling a whore?”

“No shit! You’re not the whore... she is. We both have whoring moms.” I don’t know why this is so hilarious, but we’re both laughing it up big time when I walk away.

*

I slog my exhausted body home, dragging my feet. I wonder which mom personality will be there. “I’m going to my room,” I yell as I enter.

“Come here.” Oh no... more humiliation.

I stick my head into the living room where they are reading. "We're thinking of the best for you Kathy. Understand that we want to you to be a decent young woman," says Mom all calmed down, head spun back into normal position.

Dad looks up from his book. "We worry about you. We don't need to talk about this anymore... behave yourself."

Yah, you're thinking I'm going to get knocked up like you knocked up Mom. "I am," then I back away from the judge and jury. I'll put the parents on ignore as much as I can, but I have to follow the rules and be on best behaviour for a while longer. I'm getting out of here.

*

In the bathroom I notice a glint in the wastebasket. The razor blade looks brand new, inviting, tempting. I've heard of other girls doing it. In my room I put it against my upper arm, above my sleeve line. The edge bites against my skin, I press a little harder. It would be so easy to feel the blade break my skin, letting out my fury in a red stream of pain.

My reflection in the mirror stops me from going further. I return it to the bathroom garbage, rechecking my reality.

Glen loves me. I've got him and I love him. He's so much more supportive than shit head Brad and the controlling, manipulative way he treats Sandra. I'm the luckiest girl in the world to have an incredible, loving boyfriend and my angel Anne looking out for me. *Kathy you can get through this homelife shit... just wait it out.*

*

Glen's been in the city every day looking for work. I see him after school on most days. Today he's in front of his house, arriving just before me.

There are plenty of lovely kisses to enjoy, and then he gets serious. "Follow me, Miss K." We head up to his room, and instead of kissing me again he says, "let's sit down... I have news."

Gurgle goes my belly. What'll it be? Are the Ugly Bugs touring? Has he been kicked out of the house? I swallow hard and wait.

"I got a job..." he begins.

"Fantastic Glen! Super cool... way to go! Where and what?"

"It's in the Arctic on a Coast Guard ship."

"The Arctic? I hate Longmore. No jobs, no hope and everyone goes away." I'm shaking hard from the hurt I can't see straight. "I lost Anne, and now I'm going to lose you." I grab my stuff and run. Glen starts after me. I'm out the door.

"Stop! Come back... let's talk about it," Glen appeals to my backside escaping as fast as I can.

"No... leave me alone." I run home, on the well-trod path.

I bang my way into the house and Mom looks at me in total bewilderment. "Is it that bad, whatever it is?" I ignore her and run into my room, slamming the door. She doesn't even say, 'no slamming doors.'

I can't lose him too. Anne sent him to save me from this moment. I can't stand the thought of being alone without Anne *and* Glen. He'll leave this lousy, depressed area and never look back – especially not to me. *Anne, **do** something,* I ask in silent desperation. *Save Glen from leaving me.* I grab Snoopy into a big ball in front of me and curl up. I don't want to see the world. Everyone can piss off. I don't want to lose another person.

Mom knocks on the door and comes in with an envelope. Her mouth is curved down in a show of sadness, like she even cares. "Glen dropped this by for you." She hands me a red envelope, with a broken heart drawn on it. I recognize Glen's artwork, and I take it. Mom retreats and I'm left to read.

Dearest Miss K.

I have broken your heart and for that my heart is broken as well. My heart won't mend without hearing the beating of yours next to mine. I love you with all my heartbeats. Please don't keep me in pain. I want to talk to you.

Love Glen

*

Somehow, I have to get my act together for Theareh's last night of basket making. No one talks to me or looks at me when I walk through the kitchen. They probably think Glen and I broke up.

I drag myself over to Theareh's. I can't let her down, even though the last thing I want to do is make baskets. I'm a post crying mess as I enter their house. I give Ben a hug and my best "Wuv ooo."

We get going, and I start sniveling. “OKAY. Spill it, Kathy... talk to me. What is it?”

“Glen’s leaving because there’s no work here. He got a job in the Arctic working on a ship. I can’t even join him when I graduate. He’s leaving me and why would he ever come back to this dreary backwater of a no nothing, no job village?”

“I see,” she pushes a plate of carob cookies in front of me.

“I got him, and now he has to go. Anne left me and now Glen. He gets a job far away and I stay here.” I blow into a tissue, trying to smarten up. She gets up, switches on a macramé covered lamp, and I struggle to stop crying.

“Kathy, what are *you* going to do?” We both hit the basket assembly again. It has to get done.

“Move to Victoria with Sandra and be miserable,” I moan, plunking a pink candle into place.

“Oh, Kathy... you’re not built to be miserable. I’ve seen you pass the misery test with flying colours... it isn’t in you to be sad. You know, if life isn’t going your way, you *do* have choices to make changes. What do you want? You must have *some* idea by now.”

“I can’t go for more schooling. It’s like I’m in jail serving a sentence and I get released this June. I don’t care enough about learning, and I haven’t had huge success in school. My brain can’t concentrate well on schoolwork. There must be something out there for me, but I don’t know what that is. I need to work... I like art and people... I don’t have much money. I know I don’t want to take my life for granted because if anyone knows how short life can be, I think I’m a worthy candidate for having first-hand knowledge. There you go... my life’s going nowhere but wanting to go somewhere.”

“I want you to think about something and don’t answer right away. What if you went somewhere for the summer to work? You could find a girlfriend to come along. Go and get out of here for a little while. Glen doesn’t have to be the only one having an adventure.

“Me leave? How would I make that happen? My mind’s whirling with Thearah’s idea.

*

It’s early enough for me to see Glen and explain my sissy behaviour. I phone and ask him over. For privacy, we’ll meet in the backyard.

I hear footsteps, and he joins me on our rickety picnic table.

“Glen, I’m sorry I flipped out on you. I was a drama queen and I don’t mean to be angry at you.” I wait in the dark for him to say something. Agonizingly, he doesn’t say anything for what seems like a very long time.

"I would never try to hurt you, Miss K., I'm sorry I got this job too, but I have to take it... the parents expected me to agree. It's a *preemo* job... with decent pay. I know I have to leave, but it's only for the summer... I promise you." His arms go around me, making the picnic table jiggle.

"Tell me about the job then." I put my arms around him, snuggle in and try to be open-minded.

"I'll take training in a classroom, starting right away, and it goes until June. We leave at the end of June for just over two months. I'll be collecting weather data and counting whales. There's more to it than that, but I can't remember every detail they told me today."

"You'll be here for graduation! It sounds like a far-out job... how'd you get it?"

"Who you know worked this time. Mom knows some government dude and she's been asking him about work for me. It's a special program to help young adults get job training. He helped get me in the door for the interview... I was chosen with a few others."

"I hope you get me when I say I'm afraid of losing you too."

"I get it... I won't leave you... I'll be back.

*

All this week I think about leaving Longmore for a job. Maybe I *could* do it. I finally pass the idea onto Sandra. "What would you think of us leaving for the summer to work somewhere else, like a tourist place where they hire people for the summer months?"

“I’d do that! I could work and focus on writing without Brad being around getting jealous. He doesn’t like me writing because it takes me away from him. I’m getting tired of him complaining all the time... he doesn’t respect my passion.” She’s smacking her hands on her knees over and over. I see her exposed wrists.

“Jeez Sandra, your wrists are all black and blue. What the hell?”

“Oh, shit... you’re not supposed to see that. Brad got a little physical about the writing.” She tugs down her sleeves to cover her wrists.

“You can’t stay with him! He’s mean to you! You deserve a nice guy! We have to leave!”

“I know, I know... he’ll get better... I know he will. He’ll be fine... he loves me! But how do we get a job somewhere for the summer?” She’s tapping her hands together, thinking.

“I don’t know.” I have to get her away from dick head asshole.

“I’ll ask Dad. Ask your parents too?” She’s up, pacing around in front of me.

“They’ll be happy I have a plan cooking up.”

*

We make our way through Mom’s yucky, homemade, scratch version of Hamburger Helper, or as I like to call it, ‘corn filled sewage,’ and I start with my idea. “I’m thinking, if Glen’s leaving, then maybe I should too. I could go somewhere else to work.”

“You sure as heck aren’t going to Alberta with all those drunken rednecks,” Dad snorts. He’s been sober a lot lately, so there shouldn’t be a fight... I hope.

“I don’t know what to do, where to go, or how to go about getting a job somewhere else... I’m asking for your help.”

Alan looks like he’s about to birth a chicken. He’s goggling at me like I have ten heads. Too bad. My life, my plan.

“I may be able to help you. Your cousin Gwen worked in a tourist lodge in the Yukon years ago. You could talk to her.” Mom’s on board?

“I don’t know her... she’s way older than me. Would those kind of jobs exist anymore?” I ask, trying to ignore the look on Alan’s face.

“Probably... where would the jobs go? I’ll call her and ask, and then you talk to her.” She looks at Dad, both are smiling.

“Okay... are you two cool with this?” I wipe sauce and wonderment off my face.

Dad and Mom both nod, “a summer away could be good for you,” Mom says. They want me gone.

*

Could this happen? What am I getting myself into?

“Hi Gwen, it's Kathy. I haven’t seen you since I was twelve years old, and now I’m graduating high school! So... Mom told you about me trying to get a job in the Yukon.”

Gwen sounds cheery on the phone. "Sorry I haven't kept up with your family. That's what happens when you marry and get a job in Victoria! Life's busy... but good! Yes, the Yukon... I had the best summer! It's a place completely different from here. It's wild... the sun's up most of the time, and it's full of interesting people from all over the world. You'd have fun working in a tourist lodge."

"How do I find out where to apply?" This seems impossible. I tap my pencil on the waiting paper, ready to gather information.

"Go to the main library in Victoria, get the Yukon telephone book from the reference section, and apply in all the tourist accommodations listed in the yellow pages. You'll have to mail a lot of applications."

"Really? That works?" I drop the pencil on the floor.

"It does! The businesses don't have a lot of ways to find staff for the summer season. They rely on people like you to apply through mail."

"What kinds of jobs are there?" No need to take notes. There's no way I'll forget this conversation.

"You'd probably get a job as a waitress, or a chambermaid... I'm envious of you. I loved being up there... you'll have a fantastic summer!" Gwen's enthusiasm is *supreemo*. She makes me think I can do this, and it'll be fun. She pours on, "We met geological crews, surveyors, gold miners and plenty of tourists. It opened a whole new world for me.

“Hey, thanks loads Gwen. You’ve helped me figure out what I should do after grad. Great talking to you after all this time!” I hear her laughter over mine.

“Please let me know how you get along, and where you end up,” says Gwen, and I promise to stay in touch with her. I hang up the phone; my brain’s exploding.

*

After I relay the conversation to Mom, she says with a sigh, “I never had a chance to do these things when I was your age. Women didn’t travel like that. We were all supposed to get married and have children. The women’s place was, or is, in the home as a homemaker.”

Maybe she resents Alan, Dad and I and that’s why she’s psycho. “Thanks for helping... maybe it’ll work out. I have to write up some kind of resume, go get the addresses, mail it all and hope something happens. Oh ... I also have to tell Sandra! What am I going to put on a resume? I haven’t worked.”

“Yes, you have,” Mom gets some writing paper and hands it to me,” you at least worked at Chan's one night, and you have all of the craft experience with Theareh. You sold crafts, took cash and gave change. You’ve worked with the public. Make all that stand out in your resume. The employer will see you have skills that translate into any type of job.”

“Okay.” Well, look at Mom being all helpful and one hundred percent positive... not even a bitch. She’s never going to say sorry about going all underwear freak show on me, so I’ll play along. “Thanks again Mom, I appreciate it.”

*

I call Sandra; we plan to work on resumes during lunch. We're not saying anything until we get some kind of job. We have a lot to do in between all our other stuff. "I'm not telling Brad... keep it quiet around him. We can do most of the resume writing, printing and envelopes at lunch. We'll go down to the Victoria library on the weekend."

"I have craft fairs with Theareh both days. Can you go?" I wish I could go, but I want to get the addresses as soon as possible and get going. Jeez, I need to go to the clinic too.

"I'll go on the bus... I want this as much as you. Think of how much writing inspiration I can get from a new perspective." Sandra's brain has already moved her away. Hopefully, this summer will end her relationship with crapstick Brad.

Next, I zip to Glen's house and throw a pinecone at his window. I still don't want to see his dad, even though he should be happy Glen's going to be working. He comes to the window like some reverse Romeo and Juliet scene and meets me outside. We go for a long walk and I explain my plan.

"Far-out... you're right-on about getting out of here. Nothing's going on in this dump of a village, and it'd be righteous to leave at the same time. I won't miss you as much... you'll be having your own hip summer."

"I love you Glen... you're the coolest dude." We walk around, dreaming of what's next.

"I don't want to get my hopes up too high, but Gwen was super cool and made going there sound like a rad experience."

"You'll get a job."

"I've been thinking a lot about Anne. She lived for such a short time. Most of it as little kid doing what her parents asked her to do, and then she had teachers *and* parents telling her what to do. She never got a chance to plan a future or follow a dream. She never got to have other life experiences. I don't want to sit here any longer having none myself. Everyone says to never take life for granted."

"What's life all about anyway? What are we here for? Anne and Rod's lives were too short," Glen's voice is soft, contemplating.

"I want to remember and honour her life. I want to keep her memory with me *always.* Her spirit's with me and I want to not only live my life to the fullest, but also live life for Anne... the one she never had a chance to live. I'm scared... but I think I can go out into the world... for Anne and me."

"That's why I love you Miss K."

TWENTY-SIX

"I think we can get the resumes done by this weekend."

"You're making us look good... it's *supreemo* bs!" I take my copy and read how fantastic I am on paper.

"Brad thinks I'm hiding something from him. I had the *Write your Winning Resume* book sticking out of my purse and he saw it."

"He didn't hurt you?" Scrunching my face, not wanting to know.

"No! No, but I had to lie about the book... I said it was to help you get a job... I think he bought it."

"Okay... if I see him, I'll play up getting you to help me."

"Let's get everything mailed out by next week."

*

The weekend's here. Thearah and I head out to the craft fair. It looks like spring; flowers and blossoms are everywhere.

The booth's on a corner, so we put the baskets along the two sides. The lighting's bright; the baskets look gorgeous!

"I was here at Christmas... now I'm back for ten more," a woman in a grey three-piece suit tells me, "they're for my clients."

"Wow... decent! What do you do?" I ask.

"Real Estate Agent, here's my card." She fishes a card out of her bright, red leather purse.

"Thanks... I'll give it to my parents. I'm not rich enough for a house... yet!" This gets me a good laugh and two more basket sales!

Those Christmas sales weren't so long ago, and now I think of this weekend. I was such an immature idiot back then, but I thought I *was* mature. The obsession with hair, makeup and clothing improving or ruining my day isn't there. I never get on that awful scale anymore. Glen's erased so much of what I was hung up on. He loves me for me, and it has rubbed off on me.

*

On our way home, after completely selling out, I realize this is the last fair; no more basket assembly nights, and more importantly, no more talk, talk, talking! "I won't see you as much anymore... that's a bummer."

"Come over anyway! Would you like to learn how to spin and weave wool? I have a new bag of raw, sheep wool coming soon and I remember you seemed interested in learning. It's pretty easy once you get the hang of it."

"Theareh... thanks! I've been stumped about what to do as my final Arts and Design project. This'd be rad!"

"I'd miss you too... come next week!"

"Sandra and I are looking for work in the Yukon. Thanks for putting the idea in my head about leaving."

Theareh hands me $100.00. "No way... that's too much," handing it back.

"Take it as a hand up. You'll have to pay for a flight to the Yukon, and it may be expensive."

"Jeez, I didn't think of how much that'll cost. Thanks!"

I phone Sandra when I get in. She's been successful with the list of places to apply. The list includes everything along the Alaska Highway – thirty in all. I'll have to get a map out; I don't have a sense of where the highway goes.

*

Dinner hour is calm. Mom tells us when the music band, The Beatles came out, people thought they were degenerate, hippie freaks because their hair was past their ears. Even though they wore suits and ties, people thought the world was coming to an end. Now it's totally different. Jimmy Page and ZZ Top are hairy rock gods, and we're grooving on them!

Alan pipes up. "I'm leaving after grad."

"Where to?" Dad asks.

"Into the forest. I need to live where I can be with nature." He stops patting down his mashed potatoes and reaches for the margarine.

Oh no, he's being weird again! "How will you get to work and back?" I ask.

"I don't need to work. I'll live off the land," he shrugs and starts shovelling food in.

"Get real Alan... it's not going to happen," says Mom, squaring her shoulders.

"Get a God dammed job for Christ's sakes," Dad tapping the words out.

"Don't take the..."

"Well, maybe you haven't worked out the details," I cut him off before he tells Dad not to take the lord's name in vain. "Very funny Alan. Tell us more when you have a better plan," I smooth over, not wanting to create more tension.

"I can too live off the land. I don't need money... it's evil." He looks down into his plate and moves to the rubbery chicken.

"Far-out, you won't need Mom and Dad's dough then!" We all laugh, the moment passes and we don't press further. He's dreaming if he thinks he can live outside in the forest, with no money.

*

I meet up with Glen at the lake; we sit on the cement block amongst Canada Geese milling around staring at us like we've intruded on their secret meeting.

"Miss K., my love, do you want to see the Ugly Bugs this weekend? We'll get your fake ID. I'll get us a ride to the gig, there and back. We'd be out until midnight."

"I'll have to ask. I don't want to ruffle the parent's feathers especially with you in the picture." He nods–we've had this conversation a lot.

"Come here babe..." he puts my hand there, "you make me horny..."

I think about getting pregnant, and I picture myself big and fat. No babies for me. I won't take a chance – no way. I'd ruin my life. "I'm going to the clinic... I can't get pregnant... you know how I feel."

"Yah, I want to feel all of you." He undoes my pants button.

"I want the first time to be perfect. Candles, dreamy tunes, romance and no parents lurking around."

"Sure babe... we'll figure it out." He continues with my zipper.

*

I look conservative and keep the makeup light. I hand the Camosun College student union guy the $5.00 for the ID hoping he doesn't see my hand shaking. "Fill this form out," he passes me a sheet of paper.

I fill out my new fake date of birth. I give a false address and phone number. "I'll volunteer," I offer, in the hope this helps him not ask for my birth certificate.

"Cool man... we need the help."

"I'll stop in another time." He takes my photo, laminates the card and photo together handing it to me without any other questions.

"That was flipping easy," I say as we leave. The bus is pulling up, so Glen and I run for it.

*

“Mom, Dad, can I have my curfew extended to twelve thirty on Saturday night?” Interrupting their conversation about what to watch on TV tonight.

“No. Nothing good happens after midnight. Curfew is eleven. Our house, our rules.” Mom looks at me, her face in a ‘*don’t push me*’ straitjacket.

“What’s the problem?” I push, standing my ground.

“We’re protecting you from doing bad things... listen to your mother,” Dad’s head is down, eyes shut and wagging a ‘*no*’ signal. HA! He doesn’t agree with Mom but isn’t rocking a boat that isn’t worth rocking.

“Fine.” I back off. We could sneak around any old time and do ‘bad things’ – I don’t get what the ‘after midnight’ reference is about. At least Glen understands that my parents are a real drag about curfew. I put on Genesis, *Selling England By the Pound* very quietly and think about the possibility of making love to Glen. I think I’m ready. I want to experience this with a person I love. It’ll be romantic and perfect.

*

I tell the parents I’m going into the city to find accessories for my grad dress, but I’m going to the birth control clinic. Sandra hops on the bus three stops later.

“You’ll fill out a form about your general health. They’ll ask you if you’ve ever been pregnant, had an abortion, had ‘the clap’ or any other sexually transmitted disease. Luckily, you’ll have an easy time ticking the ‘no’ boxes.

“Eww, ‘the clap... it’s all disgusting!’

"At least there are no sexually transmitted diseases that can't be fixed with a shot to the bum!" I let out a big Kathy laugh.

*

I hum nervously as I enter a pale yellow patient room, it's walls covered in venereal disease information posters. A fat, grouchy-faced nurse points to a chair. The doctor stares at me while shoving his smudged glasses farther up a skinny nose.

"Are you married?" He has the baldest, shiniest head I've ever seen.

"I'm not married but want to be prepared." He looks at me with a bored expression.

"Hop up," scowls the fat, lumpy-faced nurse, "We'll do an internal exam." She points to the bed.

"No... I'm a virgin. I couldn't get a disease. I don't want an internal exam," I state as firmly as I can. I don't want to be looked at down there.

"That's fine." He writes on the little notepad and gives me a prescription for the pill. "Here's what you'll need for the first month," and he hands me a pile of condoms out of a clear plastic bowl as if they're party treats. "The pill won't be effective right away. Follow the directions and be responsible about keeping your knees together."

Keeping my knees together? Who does he think he is, a preacher? I say nothing to him, and the nurse keeps her nasty face blank.

The pharmacy is beside the clinic. I pick up six plastic discs with the pills sorted into individual days. It comes with instructions and cautions. I'll have to hide it all somewhere at home.

I tell Sandra about the knees shut comment. "Sounds like a prick... sorry it went that way."

"Yeah, what an old-fashioned jerk. Doesn't he know, women today want to be modern and not get pregnant and married?" I whisper, getting on the bus taking seats at the back where no one else is right now.

"And the truth is, Glen's been trying to shove your knees apart for months." I swat her on the arm and laugh. She winces and holds the spot.

Sandra... what's with your arm?"

"Umm... Brad wanted to make a lover's promise." She pulls up her sleeve and peels back a bandage above her elbow.

"Jesus crap Sandra." Brad's initials are thinly carved into her skin. It's a crude etching, still bloody.

"He has mine on his arm. We did it with razor blades." She touches the area lightly, the sore oozes.

"WHY?"

"I was scared about him finding the resume book, so I went along with it so he won't suspect me doing something behind his back."

"Tell him what you're doing!"

"No... I'm not. He'll freak, and then if I don't get a job in the Yukon, telling will be for nothing.

“We’re getting the jobs, and if not the Yukon then we’re moving into our own apartment. He’s not good for you... don't you get it?” I’m trying to keep my voice down, but it’s hard not to wig out.

“I know... I know. I’ll fix him up. He’ll be okay. I’ll work on him... he has horrible alcoholic parents. That’s why I need to help him. We’ll get there.” She puts the bandage back on, pulls down her sleeve and looks me in the eye. “I promise you, he loves me, and everything will be perfect.”

“I hope so.” I don’t see it. At first he yelled, which was bad enough, then he bruised her wrists. Now he wanted, and did, brand her.

TWENTY-SEVEN

It's been three weeks watching the mail. I keep busy making my grad dress, Ugly Bug posters with Glen and hanging out with the gang. Alan has calmed down again and hasn't mentioned bolting to the forest. I'll talk to Theareh about him.

*

I'm to deal with a pile of raw sheep wool. I manage to comb it out between two big square brushes. The spinning part is a lesson in hand-eye coordination. Draw the wool through the tiny hole using my hands and with my foot, push the pedal up and down to create the spin and keep everything moving along.

"Don't worry," she sees me looking at the messy pile. "The texture will make the wall hanging look interesting."

"I'll have to pull off a good sell job to the teacher. It looks like an alien disease," I pick up the bumpy, uneven work.

"Take a break," Thearah says. I sit on the couch made of driftwood and hand stitched pillows.

"Can I ask you about being a hippie?"

"Sure... I've all but hung up my hippie beads, but I think I can remember some of the finer points," She smiles her infectious smile.

"Alan wants to live on the land, like a hippie. He has no money and no job. Do you think he could do it?"

"Look... it isn't an easy life. It's hard work getting food, building a fire, getting clean water and protecting yourself and your belongings from bad weather. But plenty of people do it. He's young enough to try it and see if he likes it. Would he go to Sombrio Beach?

"He said the forest... what's Sombrio?"

"There is, or was, a hippie commune there. Everyone shares their skills and whatever food, while they live on the beach for free. Hang on... I'll play a song." She slides out Joni Mitchell, Blue and puts on 'Carey.' Thearah says Joni lived in Matala, Greece, in a cave, and while there, she wrote the song.

"Jeez. I suppose if she could live that way, anyone could! I don't know what his exact plans are... I didn't know we had hippie commune around here. I'll ask him if that's where he wants to go instead of being alone in the forest." His plan isn't sounding too crazy.

*

It's April 30th; there's an envelope addressed to Sandra and me.

I tear it open and start reading a letter from Gold Miners Lodge, Mile 1095, Tigwash Landing, Alaska Highway, Yukon Territory.

Dear Kathy and Sandra,

Thank you for your letter of application at the above lodge.

We would be able to give you both employment starting June 19th. It would be either waitress, or chambermaid, or a combination of both. The rate of pay is $3.00 an hour plus room and board, six days a week.

I would like a quick reply to this, but please be quite certain before accepting that you will come because if we hold these jobs for you and you let us down, it will be very difficult for us to fill your places at that time. We and all other tourist businesses are very busy by mid-June. We will look forward to hearing from you, by post, as soon as you are able to send a reply.

Yours faithfully,

M. Kay Rhodes

for

Leo Allen

"WE GOT JOBS," I scream at the top of my lungs!!! Mom cheers for me as I race to the phone. I yell the news to Sandra, and I tell her where, which is a mystery location at this point, but who cares!

"WE'RE LEAVING!" She and I yell and laugh at the top of our lungs. Both of us have been handed a chance for an adventure this summer. Neither one of us can believe the rate of pay. It's double what we'd make here for the same job. We'll be rich! No more Longmore for over two months! I'm reeling with the promise of an unforgettable summer.

Sandra and I plan to see each other as soon as possible to talk about how we'll get to Whitehorse. I write our confirmation letter asking for details on how to get to the lodge. Tigwash Landing is not on the map we have at home. The school library has a better map.

I stamp the letter and post the most important piece of mail I've ever sent, and then I race off to Glen's. I'm hopping around like some sort of idiot; I jump up the stairs to Glen's room.

"We got job's," I say breathlessly. Glen swings me up in the air and around in circles.

"Righteous!"

"Will we stay in love?" I ask, detaching myself.

"Of course," his breath sends gentle heat across my lips, "You know I'll love you forever."

"We'll meet back here in September, and I'll have loads of love and want for you, it will make you blush," I whisper in his ear.

"Babe," his knees cave. "I got news for you... May long weekend... the family's going to White Rock. I'll be training, so I'll stay here and we can..."

"Make love!"

"What I want to do is fuck you, nice, and for a long time," devilish grin.

"That's not romantic you nutcase! I want romance, candles, music and you."

"Ms. K. It'll be making love."

*

Now that I'm leaving, there's fresh energy boosting me forward. I'll graduate on June 18th – we have to be in Whitehorse June 19th. I have six weeks left of school and Longmore.

*

Glen and I are full of plans. Lots of candles, and he'll get baby champagne. I've been on the pill long enough, so no condoms needed. It's going to be one hundred percent romantic!

Glen hasn't peeped a word about his family leaving for the weekend. Mack and everyone would be over, hanging out in a parent free house. Mom and Dad don't know Glen's family's going away. I keep my nose toward finishing school and staying out of trouble.

*

I leave right after dinner on the night of '*The Big Event.*' I have to be home at eleven; we want as much time as possible. The house is dark and looks like no one's home. I go in and lock the door behind me. I see a candle at the top of the stairs and follow the flame to his bedroom.

Glen opens the bubbly wine, and he hands me a glass. I feel sophisticated, with wine and candles, in a house we're pretending is ours.

"Is there any chance your family would come back tonight?"

"No chance... it's just us Miss K." He looks gorgeous in the candlelight.

The music's a mix cassette tape of romantic tunes. We're listening to "Kiss You All Over" and "Three Times A Lady."

"Want to make love?" Glen glides over.

"No...I want to fuck you." I pull off my top slowly over my head. He draws my bra straps off my shoulders and unwraps me like a present. The button on my skirt undone, the fabric slides down my body. As I kiss him, underwear is slowly pulled down my legs and cast off. I pull off his t-shirt and remove the familiar jeans... he hasn't worn underwear. I have all of him.

Hands and lips are touching, caressing and loving. He's taking his time, stroking and kissing. My pleasure rises; I arch forward, pressing against him. I follow his length up and down.

I hear the cassette tape crumpling in the player.

"Hang on," Glen puts his elbow right beside my head.

"My hair... ouch!" I shove my hair back behind my head with a giggle.

"Sorry lover." He moves over and puts on Moody Blues album, *Days of Future Passed* onto the little turntable. I can't stop giggling!

“Not a good time to laugh Miss K,” and he silences me with a deep kiss. I’m ready again and full of physical feelings I don’t have to suppress anymore.

The album starts skipping. I’m ignoring it, but ‘Tuesday Afternoon’ is throwing us off. Glen gets up and ticks the needle arm enough to get it back on track. We regain our positions on the bed, but I’m fumbling around with my hair.

Glen and I bang the turntable, tipping it off the bedside table it was teetering on. I hear the player crash onto the floor. We look at each other, “Ignore it,” I say.

Something happens, or more like nothing happens. Glen deflates. We keep trying, but there’s no change. I feel him tense up. What’s going on?

We decide to wait a bit and try again. It’s still early enough in the evening for us to continue, without haste. We take it slowly, stop drinking wine, and things are back on track. We try it when ‘Crazy on You’ is halfway through the chorus and once again Glen loses it.

I never in a million fantasies would’ve thought my first time wouldn’t happen for this reason. The little I know about the subject depicts men as virile beasts wanting to ‘get it’ as much as possible. This scene never occurred to me. He’s never had this happen in past fooling around sessions.

I tell him, “It’s nothing I’m getting bent over. I love you, and that’s all that counts.” He can’t give me any reason why he lost his erection.

"Sorry Miss K. I wanted it to be special for you... I fucked up. I don't know what happened... fuck it." We spend the rest of the evening lying in bed, watching the candles dance off the walls of his room. We listen to Pink Floyd, *Dark Side of the Moon* album. The music goes deep tonight. I love the song Eclipse. The song pulses through all that we are. Glen is love to me.

He seems fine on the walk home. Well, maybe he's a bit quiet. I wonder if it bothers him that he couldn't do it. He kisses me goodnight and tells me he loves me.

"I love you Glen... I love you."

*

I lay in bed confused. Tonight was supposed to be the big night of lovemaking, but Glen couldn't do it! It was totally weird. Did I do something wrong? Does this ever happen to other couples? There's no one I dare ask. The only book I've ever seen on sex is, "Ann Landers Talks To Teenagers About Sex" but it was written in 1963, and her advice is to keep sex for marriage. Not much help there for young people to find out anything about how sex works. The school sex education covered anatomy and diseases, then pregnancy. No help there either. I'll never know what happened unless Glen figures it out. Maybe next time – if there is one –we'll be successful.

All this waiting and dreaming about my special gift I would give, and then it's nothing like I imagined. No fireworks, or 'bodies moving as one'. I'm alone here. I won't talk to Glen about this and for sure, not Sandra... too personal... too embarrassing. Everyone else is probably having fantastic sex except Glen and I.

*

Steve, Alan, Glen and I play Cribbage on this rainy Sunday.

"Alan, Bob Seger's new album *Stranger in Town* has a righteous vibe. Have you had a boo yet?" Glen asks.

"Nope, not yet..." Alan's interrupted by Steve.

"He's on TV next week... can't remember what show... I'll find out."

"Cool," says Alan returning to the game, "Fifteen two." Alan seems normal when we play board games.

"And the rest won't do..." Steve the poet.

"Glen, we should watch it together," I say.

"Sure," he shrugs, glances up and then back to his cards, "Thirty-one for two," ignoring me, moving his peg along the board. Is he mad at me? I told him I loved him. That should count.

When he leaves, he kisses me in front of everyone. I walk out with him and stand under the porch, just out of the pelting rain. "There'll be a next time Miss K."

*

Glen's going for a tour of the ship, and I'll work on my grad dress. Considering the dress pattern is a wedding dress I've been successful re-making it into a gorgeous dress fit for grad. Mom and I have taken turns hemming the yards of ivory lace that make up the floor length skirt. The bodice fits perfectly. I hand sew on the brown velvet straps and then add little red silk roses on the bodice front. A brown velvet choker gets red roses as well. Glen will wear a red rose boutonniere, and I'll wear a matching wrist corsage. I found ivory coloured gloves and trimmed them with the lace. There's even enough fabric left over to make a small bag to hang off my wrist. I didn't need a stupid fashion magazine to come up with that idea. I pick up the dress, hold it in front of me, "dress... we're almost there."

TWENTY-EIGHT

We get a letter from Gold Miners Lodge detailing us getting picked up from the airport. "We'll be picked up by a man named Blake Grey," I tell Sandra over the phone.

"I haven't told Brad yet... maybe I won't... I'll just run away with you!" She's laughing like it's a joke.

"Let's get the airline tickets and then decide if you'll tell him... is that cool?"

"Cool... I can't wait to get out of here. "'Auntie Sue' is driving me nuts. She wants to go grad dress shopping with me... not a chance."

"I'm going to miss Glen, but I can't wait to go either. I'm so sick of my parents and all the rules."

*

Glen and I won't get another chance to make love before I go. He leaves right after me. He seems a bit shy about the whole thing. I've taken to laughing it off. We'll be ready in September that's for sure. I'll wait for him forever!

*

On Saturday, Sandra and I meet in the village to buy the airline tickets. She looks sick.

"Kathy, we have to talk... let's go here first," she says and then leads me into 'Taffy's Tea Joint.' We get our drinks, trying to avoid the jungle of ivy growing from everywhere and choose a small table made from a tree stump. We pull up smaller stumps and sit down.

"Kathy, there's something I haven't told you, because I barely believe it myself," she says, her eyes huge and bright.

"You're pregnant!" I blurt out in horror.

"What? No... god no!" This breaks the tension somewhat, but she's put me on tender hooks.

"You know I've been writing and handing in some of my work to Mrs. Cleaver?"

"Yes. Did you win a big award?" I clap my hands together.

"I won a summer scholarship at the University of Victoria. The program leads into the four-year degree I want... I can't go to the Yukon with you." She cringes as I stop clapping; my arms slip down like limp noodles.

"You didn't know about this *at all*? Mrs. Cleaver didn't mention it? You're telling me *now*? What am *I* going to do? How long have you known about this?"

"I didn't know! Mrs. Cleaver had me thinking about applying for university, which I did, but this came out of the blue. I had to hand in a sample of my work. Apparently, they saw it and offered the summer scholarship program. I didn't know – honest!"

I'm *sick* of crying. I start sobbing. "I'm happy for you and sad for me. I can't go now... I won't go by myself," blubbering more.

"Oh yes, you will! I'm not going to be the one to stop you. This was your idea so get out of this boring place. There's more to life than Longmore, and you're the one to go out and get it. Think about how Anne would never get a chance like you and I are getting right now. What about your show about being brave and independent?"

"Give me a minute... it's all too much." She hands me a paper napkin from the giant clamshell holder.

"I have an idea Kathy... give me your hands." I pass them across the stump. She takes them in hers and says, "Anne's with us in spirit... she's here with us right now. Let's ask her to stay with us, on our life journey." Sandra's hands are clammy. "We're taking a big step off the high school platform into the unknown."

"Anne, we miss you. We keep your spirit close and take you with us every day we're lucky to be alive. We'll live lives you haven't had a chance to." I say these words out loud – words I've thought and shared with Glen.

"Sandra, I'm scared," tears still rolling.

"Me too," Sandra chokes.

*

We walk into the travel agent office. The walls entertain us with posters of Disneyland, Hawaii and Australia. "Hello ladies... come sit down." We take chairs in front of a huge desk covered in bulging file folders. I buy a ticket to Whitehorse, with the return on September 9th. My hands are numb as I hand over $125.00. The lady smiles and asks me if I'm all right. I tell her what I'm doing, now all alone.

"You're going to love it up north! Don't get married! Go on plenty of adventures... don't get married!"

"Um, okay." Marriage is the last thing on my mind. I have to get through grad and then leave everything I know, for nothing I know, and go alone. "Thank you," she hands me the ticket in its yellow plastic folder. "Goodbye... and thanks for the advice!"

"When do the writing classes begin?" I ask as we walk out the door.

"The end of June. I never handed my notice to Dairy Queen. I'll work nights and weekends."

"What does Brad say about you staying now?" I don't want to know.

"I never told him our plans... I was scared he'd flip out on me."

She's still frightened of ass head and is *still* with him! "I guess you won't see him much since you sound packed busy this summer."

"Brad might leave to get better work in Alberta... I may get a break," her tone has a distinct upturn.

"That'd be great if he left! That would be super cool. I'm worried about you, and him... he needs to be nicer to you."

"He's been sweet since we did our initials."

Jeez.

I ask her to call Gold Miner's Lodge today and let them know it's only me coming to work there now. I guess they'll have to hire someone else to fill her spot. I hope they can. I don't want to let them down, and I haven't even started.

We head our separate ways, and I can't believe I have to say goodbye to Sandra in eighteen days.

I get home and let Mom and Dad know what's happened. "It'll be okay... I'm brave and want to go out into the world." They don't stop my plans. They probably want me out of the house anyhow. There'll be one less person to feed and think about.

*

"Glen, I'll have to go... I can't stay here. I accepted the job. I bought the airline ticket. You're leaving, and I have no summer job here anyways. There's no reason for me to stay... except my colossal fear. Who knows what's going to happen to me now. Do I have the guts to go through with this?" The picnic table's jiggling.

"Stop it with the fear Miss K. You're loved if you're here, or if you leave. We'll write to each other. You and Sandra will write to each other and swap stories of your summer. It'll be okay... you'll be fine. You're smart *and* funny, *and* will dazzle your employers!"

"Gee, where are your pom-poms Mr. Cheerleader," I get up and start a goofy cheerleader dance for him.

"Don't leave me for a gold miner though!" He tries to catch my imaginary pom-poms.

"Never, never my love!" A few star jumps later, I drop the pom-poms and lean in.

"I have a plan," he pulls away looking at me with a devious grin. "Let's practice using your fake ID and go see a band tonight. It's not the Bugs, but I heard these guys are *primo*."

"Okay, sounds rad! I'll ask for a curfew extension!" I leave him, and head in to tell Mom and Dad my plans for the evening.

"Glen is taking me out to listen to a band at 'City Hall.' Should be fun. I'd like to stay out until midnight."

"You know curfew is 11:00 p.m.!" Mom's in a howling mood. Maybe there's a full moon.

"WELL, I'm leaving soon enough, and you won't have to deal with me anymore. You can't have it both ways by treating me like a baby and then expecting me to be grown up. I'm going out for as long as I want! What are you going to do - ground me like a child?"

They stand there. Dad has a slight glimmer in his eyes and a touch of a smile.

"I can damn well ground you... I'm your *mother*. Don't you dare cross me..."

"Leave me alone!! I'm SICK of you being my mother... you're hateful... mean. I can't wait to get out of here." Heat and pain rise through my chest as I take a step closer to her, staring at her vile face, feeling grown up... feeling I can win.

"Adele... leave Kathy alone, please. Kathy, no drinking or drugs?"

"No, I want to go dancing!"

"Go then... see if I care about you!" Mom grabs her book on feminism and goes to the living room, out of sight.

"Make sure it's just dancing... I trust you Kathy. I'll talk to your mother," says Dad.

"Thanks Dad. I'm getting ready." I go to my room vibrating from the confrontation I hate, but I have leverage now. I'm moving out like an adult. They have to get used to it. I'm leaving this house. I want more freedom, and I think I rightfully demanded it.

*

My fake ID is totally believable. We're seeing the 'Dishrags.' It's licensed; I drink dry apple cider. The place is crowded: everyone's smoking, drinking and dancing in the dimly lit hall. The heavy rock isn't what I have on my record player, but it's fast and danceable. I'm having fun dancing with Glen, sliding up to him, teasing him. We're all sweaty by the end of the first set.

Glen leads me out the back door to visit one of the members he knows. They do a flip, flap handshake that looks like they're drumming on each other. I get introduced to Jim, a rocker, with stringy, long black hair and crooked teeth. He pulls out a joint, lights it up and passes it to Glen. Glen's never smoked pot around me; he takes a big toke and passes it back to Jim who then passes it to me. Crap. I don't know what it'll do to me, and I can't go home messed up. "Nah, it puts me to sleep," thinking fast.

"Christ on a pole... that's fucked," says Jim.

I laugh, and the joint goes back to Glen. Maybe I passed the *'Glen's cool girlfriend test'?*

Glen seems fine, "Everyone blazes up at gigs, and it's cool if you don't Miss K."

Everyone's friendly, I don't get drunk, or stoned, and we dance a million dances.

TWENTY-NINE

The day is here. It's Grad day. Alan looks like a coat hanger, with an oversized jacket draped on it. He's too skinny! He insists on wearing mirror sunglasses, not because he's trying to make a style statement, but wanting to 'stay safe' as he puts it. I'm completely past worrying about him. He's weird. I'm leaving.

Mom takes our photos before everyone comes over. Steve's dad has a giant yacht of a car he's borrowed for the evening; they're cramming in together. None of them have dates! They all want to 'play the field.' I think they're too chicken to ask anyone.

Glen and I can use his family car for the night. Glen looks super excellent in his dark green velvet jacket, black dress pants and a dark blue and green tie he borrowed from his dad.

He puts on my wrist corsage, and I put on his boutonniere. "You look beautiful Miss K. I'm honoured to be your date."

*

We meet up with Sandra and Brad at the school. "Sandra, your dress is Marilyn Monroe fabulous!" The butter yellow, body-hugging, low cut sheath shows all the curves.

"Brad helped me pick it out!" Sandra says, looking all dreamy at him.

"Did you hear Sandra's got her way paid at UVic?" Brad has his Longmore mullet tamed into a half-groomed mess. The suit is black with no lumberjack red checkerboard pattern to be seen. His boutonniere is a pale yellow rose; Sandra has her matching corsage fixed as a necklace.

"Yes, we did Brad. I barely recognize you all jazzed up," I say like I admire him for a second. "You must be so proud of Sandra!" Wow, he's acting like a decent boyfriend!

"Smart, *and* you could bounce quarters off that ass."

Glen and I walk into the building. "He's a filthy anus," Glen whispers in my ear.

*

The school gymnasium's packed with families and friends. The student council decorated it with balloons and bunting. There are speeches; I wave at Mom and Dad seated in the bleachers. Anne and Rod's families have asked there be no speech about the deaths.

“Kathy Johnson.” I walk up to get my diploma. A wave goes through me from the tip of my toes to the top of my head. I have goosebumps all over. *Anne... I feel her. She moved through me. Anne!*

I take my diploma with a smile as wide as it can go, laughing my big Kathy laugh.

*

Somehow, our school can have our dinner and dance at the classy Empress Hotel in Victoria. Most schools haven’t been allowed here for graduations. The Crystal Ballroom is elegantly decorated with massive chandeliers, mirrors to catch the lights and fine light blue drapery frothed around soaring windows. We take our yearbooks and run around getting autographs. There is a formal photo taken, and I’m the proudest grad to have Glen with me. The man who helped save me from the despair of losing my best friend is standing with me, beside me.

We eat, dance and reminisce. Alan doesn’t do anything weird except keep his sunglasses on the entire night.

After the dance, we drive to Lagoon Beach in Calling for a bonfire. Lots of people arrive, and plenty have alcohol. I have some Lonesome Charlie that Glen bought, but I don’t want to drink much because I have to leave in the morning for Whitehorse. I need a clear head for being alone and scared.

What an outa-sight night! We sing, some people have guitars, and we dance until the sun starts to show pink on the horizon.

“W,” says Glen. I nod. Hell... I’m going to lose it.

"Sandra... we have to go," the glowing pink sky finds me, "I don't know how I'm going to do this without you." Glen and Brad step back as Sandra and I hug.

"Write lots. I'll miss you... don't make me cry." We hold hands across from each other like we did in 'Taffy's Tea Joint.' "Anne is with us," Sandra whispers.

"Anne is here," a shiver goes through me like static shock.

Sandra hugs me close, whispering in my ear, "Brad's going to Alberta for the summer... it'll be a good break for us."

Strain is shaking away. I didn't realize how scared I was for her. "I'm glad for you... I know you'll be the most talented student in the program!"

"Babe..." Glen says, and I know this is it for now. We pull out of the car park and I look back until I can't see Sandra anymore.

*

We arrive home to find Mom and Dad standing by the door. Alan has a large rucksack packed to the hilt. "Goodbye," he mutters, head down, baseball cap firmly on and shoved as far down over his face as possible.

"What kind of stunt are you pulling?" I yell.

"I'm going to live in the forest for the summer." He starts to walk out the door.

"Mom, Dad... stop him!" I'd thought he'd given up on the idea. I look at my parents who are standing in the back door area, with their arms crossed, but not blocking Alan's way out.

"We've been trying. It's reckless and dangerous. Alan, cougars come in close to this area... how are you going to defend yourself?" Dad's tone is reasonable.

"Alan, this is stupid... don't go... you'll be by yourself. It's not safe!" He turns away, not paying attention to me.

"Alan, I forbid you going!" Mom is close to ballistic level one hundred.

"You can't *forbid* me," he scoffs, "I'll be fine!" He looks at them with his goggle eyes, like they're the ones who are doing something crazy. "I want to try it for the summer. I'll camp behind Scott Mountain... you can't stop me." He slaps on his sunglasses.

"How will you eat? What if it rains and you get all wet?" Frustrated, I leave the room to get changed for the flight. What am I going to do? Should I tell Mom and Dad about his made up story about nuclear testing and how he believes a possible end of the world scenario?

No. I can't betray my twin. He'll never forgive me for being a snitch. It's his well-known eccentric behaviours. He's okay. I can't say anything to Mom and Dad. I want to protect our twin bubble. *I won't tell them.* I won't do this to Alan. His life and his choice, just like Joni Mitchell.

I give Alan a hug and it feels like he's turned into a cement post. "Goodbye... come back when your adventure's over," I say.

"You too." Alan turns and walks out the door, ahead of us. He waves and walks toward the hills we've played on since we were children. Now it'll be his home. I hope keeping quiet about him being weird isn't wrong.

*

My suitcase gets tossed in the trunk. Glen and I pile in the back seat. We hold hands, staying silent the entire excruciating forty-five-minute drive. The airport is buzzing with people. Mom, Dad and Glen join me at the ticket counter to get my boarding passes. Mom pipes up and tells the lady at the counter that I've never flown by myself before and what'll I do if I need help. As much as I wince from embarrassment, I appreciate the lady filling me in on how to get around the Vancouver airport.

The goodbyes are *almost* not as bad as I pictured them. Mom's crying; that throws me off. Why would Mom cry? I thought she'd be doing a polka dance around the departure area screaming, "she's leaving!" I guess I don't know what's inside Mom. Dad gives me a tight hug, "I'm proud of you Kathy."

Glen and I cry and laugh. I kiss him, without embarrassment, in front of my parents.

I turn around, throw my daypack over my shoulder and walk through the departure doors.

PART THREE

THIRTY

I can't go back now; I'm through security. My solid self has turned to liquid. Shaking, I sit down in Gate One seating, the only gate in this airport. I feel physically ill and spot the washroom. I can't move, I'm rattling so hard. Tears are filling my eyes. I take big yoga breaths to calm myself down. This has got to be the stupidest plan I've ever made. What an idiot to think I could do this on my own.

A lady, speaking loudly, announces the flight, getting us into a lineup. She checks the boarding pass, wearing a warm smile. I swallow, still nauseous, and walk past her, pressing my shaking, watery body toward the aircraft.

The airplane's small, perhaps holding twenty people – it must be unsafe! We're going over water! What if we crash? I find my seat and pull Snoopy out of the bag. I told everyone at home he's meant to be a pillow, but in fact, he's here to save my life. I hug him and don't care about anyone staring at me like I'm a baby. I suppress a sob and hide my face in his worn-out body.

The propellers start whirring; the stewardess gives us a safety talk on how to put our seatbelts on, and where the exit doors are. The flight to Vancouver is fourteen minutes. I grip onto the armrests and ignore the person beside me, who has sat down at the last minute before the doors shut. I tell myself to calm down – it'll be over soon. But then I need to find the other plane at a huge airport. I'll get lost. I close my eyes and think of not throwing up.

The plane's moving, with me strapped in. The thundering noise is blocking out every thought in my brain except panic. I don't want to be here in this tiny plane! I could turn around in Vancouver and come back! Maybe I should... this is madness. I'm in way over my head.

That's my plan! I'll return home and get some kind of summer job.

I'm a bit better now; I stuff Snoopy back in the pack. Out the window I see blue ocean, and shards of black land, striking out of the water like fingers pointing me back home. The propellers create a thrumming noise telling me to turn around. It looks beautiful outside... I'm glad I've decided.

*

We land in Vancouver soon enough, and I walk off the plane, onto pavement, following everyone else. We head to a monstrosity of a building; large aircraft are parked along the edges. I count ten of them waiting their turn to take people somewhere else.

In the main building, I spot the airline's kiosk.

A woman, whose face looks like a jackhammer hit it, scowls and snaps, "Yes? Can I help you?"

"I want to turn in this ticket and go back to Victoria." I hand over the ticket; she flips through the filmy, carbon pages.

"This ticket is non-refundable, non-transferable and non-negotiable." She hands the ticket back, returning to the paperwork in front of her.

"Well, I'll buy a one-way ticket back," leaning over her counter, making sure I'm heard over a flight being called on the loudspeaker.

"No such thing as a one-way ticket. You must buy a return ticket. It'll cost you $100.00. Not even this department. Leave this arrivals area, go to the departure check-in at the other end of the airport and if there's a seat available, you have to pay cash. Also, your luggage will be transported to Whitehorse and will cost you $50.00 to fly it back."

"Oh, thank you," I say, trying to get everything she's jackhammering about. It's going to cost me $150.00 to go home on a fourteen-minute flight? The entire student discount fare of my current ticket is $125.00. My luggage could get lost or stolen if I don't get it myself. Who knows what it's like in the Yukon. There could be thieves ready to steal my bag. I drag my carry-on pack and myself to a seating area to consider my choices. I thump myself down like an elephant.

"Whoah girl, everything okay?" A pile of white teeth flashes before me. A man, who looks as old as Dad, is peering at me with concern. His tanned face is wrinkly, grey hair swings wildly to one side of his head. I see he's wearing a black jacket; the yellow stitching on an arm patch reads, '*Whitehorse Copper Ltd.*' I explain my predicament while watching his hair bob up and down in agreement.

"Listen, young lady, I can't tell you what to do, but I'll tell you the Yukon's a wonderful part of the country. It's friendly and easygoing. I can pretty much guarantee you *will* have a fun summer. I'm heading to Whitehorse right now. Where are you working?"

"Gold Miners Lodge," I mumble, scuffling my feet across the beige, bubble gum splotched, linoleum floor.

"Har! The Tigwash Airport is a short walk away. I'll give you my name, and you pass it along to Norm, my buddy. He'll show you around the area." I stare at him, lower jaw flapped open like a bozo.

"Now young lady, there's a big concern if you go home now. There's the business of letting down the folks at the lodge. You bailing out would be very upsetting for the owners. Trying to re-hire at this stage of the game is difficult. Most workers have secured a job for the summer. You wouldn't want to leave them hanging, would you?" He's shaking his head; the hair's getting crazier looking. I almost feel a smile breaking out on my face and tell him I wouldn't want to let them down after they took a chance on me. "There you go girly! Everything's going to be fine! My name's Dan the Mountain Man," he extends a rough, calloused hand, we shake.

"Kathy Johnson scared as heck and pleased to meet you," and there it is – a smile on my face.

"Listen girly, you go to the Yukon and eat up your summer like it's your last. Life's number one fun in the north. You're a ballsy woman to be on your own. Don't go home... you'll regret it forever." His unwavering affection for the Yukon gives me a chance to reconsider.

Would Anne go home if she had a chance to choose? She doesn't get a chance; I have to decide and be on my own two feet. "Okay, Mr. Dan the Mountain Man, I'll go, and if I hate it, I'll find you and tell you off!" I laugh a big Kathy laugh.

"Come on Kathy, let's go to our gate." I follow Dan who I think sounds logical and practical. I'll go to Whitehorse and swallow my fears. I'm not quite as frightened anymore, because I've made a friend.

*

We board a Pacific Western, Boeing 737 jet and arrange with the stewardess to be seated together. Dan tells me about the plane and how safe it is. He entertains me with stories of his travels around the north using different modes such as floatplanes, ski planes, helicopters, and even snowshoes. He says, "You'll probably fly in planes and maybe even a helicopter this summer."

"How will I get a chance to fly? I'm working in a tourist lodge," I say, taking a sip of the lukewarm coffee put in front of me.

"Are you kidding me? A girly like you working up north? You'll have plenty of opportunities... mark my words," he raises his hand as if an oath is being taken.

"I'm to meet a man named Blake Grey. Would you know him?" He seems to know everyone in the Yukon.

"Blake! Sure I know him. He's one of the best bush pilots in the north. You're in safe hands!"

THIRTY-ONE

We fly over Whitehorse on our descent into the airport. It looks like a small town, with no large skyscraper buildings. The downtown streets are set on a grid design. We fly low over a paddle wheeler boat... cool, I've only seen one of these on a TV show. Maybe I'll get to go on one! The sound of the plane becomes earsplittingly loud. We're about to land... I'm gripping my seat.

Our plane lands hard on the airfield, the braking shifts me forward against the seatbelt. The ground crew wheels up a staircase; a stewardess opens the plane door. There are lively exchanges between crews. Dan and I walk outside into the crisp air. Dull sandy surroundings are dotted with tiny trees. The sky is astoundingly blue; I gawk up at it.

“The air’s perfectly clean, making the sky bluer than blue!” Dan informs as he leads me to the entrance door – we enter the small, square, nondescript building. “Blake, over here you bush man!” Dan’s voice booms across rows of chairs in the seating area. A dark haired, massively-bearded man strides over.

“Dan! Who do you have here?” Blake flashes a welcoming smile.

“I present to you one Kathy Johnson ready to work at Gold Miners Lodge,” says Dan; I shake Blake’s hand, with the firmest grip I can muster.

Where’d you meet this old geezer?” Blake’s eyes dance, “didn’t fill you with stories of his misguided adventures did he?”

“I don’t think so! I met Dan in the Vancouver Airport, and he’s been telling me about the north... I’m scared, but excited to be here.” I turn to Dan, look up at him, and gush out, “thank you for getting me this far. I’ll appreciate it for forever.”

“Kathy, I hope we meet again,” he passes me his phone number and tells me to call him if I ever need help. I see my bags on the cart parked inside the big door. Blake lifts them from the pile for me.

“Gotta make tracks now!” Blake is already walking out; I scurry behind him waving at Dan.

*

We’re heading to a wreck of a truck. It looks like a metal patchwork quilt, all brown, white and dark green. It’d better get us the two hundred miles to the lodge. This heap looks like it isn’t going anywhere.

“Jump in.” I do, while he flings the bags into the back. “Kathy, we have to pick up the other person you’re working with, and then head over to the floatplane dock. If we fly there, it’ll be a lot faster.” He hops in the driver’s seat, and we tear off, out of the airport, down a wide, gently sloping hill into town. “This is called Two Mile Hill, built at the same time as the Alaska Highway, in 1942, to connect with the downtown area.” We bump along the so-called road. It’s paved but pot holey. At the bottom of the hill, we skirt along the edge of the town. There are houses mixed with businesses, and everything looks a bit worn out, as are most of the rusty vehicles we pass along the way. The houses all seem a bit like Blake’s truck – sort of patched up with metal siding, wood and whatever else found for such buildings. There are plenty of people to stare at, and they all *look* normal. Families with strollers and trailing toddlers well-dressed women and men, laughing and talking as they walk down clean sidewalks.

We pull up to one of the largest buildings I’ve seen so far. There’s a sign stating we’ve arrived at the 4th Avenue Residence. Blake hops out, “Elke is your workmate.” The place looks like an apartment building, but I read a sign saying, ‘Dorm rooms, single, double and quads. Nightly weekly and monthly.’ It seems like a groovy idea for people who need a place to stay in town. I’ll keep it in mind for September.

Blake walks out the main door with a striking-looking young woman. I get out of the truck. “Hi, I’m Kathy,” I smile, with my hand extended yet again.

“Hi, I’m Elke.” She has an accent of some sort but speaks perfect English. “Are you ready for the new job?” I nod and look at Elke a little more closely. She’s taller than me and a bit sturdier built. Her brown hair looks sun bleached, and her skin is slightly brown. She has piercing green eyes – beautiful. “What’s this about a plane?”

We both look at Blake. “You ladies are going to the lodge in one of the Yukon’s best workhorse planes, a de Havilland Beaver floatplane. One of the greatest bush planes in the world.” Elke and I look at each other.

“Okay.” I manage. First day and I’m already going to fly in a tin can. I keep my mouth shut. I won’t be a baby about this, even though I’m tripping out.

*

Blake is careening down a dirt road beside a river that seemingly runs through Whitehorse. Ahead, there’s a dock loaded with planes; we park in front of a yellow contraption of an aircraft. The one propeller sticking out the front indicates we’ll have only one engine, which is not inspiring confidence. The whole plane’s perched on pontoons stuck onto where the wheels should be. “There she is... a beautiful machine! Get in ladies... it’s time to go.” He opens the small door, and we climb in. The seats are worn canvas that release puffs of dust when we settle into two places behind the pilot’s seat. The seatbelts are on top of my mind, but when I pull them out, they’re nothing I’ve ever seen before. There’s a metal hook, latch-over system that looks like it wouldn’t keep Snoopy safe, let alone me. The straps are thick, old and frayed. Elke and I figure out how to use the buckle gadget.

Blake gives a young man in dirt-streaked, beige coveralls a thumbs up while starting the engine. The massive wooden propeller is swung manually, and then turns on its own accord. We're untethered from the dock, and like or not, I'm going to fly in a Beaver floatplane two hundred miles to the lodge.

The plane is a barrage of noise, from the engine drumming to the propeller droning. Slicing the rippled water, and then with a slight lurch, we're airborne. Elke looks over at me and starts to laugh. I do too. I can't escape this wonderful feeling of being lifted off the water and into the biggest, bluest-ever sky. I hope I never forget the exhilaration as we whip along treetops, slowly gaining attitude. We tip from side to side, allowing me to look down at the earth from our noisy perch. There are a lot of trees and not much else. There's a ribbon of highway we're following. Blake screams, "it's the mighty Alaska Highway we're tracking to our destination." Soon I see a range of snow-capped mountains in the distance. Not long after that, an immense span of lake, much bigger than Longmore, comes into view.

"That's Kluane Lake below you. We're almost at the lodge." He turns back to his position and starts descending to the lake. We barely got up here, and it's going to end. I hope I fly again this summer.

Slowly, we fly to a dock. To the left, I see a group of houses, which I'm sure are miniature. A fellow is waiting for us to land, which we do with a gentle splash. The plane motors up as if it's turned into a boat. Blake stops the engine: we silently drift, and then he jumps out of the plane, stands on the pontoon, and throws a rope over to the young man. They tie up, and we jump out. I'm a bit wobbly, and then I remember, I didn't sleep the night of graduation and haven't even had a nap yet. Jeez, was grad only yesterday?

There are more handshakes and greetings. Karl, who has tied the plane up, seems shy – he looks down when I ask him how he's doing. He shrugs a bit, so I don't push him with more questions. With waves good-bye, Karl unleashes the plane from the dock and Blake flies off to his next destination. Karl drives us, in another banged-up vehicle, the short distance to the lodge. I see our home for the summer.

THIRTY-TWO

Settled on the edge of the lake is a drab looking, brown building. On the left of the structure is a two-story section outfitted with small, equally placed windows. Attached, on the right, is a long, lower set building with larger windows. A hand-painted sign on top says 'HOTEL.' Strewn along the gravel parking lot are more beat up vehicles corralled in by two sheds made of rough-cut planks. Around the large building, I see small cabins on one side, with a hand-painted sign, 'Guest Cabins' in front. Beside this, a set of clotheslines with white sheets billow in the wind, as dust lazes over the land settling on tall grasses beyond. An old, rusty tractor completes the appearance of neglect. Threads of cloud intermittently dull the view into a sad existence. It looks as if this place may have never had glory days.

We enter the front door in the lower part of the building, stepping onto ugly, dark green linoleum and into the central dining area. There are 1940's era chrome and beige vinyl chairs set around matching Formica tables. Beyond this room, is a sun-filled dining area filled with potted flowers resting on window ledges. The view is the redeeming factor – the lake and mountains across the water, are wilderness perfection.

*

"Hello!" We're met by three older folks, who emerge from the two-story section, via a small set of stairs. "I'm Enid, and this's my husband, Leo. We're the owners of Gold Miners. Here's Kay Rhodes, whom you will report to."

Enid and Leo look way past retirement age. Both have gray hair and stooped posture. Enid is wearing a shapeless, floral cotton dress, and Leo's wearing jean overalls, covered in oil and dirt. "I think you'll have a fun summer here with us," says Enid cheerfully. She looks like a classic grandma, smudgy glasses and all.

"Heh," chuffs Leo, "but not too much fun," he adds, sarcastically. He looks at his blackened hands, rubs them together, and excuses himself to go fix something broken. By the looks of this place, fixing broken things may be a full-time job.

"Come eat lunch…we'll explain in more detail what your responsibilities are. There are sandwiches bursting with chicken. Kay places a thick, brown hearty looking soup in front of each of us. It's incredibly delicious – rich broth, layers of flavour, generously loaded with meat and vegetables. The meal's excellent – I'm starving!

I apologize for Sandra not coming. Kay says they were lucky to get Elke at the last minute. I'm relieved that, in the end, Sandra didn't leave them in a lurch.

*

Kay must be a million years old. She looks it, with white hair formed into a combat helmet, black cat eyeglasses and a wrinkled up face, adjusted with foundation, paired with an unnatural shade of lipstick in pale orange.

Kay goes into 'Official Boss' mode, speaking in a crusty British accent and a clipped way of explaining duties.

I think I've been conscripted into the military. "Your jobs will be posted in the kitchen, but the list is basic. We serve dinner and breakfast for bus tours and have work crews in who'll need packed lunches and meals as well. They usually don't come at exactly the same time as the buses. Therefore we can stagger the service. You'll be responsible for setting up the dining room, tearing down and hand washing all the dishes. There usually isn't much business outside of mealtimes. Occasionally we'll get people in for coffee. Your shifts will be split into morning, with a break in the afternoon, and then dinner service. The day ends at approximately 9:00 p.m. Let's now go look at the kitchen."

It's stacked with dishes, on shelves, all over the place. Heavy-duty coffee cups and thick, white plates by the hundreds. The kitchen sink is in three sections, and we get a lesson in the cleaning process. There's hot, soapy water in the first: then, in the middle sink, hot, clear rinse water, with one tablespoon of bleach, and lastly a sink of hot water, for the final rinse. I'm used to hand washing dishes at home – I'll cope.

The toast station has two, four-slice toasters, with an explanation the electrical breaker will blow if any more toasters are being used at one time. The coffee maker is something out of a mad scientist's lab. The glass coffee pot is on the bottom, and there's an additional glass pot that fits on the top. This upper pot has a glass pipe coming out of the bottom into the lower carafe. Kay sees we're both looking over and around this mystery appliance. I don't have a clue how it works.

"This is a 1940's Silex Double Bubble Pyrex coffee maker. You put the grounds in the top section, the water in the lower. Put the pot on the element to boil. The water goes up the tube, the coffee and water mix, and then the coffee comes back down the tube, without grounds, into the bottom pot. It's ready to serve at that point."

"Wow... that's super cool! I've never seen anything like it." I say.

"Fingernails please." Kay suddenly sounds like a Drill Sergeant. We show her our hands. "Kathy you'll be trimming those before the first shift... they look hideous. No nail polish and keep them trimmed back and neat. We don't tolerate a slovenly look. Put your hair back in a tie. Light makeup is fine, but not red or dark lipstick – it's cheap looking." My eyebrows raze my hairline. Now she sounds like a *mean* Drill Sergeant. Elke has a look of shock on her face. "Ship shape and Bristol fashion is what we are achieving here!" I nod to look agreeable.

After the kitchen tour, we walk up to our cabin. It's another ancient-looking wood building. There are two windows in the front and two on each side. We enter and find it clean and cozy. Two bedrooms are already made up for us, and a small seating area grouped around a wood stove looks inviting, but there's no kitchen or bathroom to be seen. Bare bulbs hang from tangles of wire, strung from a water stained ceiling. Curtains in faded blue, match the linoleum floor. There's a small hand mirror hung off a nail, the only mirror I see. I look around... no TV!

"It can get cold at night. Maybe you could get a fellow from the crews to chop wood in exchange for doing his laundry," Kay offers. There's no way I'm doing that. I hate doing laundry and I always liked chopping wood when our family went camping. "I'll leave you two for the rest of the day to explore the area. Oh yes. The Tigwash Landing village is where the post office is. The mail comes in and out on Tuesday's and Friday's. That should be all for now. Make a decent fist of your summer job." She marches back down the gravel to the main lodge.

We close our door, and I start prancing around, "Now ship shape and Bristol fashion. No lipstick in 'Slutty Red!'"

Elke salutes and marches around. "Hair tidy... not shitty!" We laugh hysterically.

I confess I need a nap before exploring. Elke puts on hiking boots, saying she'll be back in two hours. I lay down on the squeaky, iron bed, and fold into the saggy mattress making me feel like a human hot dog. Sleep is immediate.

*

Elke rousts me up two hours later. "Get up... you have to see the village!" I shake myself out of a stupor and wander out for a pee. I'm a little wary of the outhouse, but it's perfectly clean, painted yellow, and someone's artistic pink flowers dot the walls. It doesn't smell like anything. We'll have to learn how to keep it from stinking.

*

"What village?" I ask as we set off.

"The Indian village where the post office is. Have you ever been on an Indian reservation?" Elke is stomping the ground in apparent anger, sending up wisps of dust.

"Sure. Where I live, there are two areas where farming and fishing are a big deal. There are places to go to for fresh produce and fish." I don't understand Elke's under the breath hissing.

"Wait until you see it. I turned around and left... I felt like a trespasser." She leads me down a dusty road, barely wide enough for a vehicle. A wooden sign in disrepair, propped up on a big, metal drum, covered in dried mud, says, "Tigwash Landing."

We enter the village slowly and quietly. This is nothing like the Vancouver Island reservations I've been to. I remember them from when I was little... Mom going to buy fresh-caught fish or vegetables while I sat in the car watching the kids riding bikes and people fixing boats.

I try to keep my face forward and impartial. People are sitting around on broken chairs. Their vacant stares don't acknowledge us; we don't say hello. The houses are all the same. Bare plywood, no paint, or any semblance of finishing a regular house would have. There must have been glass windows, but the three windows on each house I see are covered in dirty plastic sheeting. On some windows, the sheeting's tattered and flapping in the breeze. The doors look like a piece of plywood and nothing more. They're living in houses unfit for humans, as far as I can tell. We walk by a larger building, with a sign hanging on one nail, 'Shower and Toilet Block.' The shacks don't even have washrooms? This is how these people live all year round? Trash blows by us. There are skinny, shifty dogs lurking in the surrounding bushes. How could this happen in Canada? Why do they live in such disastrous conditions? We spot the post office and go inside. At least this little building looks half decent. The person serving us looks about my age. Her long, black hair hangs down her back like a luxurious blanket. She has perfect skin, lighter than the other people we saw along the way. "Hi. Could we buy some stamps please?" I try to smile, unsure of how this is going to go.

Her brown eyes light up, "Yes, of course, I'm Betty," she introduces herself, "welcome to Tigwash! I'm guessing you're working at Gold Miners."

"We arrived today and start tomorrow. Do you live in the village?"

"Not really. My mom's here, Dad's in Whitehorse. I go to school in town and work here in the summer... I'm going to university in September. I'm getting an education and then I'll come back to work with our people to build better lives here. It's my future... I can't wait!" Her voice is firm and passionate. I don't blame her. It's appalling here. Someone has to do something.

"Deal," I say, "I hope we see you this summer." I stop myself from sharing my feelings about her village and its people.

"Enid and Leo are my godparents. They're salt of the earth! You'll have a fun summer!" She turns her attention to the ringing phone on the wall. "It's the phone we all use, and I'm in charge of answering it," she reaches for the receiver as we leave.

"There's only one phone for the community?" Elke whispers. It's beyond my understanding. We walk back in the direction of the lodge and see a small campfire being lit. There's a large bottle of something being passed back and forth amongst the rough- looking trio. We walk as fast as we can.

"It's a total hole. It's going to give me nightmares." I shudder.

*

"There's Leo. Let's ask him about the village." Elke marches over. He spots us, and the direction we've come from. He lays down a large wrench and wipes the sweat off his forehead. The tractor has a couple of its pieces lying on the ground.

"Mr. Allen," Elke starts, "tell us about Tigwash Landing."

"Huh. They don't work, don't want to and they drink to get drunk almost every day they can get their hands on the booze. Don't hang around there girls. They keep to themselves and don't like intruders."

"They live in shacks, Mr. Allen." I say.

"Call me Leo. I've lived here, every summer, for almost twenty years. They don't live with any kind of pride. They'll burn furniture instead of chopping firewood. They get money to buy a snowmobile and then spend it on booze. They could work on the roads or construction, but they get a handout from the government which they're so used to getting, it stops their reason for needing, or wanting a job."

"You mean our government hands them money so they can sit and drink? Who comes up with such a bad idea?" I feel my face burning.

Leo sighs and shakes his head, "It's a long and complicated history between our native people and the white people here in the north. I would need a degree in diplomacy to tell you the story without getting hot under the collar myself. One day situations may change, but right now things are depressing for them."

"I hope something changes because that way of living is horrible," Elke blurts out. I don't know what to think about Leo telling us all this, but we thank him.

"Best to stay out of the village unless you're going to the post office... I mean it." Leo shakes his head and picks up the wrench, turning back to his work.

“I’m embarrassed for our country Elke. We need to do better by our own citizens! What’s wrong with us? You’d have to be cold hearted and blind not to see how gross it is.” She laughs and says she’s seen worse. Seen worse? I’ve got to hear about that sometime.

Our little cabin gets some personal touches. We move the two couches, so they form an L shape around the little wood-burning stove. A wood crate will serve as a coffee table. We move a well-worn, blue rug from the empty backroom to our front door. There are hooks for our coats. The only two pictures on the wall are of the Kluane Mountain Range. I pull back the curtains clearing the way for sunshine and dust motes.

We have a jug to fill with drinking water from the stream in the back, and decide we could easily wash up and brush our teeth there. I feel rugged and outdoorsy living in a cabin way up north.

The sun’s still high in the sky, and since the official start of the lodge’s season is tomorrow, we have time to get used to our new home. There’s a ladder set up alongside the cabin, so we climb onto the roof and check out the surrounding area. The stream creates a natural barrier between the grass covered rolling hills and us. There are large nondescript, white tanks in the back of the property, and those same small pine trees I’d seen earlier. Little mites of trees compared to home. I’m looking forward to experiencing the mystical ‘Midnight Sun’ where the days go on forever in summer.

I ask Elke about herself. “I’m from Germany but have been travelling for a year now. Before travelling, I went to England to improve my English language skills and then went to Paris to learn French. I was in school for business and marketing. Languages will be helpful for international work I want to do.” I love the way she says this in an old-fashioned, formal way.

“How old are you?” I lay down on the black, tar-shingled roof and look up at birds circling in the distance.

“I’m twenty-one. I want to travel for another year... then go home to find work.” She lays down on the scratchy surface.

“Two years of travelling? How can you be gone that long? Don’t you miss your friends and family?” A massive black bird lands on the roof and stares at us like we’re road kill.

“They’re there for when I get back. I write lots of letters and sometimes phone, except it’s expensive. My parents were sad at first, but now they’re happy. I’m living a busy life, working and learning languages.”

“You are *too* cool! I wish I could do that!” Rolling over onto my side, I face my new friend.

“Why couldn’t you? Are you married? Going to school in September? Caring for a sick relative perhaps?” She counts these points on her fingers.

“Zero for three. I can’t see how I *could* go. I have a boyfriend! I don’t have a passport,” sliding over to my back, sighing.

Elke's voice ramps up, her finger counting starts fresh, "Go on a short trip. Here's what you do: get a passport, make money, and get on a plane to another country. Maybe pick a country you could work in that isn't too difficult to travel in. England is easy. You can stay at International Youth Hostels and meet other travellers while you're looking around. Then you'll have the guts to take the leap and go further. It's hard at first but you'll meet lots of cool people."

"Thanks, Elke, you're *super* rad!" I'll think about what she's said. I'm not married, but Glen's my guy; I won't abandon him. Three months is long enough to be apart.

"What about you Kathy... what's your story?" I tell her everything about Anne and Rod, the final year of school and how Glen helped save me from the pain of Anne's death. I don't talk about my family, except to say I have a twin brother, a mom and a dad. I explain how I ended up in the Yukon and how she's Sandra's replacement. I rationalize staying put, "Sandra's an important person in my life... I can't abandon her either."

*

Kay appears at the lodge door and waves at us to come down. We wash our hands in the stream and keep the soap in a rock shaped like a bowl. It takes a minute to walk down.

Elke and I introduce ourselves to the two new people hired as chambermaids.

Monique is fresh from and doesn't seem to have a good handle on English. She looks like one of those dogs with the punched-in face. Her nose is upturned toward bulgy eyes and wiry hair. Elke speaks French to her, and I have no idea what they're saying.

"Jane where are you from?" I ask.

Her thin shoulders fold in on themselves like she's apologizing for existing, "I'm escaping my Toronto life," she squeaks. Maybe she got kicked out of the city for having the worlds ugliest hairdo. The partially grey hair looks like a cat crawled on top of her head and died. She has the thickest lenses I've ever seen set in a pair of glasses; they look like pop bottle bottoms. At least they hide most of her face, which looks like the sole of a running shoe. Everyone smiles politely without asking why she escaped.

"Monique and I met at the Church of the Spiritual Way and we'll be sharing our friendship this summer to reflect and meditate after work... you won't see us much," Jane says gently, sharing a watery smile with me.

"Cool... you know where to find us if you need anything!"

Kay has us help bring the platters to the table for our staff meal. There's delicious fresh whitefish caught in the lake this morning! We have mashed potatoes, peas and fresh baked buns. I'm going to get fat if I eat like this!

I find out Leo worked building the Alaska Highway when he was a young man. Enid was a 'bull cook,' which apparently is a camp attendant, cleaning rooms and doing other chores. They met here in 1942, went back to California to work on cattle ranches, but returned to open this lodge in 1960. Enid does all the talking, while Leo gives the occasional grunt. He seems grumpy, but I think he's a sweetie deep down.

Kay's a British citizen, who came over to work in the military. I'm correct! She fell in love with the north and has stayed ever since. She lives here all year round as the caretaker while Leo and Enid go back to California.

I tell a bit about myself, but not about Anne and Rod. I don't want everyone to know about it. People may look at me differently and I want to fit in.

Elke and I get a practice run cleaning up and resetting tables. The kitchen's small so we have to try not to bang into each other. We decide to take turns each washing and drying.

*

Tomorrow, we have a ten-person road crew coming in, and then our first bus tour! I know the sun's going to be up all night, and I'd like to see it, but I beg off and hit the bed. I look at the blank writing paper waiting to be filled. Not tonight, I'm beat. I nod to Snoopy, who's sitting on the water stained dresser; the sun creeps around drawn curtains, lighting the room and my sleep.

THIRTY-THREE

"Get up Kathy!" Elke calls. I quickly dress and run to the stream for a literal, breathtaking face wash in the freezing cold water. The sun's way up in the sky and I've slept in.

"How late are we?"

"We're not, it's eight o'clock!" Elke laughs, and agrees that seeing the sun shining all the time is going to take some getting used to. The air's fresh and scented with an unknown herb.

"It's beautiful here," I say as if I've always known it. I'm full of happiness, and a full-night's sleep.

*

We head in for a breakfast of some sort. I get to make coffee in the mad scientist coffee makers. It's rad how the water bubbles up into the upper chamber, swirls the coffee granules around, then by some mystery, the water decides to head back down into the bottom carafe. It tastes strong – I add sugar and milk to it. We make toast using the slowest toasters in the world. The locally made Low Bush Cranberry Jam is tart and tasty. We finish the breakfast creation and get to work.

"You need to empty everything out of the pantry, wash and dry it all. Then wash the windows with this newspaper and vinegar," Kay barks her orders at us. I've never washed a window with a newspaper, and when Leo strides through he comments on how he has the cleanest windows in the Yukon. They were cleaned last week. Maybe Kay's making work projects for us, to keep us busy. The pantry *is* dusty and greasy – it's a chore to get at the piles of plastic containers and baking pans. Everything looks, 'ship shape and Bristol fashion' by noon.

*

A large truck drives up and we're asked to help load in provisions.

"Damn moose on the highway at mile 1000... almost hit him. Not sure who'd have fared worse." The driver's covered in a chalky film. When he takes off his sunglasses, there's a raccoon look around the eyes where the dust missed. He hops down and opens the large back doors.

We're handed twenty-five-pound bags of flour, which seems a lot, but Ben weighs at least that much, and I hauled him around no problem. We load in flour, sugar, milk powder, baking supplies, meat, and boxes of other food items. The cartons of milk aren't refrigerated. I read the label. "Ultra Heat Treatment Shelf Milk – safe for six months – no refrigeration required. Cool. "Leo, why don't we go to the store when we need something?"

"Heh, heh, heh. The closest store is 200 miles away."

I keep on hauling supplies in the door. Every week Kay will put in an order, and we get the delivery two days later. No wonder the menu's small and expensive.

I'm a bit shocked at the menu prices. Bacon and eggs with toast is three dollars! Coffee's forty-five cents – that's crazy. At home we can get a breakfast special for $1.99 including all the coffee you can drink. There are four items on the dinner menu. Trout, pork chops, lamb chops and liver and onions. People must make more money up here because dinner is five dollars. I'm relieved we get our food for free.

After another great lunch of Kay's chicken noodle soup and fresh rolls slapped with butter, we go down to the lower level and meet the women who look after the laundry.

*

A heavy door to the basement needs a good shove to open. We're met with a blast of warm humidity. The air smells like laundry fresh out of the dryer. The room's long narrow windows bring in sunlight.

Two ladies, I understand are from Construction Bay, population fifty-seven, greet us.

Alberta is from around here. She has the same brown skin colour and long black hair as Betty. Her tiny chubby frame and easy smile make her super cute. Marina is tall, lanky and blonde, she's wearing loose fitting jeans and a sweatshirt declaring "Dawson City, Diamond Tooth Gerties Canada's First Casino."

They show us around the ridiculously prehistoric laundry system. Hot water and detergent are filled into large metal tubs where the sheets and towels get placed for washing. This cleaning's done by pushing a big, wooden stick, back and forth, and up and down. The rinse is done in other metal tubs, with clear hot water. After that, they get put through The Mangle.

"The what?" I ask. The machine has rollers and a large cranking wheel.

"It's a heavy-duty wringing machine. It takes most of the water out of the washing. We hang everything outside on the lines. If the weather's fine, everything dries in no time."

"This's a lot of work. You two must be super strong!" Elke points at their arms. They comically strut around baring their arms.

"Our husbands are impressed with our sexy muscles," Alberta jokes and both give us a show of pumping muscles.

We help them finish off the laundry and I enjoy hanging everything up outside in the warm breeze. Mom hung everything outside in okay weather. I love the smell of bed sheets dried in the sun.

“Oh look... there’s Jane and Monica by the lake. The ‘creatures’ are sitting cross legged while their arms are reaching skyward and swaying back and forth.” I can hear singing, although what tune is a mystery. “They’re too weird for me,” I whisper to Elke.

“Too weird... thank goodness we ended up together and not with them.”

A vehicle trundles down the rocky road, sending up dust behind it. “Oh,” Marina says, “It’s Nurse Colleen and Constable Davies. They’re not a couple,” she turns to us and gives a giant wink and a nod. “Why don’t you go over and make fresh coffee. Maybe Kay has made a cake.”

*

Elke and I walk the short distance to a half-decent pickup truck all painted in one colour: black. We introduce ourselves, they do in turn, and we offer to put on the coffee.

Nurse Colleen strides across to the table. Her brown hair, tied in a high ponytail, swings in the air. She looks more like an athlete than a nurse in her Adidas triple stripe tracksuit and matching runners. Constable Davies pulls a chair out for her. He looks the part in his black RCMP uniform. Gold patches on the shoulders confirm he’s police. I get why Colleen would like him, but I don’t know why the possible romance isn’t public. Who wouldn’t like a tall, muscular, brown-eyed blondie?

“How do you cope, living in such a small village with nothing to do?” They stare at me.

"Kathy, there's plenty to do! We work long hours and are always on call. There's fishing, hiking, hunting. The community always puts on bingos or potlucks. It's a friendly village which makes my job much easier," says Constable Davies.

"There's a Canada Day dance too. You'll both have to come," Nurse Colleen says.

*

The two drive off; we clean up and then compliment Kay on her chocolate chip oatmeal cookies. A hint of a smile cracks her already cracked face.

"Pish posh! Now... you have two hours free time before the crew comes in. Be back at 4:00 p.m. *precisely,* to set a table for ten people. They may want beer. Go to the bar and put some in the fridge now before you leave."

"There's a bar here?" Elke looks around.

"Yes. We don't open it because the villagers think they can come in and sit down. They can't. We keep it closed except for crews. The outside door will stay locked all the time. Don't dawdle Kathy!" *What's up her butt about me... I'm not dawdling.* She goes back to her kitchen labours, and we see the door – on it, a small, hand painted sign says, 'Bar.'

"Did she say what I think she said?" Elke stares at me.

"If she means villagers are banned from the bar because they're Indian, I think I heard the same thing. The prejudice is one hundred percent complete as if we're in South Africa, not Canada. What a pile of crap. I'm going to tell them that."

“Wait awhile Kathy,” Elke cautions, “they probably have some reason we don’t know about yet.” I agree, and we put beer in the disaster of a fridge. It has a large cylindrical, cooling system attached to the top, instead of the back, like all other fridges I’ve ever seen. It’s rattling and clinking, like everything else around here.

“I’ve never used a tray to serve drinks. Could you teach me how?” Elke gives me a lesson on how to load and unload the drinks and bottles in a balanced manner so the whole tray doesn’t tip over. She shows me how to keep it level when leaning over. I’ll have to give it a try, but for tonight she says she’ll handle the beverages if I do the meal order.

*

We finish up and decide to walk the other way down the lakeside. We don’t want to end up in the village again. There’s an old road, somewhat grown over with grasses, but we can see where it goes. After forty-five minutes we end up on a paved road. In the distance, we see a plain metal building, and an airstrip.

“Cool! We’re at Tigwash Airport. Let’s go in and see if Norm’s here!” I’m jogging now to the door. Elke’s right behind me; we cautiously enter.

A man older than us by at least ten years turns around and greets us by name.

“Hello, Kathy and Elke! Welcome to Tigwash Airport. The name’s Simon.”

“You know who we are?” I ask, trying not to stare at his revolting bowl haircut.

“Hey, it’s a pretty small place, and word travels fast. I know everything! Actually, Marina’s my wife, and I happened to call her this morning. She said she’d met two fun-loving, young women. Must be you two!

“That’s us... but we can’t stay... don’t want to be late for work,” says Elke. “We’ll be back!”

*

We change into shapeless white dresses and throw on very ugly red and white-checkered aprons for our first official dinner service. This uniform is what we’re to wear while on shift? It doesn’t say ‘snazzy’ by any stretch of the imagination.

The ten men come in and sit at the table we finished setting two minutes ago. A gaggle of scruffy hair, jean jackets and matching seen-better-days-jeans make up the group. One thing they all have in common is smoking. I grab a bunch of ashtrays and send them around. Everyone lights up and takes a long drag. They’re all laughing about something.

Elke appears in the cloud of smoke and asks who wants a beer. They all lift their hands and she heads off to the bar. My belly’s going flip-flop as if I’m about to go on stage. I gather up some drama skills and decide a one-act play ‘opening scene’ will be my tactic.

“Good evening ladies and gentlemen,” I boom. “Here, for your eating pleasure, I have these lovely red menus for your perusal. Kindly note the four fabulous dinner choices on the right side of said menu. You’re all in for quite an evening of fine dining!”

They all kind of gawk at me and then burst out laughing. I relax now that I've made them happy. Elke returns with beer having caught the last of my speech and winks at me. She puts the beer down without tipping any of them over. I take the food orders and pass them to Kay.

"Was that necessary?" Kay glares at me.

"They laughed didn't they?" How bad could it have been?

"Wipe that cheek off your face. Watch with whom you joke around... not everyone will think you're funny," snarls Madame Sour Puss who looks like she'd chew the head off a bunny.

She turns to start the meals; Elke makes a face behind her back. "*Whom,*" she mimes. I put a hand on my mouth, stifling a laugh.

The meals look incredible. Kay makes them look like homemade dinners for starving men. The plates are heaping with fresh looking vegetables, mashed potatoes, and grilled meat in generous piles.

"This's why we like staying here!" Says one of the men, while staring lovingly at his meal. "Way to go Kay, a lovely scoff!" he yells at the kitchen, as they attack their plates.

"Ladies, we're doing a campfire by the lake if you'd like to join us. Guitars and bad singing's all we can offer," says scruff ball, big belly guy.

"Sure, we can come along," I say speaking for both of us. I look at Elke and she agrees.

We clean up the kitchen and prepare for breakfast – there isn't a whole lot to do yet. Kay dismisses us early.

*

We change into jeans and sweaters. I can smell their campfire from our cabin.

"What if the boys get flirty with you?"

"Boys don't flirt with me... I'm boy repellent."

"I doubt it."

"I am. Glen was the first and only guy to like me special... no kidding."

"Are all the boy's idiots where you live?"

"Ha... I think I'll keep my repellent on tonight. You?"

"I didn't see anything so far."

*

We find them sitting on hand-made benches, around a small fire. Big Belly introduces himself as Frank, hands us a beer and then introduces us to everyone. I'm sure I won't remember their names.

"Hey there Kathy... who knit ya? Mr. Wire Framed Glasses asks in a thick accent I don't get.

"Sorry, not getting your question." I tilt the beer bottle at him.

"Kathy, me doll... who knit ya. Where ya from?"

"I'm from Vancouver Island... the land of no jobs." Is he being rude?

"I'm a Newfoundlander... land of no jobs. And do you always look like that Kathy my love?"

Now I'm pissed off. "What do you mean budzo?"

"Oh me nerves... do you always wear that beautiful smile?" Asks Mr. Wired Framed Glasses. Everyone smiles a giant fake smile at me.

"Yep I do! So there you..." I say.

"Okay... we're having you on... don't get crooked. Frank... you owe me a dollar. I guessed right you'd say yes. One more. How old are you?"

"I'm a hundred and thirty-five. You're all bonkers! Go pick on Elke!" I jostle her and achieve an overachieving smile.

"Never mind... I'm off limits!" Says Elke, "I'm never going to get the better of a Newfie... too sharp for me!"

"We're not all Newf's," Frank points to the guy with wire framed glasses, "Ray and I are from around the bay... we're real." He nods to the guy with a guitar, "Wade's not a real Newf... he's a townie and Jimmy comes from away, so he doesn't count."

"Frank... Newfoundland is still number one," Jimmy raises a middle finger, smiling.

"Fuck you bay boys," says Wade without malice, "stunned as your arse."

"Now boys... that's enough of that... no cursing!" Mocks Frank, pulling a jacket over his expansive belly. The others laugh, but no one swears again.

The guys tell us they work on the roads during the summer and live in 'town,' which is Whitehorse to everyone around here. It's ten thirty, the sun's barely going down. The sky looks like it's on fire. It's ten shades of orange, covering us in a glowing blanket. It's the most beautiful sky I've ever seen.

"Now Wade, give us a song," says Ray.

"'Sonny's Dream' here." Wade picks up the guitar lying next to him and starts strumming. His beautiful voice fills the campfire circle telling the story of a mother not wanting her son to go away to sea.

Everyone claps after the story filled song. "Goodnight everyone," Elke and I say, and get up to leave.

*

We walk back to our cabin humming the tune.

"Elke, do you have a boyfriend?"

"No, and I don't want one. Men don't like girlfriends who don't stick around and I don't stick around. What are you going to do about Glen?"

"What do you mean? I'll be back with him in September."

"Yah, sure Kathy. You had all those men wrapped around your fingers with your big smile and sassy attitude," she says.

"What?" I open the cabin door and shake off my sweater.

"Kathy, you have the gift of making people laugh. You're funny. Guys dig that." Elke finds the light switch, which bathes the cabin in a dim, yellow hue.

"Never heard that before. I'm Kathy... Alan's twin sister, drama kid, Anne's best friend and Glen's love."

"Now you're 'Kathy of the North,' putting magic spells on men and making everyone laugh."

*

I pile the quilts around me staring at the blank wall. Am I seen as different to my Longmore life? Is the fun magic Elke sees in me, the me I want to be? My stomach is never in a knot anymore. I don't walk in fear waiting for the next blow out. It's rad not having parents breathing down my neck, especially about the curfew issue I've been living with. I'm not living with the harsh judgment and criticism Mom and Dad dish out... especially Mom. Alan doesn't worry me, I guess because I don't see him and I think he's made a strange choice, but I believe he'll be okay.

But what about Glen? I stare at my writing paper, deciding not to fill it. The small cassette player from home is sitting beside my bed. I didn't even ask if I could bring it with me – I took it since no one used it at home except me. I put on Elton John, *Goodbye Yellow Brick Road.*

THIRTY-FOUR

We set up the dining room for thirty bus tour guests. The road crew left and will be back in two weeks. Now we have a group of Americans' going through to Alaska.

Big dinners are served simpler than each person getting a menu. We serve soup and baskets of freshly baked buns, and then lake trout. For dessert, Kay has these weird squares. It's milk, sugar, cornstarch and vanilla with the low bush cranberries mixed inside. Its called Blancmange and apparently, it's a bus tour favourite.

A weary group of gray haired travellers alight from a snappy looking 'Earth Tours' bus. The long-legged, redheaded bus driver, in a drab brown, double-knit polyester suit, is getting the luggage from the underbelly of the bus. Karl, our shy helper, assists with the unloading.

Elke and I are taking it all in when Brown Polyester turns around and looks at us. He looks shocked, and then promptly falls over a suitcase. It's hard not to laugh at his misfortune, but everyone's laughing loudly. Leo pipes up, "Never seen women before? Heh." Elke and I are feeling bad for this fellow, but not really!

*

The guests head to their rooms to freshen up before dinner. Brown Polyester comes around to us in the dining room, while we're setting out bread and butter. "Hi. I know I made a big entrance. Please ignore that smooth move, and I'll be indebted to you two forever. My name's Shawn, and I know you're Kathy and Elke."

"GIRLS... onward and upwards!" Kay yowls; we excuse ourselves, with eye rolls. "Kathy, keep your voice down... you sound like an elephant trumpeting!" Jeez, what a bag.

The dinner service is hectic because we try to serve all the soup before it gets cold, and then we try and do the same with the fish. There's almost no room to work. We do our best, but it's almost too much for the kitchen to handle. After clearing dessert, we're left with a satisfied tour group, and hundreds of dishes to clean. Everyone loved the meal. The dessert, indeed, was a hit. They probably don't know what's in it.

We're dancing to no music around the sinks when Shawn pokes his head in. "Great job ladies. I have three cold beers and nowhere to drink them. What do you say?"

"Come to our cabin... if you can handle two rad women," I say, with a flair for the dramatic.

“Yes for beer! You’re winning over a German girl’s heart!” Elke hangs up all the drying cloths, and we’re ready to leave, having done the breakfast set up before dinner. That’ll be coffee, and muffins, on side tables that get moved into place in the morning. The group gets a breakfast menu also. That should be a trip.

We head off to the cabin, getting seated on our two little couches. I spark up a fire, and we crack the beers. I pick Rolling Stones, *Miss You*, cassette.

Shawn is twenty-one and going to university in Toronto. “This’s a good summer job,” he says, “there’s a great salary and plenty of tips. You gotta be a real people kind of person. Don’t get me wrong though... the guests are all nice! Nice like you two. To Kathy and Elke in the north!” He lifts his beer, and we all do a ‘cheers,’ drink and talk until our beer is finished.

After he’s back in the main lodge, Elke says, “he’s all yours honey.”

“Elke, no – you take him if you want,” defending my current relationship status.

“Not a chance for me. Not my type. Anyways, did you see the dreamy eyes he was making at you? He’s got it hard for you.”

“He’s cute.” Stop it, Kathy. Glen. Remember Glen.

I climb into bed without starting a letter to Glen.

*

Breakfast is all about keeping the mad scientist coffee makers running full tilt. We have a big coffee urn to pour it all into, but people sure like their coffee hot, and ‘keep it coming.’

We have to start making toast before anyone's in the dining room. Sixty slices at least to make, in the turtle slow toasters. The toast then gets stacked in long lines. By the time people get it, the bread's dry and cold. There's no other way to do it.

Most people want eggs in all different ways. Alberta is in the kitchen getting the food out as efficiently as possible.

"She cooks, she cleans – she's Wonder Woman," I cry as she passes over five bacon and egg orders.

Of course, we get through it. We're a super team! The bus is leaving for the next leg of its journey. Shawn pops his head in the kitchen and tells us he'll be back soon. He whispers in my ear, "you're going to be my girl. You're the best." Then he walks away. I swallow hard and say nothing.

We clean our way through the pile of dishes. "Shawn said something sweet to me," I whisper to Elke, "he's a charmer."

*

After having the morning off, Kay arrives in the kitchen with a very large man by her side. Big black robes cover his girth. The telltale white collar of a Catholic Priest is choking his blubbery neck.

"Girl's, this is Father John, our local Catholic Priest." He slowly drags his eyes up and down our bodies, his gaze lingering, unhurried. His tongue darts out and fidgets across red, chapped lips. I step back from the handshake, I want to say something to him about how he's looking at us, but nothing comes out. I look at Elke who's giving him a defiant stare down.

"Are you ladies coming to church today?" He asks kindly enough, his tongue back in his mouth.

“I’m a Protestant, so no,”

“We take anybody,” he laughs deeply at his own joke. We all laugh to be polite.

“Well, you never know,” Elke says, not offering to show up either. Kay and Father John leave, wander up the hill and down a barely visible pathway to where the church is. Neither Elke nor I, have seen it yet. The last church I was in had my friend’s bodies lying in it. I’m not in a real hurry to see the inside of another church.

“What do you think of our local priest?” Elke inhales, her teeth gritted. I think I know how *she* feels about him.

“Slimy. Did you see how he stared at your boobs? I’m going to stay out of his way,” I can’t believe a priest would act so creepy.

*

Since no one’s checking in until three o’clock, we decide on a walk to the airport. It’s another glorious day of sunshine; breezes blow across the cattail grasses. “Have you written to anyone yet?” Elke asks.

“No and I’m starting to feel guilty about it. I don’t even know how to explain Tigwash. I thought I’d be in a quiet, remote place with nothing going on, but it’s non-stop action, with tons of fun people to meet and hang out with. What am I going to tell Glen?”

“Kathy, you’re here... have fun, and don’t feel bad about it. You’ve already won the hearts of everyone... except for Kay! Enjoy your new life! Be happy wherever you are.”

“Well, I suppose I could tell Glen about the general stuff... but not about the guys we’ve met.”

“Tell him what makes you happy about being here. Other news – what about that Shawn guy?”

Nothing!” My voice cracks. It’s *so* not true. He’s funny, cute, and I like him way more than I should. He’ll be back with a fresh tour on July 3rd, and I can’t wait to see him again.

*

We quietly walk into the airport office and see a new face. “Hi. We’re Kathy and Elke,” I say.

“Of course you are!” I’m Norm! Dan told me all about you. He plugs in the kettle and gathers three mugs. I notice a slight limp as his slender frame moves across the room. He certainly looks better groomed than most of the people here. Neatly combed salt and pepper grey hair in an actual style, clean khakis and a new looking sweatshirt that says, Faro, YT.

“There’s a plane coming in shortly. Sit here,” he motions to chairs near the large window. The runway is dirt, fenced in and surrounded by the ever present grass.

Norm sits at a desk overlooking the runway, puts on a big headset and starts speaking to the approaching plane. There are smatterings of technical talk and a few names interjected. They report their ‘call letters’ and Norm lets them know the wind speed and direction.

The plane, still airborne, starts to wobble. The engine sounds alternately loud and then almost nothing.

“Scheisse,” says Elke grabbing my arm.

"Jeez... not good," The plane looks ready to crash. We hold our breaths and can't take our eyes off the small, coughing plane.

Norm speaks, in a calm voice, with no real equipment except the radio and his eyes, while the plane lands in a lurch, bounces along the airstrip, stopping just short of the far fencing.

"I don't know what happened... we'll find out. Want to come meet them and see how the plane is refueled?" We jump up and follow him. Two people come out of the tiny door, perched above the wing. They step very carefully onto the wing and then hop to the ground.

"Norm, you old bastard! Sorry about the abrupt landing... I'm out of fuel." A man, sporting a frazzled, graying beard, and not many teeth, gives Norm a big hug.

"Christ, I don't need that much excitement," Norm says.

"Who are these ladies?" An older woman, with the same drab, beige outfit as the man, follows right behind, grappling Norm. She seems unfazed by the scary landing.

"This is Kathy and Elke. They're the gals at Gold Miners Lodge this year. Sal and Doug work a gold claim near here. Any gold yet?"

"Never going to tell you," jokes Sal. She asks us questions about ourselves, and our impressions of the north. We have questions for them about being *actual* gold miners. They say it's not as romantic or as unbearable as the gold rush. "We use a backhoe to load the riverbed gravel into the sluice boxes, and as long as the equipment doesn't break down, we're in business. The gold shakes out to the bottom... it's a treasure hunt every day."

They get a full tank of fuel and continue their flight. "Fuel up more often!" Norm yells and waves them off as they taxi.

We get a tour of the building including radios, charts, phones and a Teletype machine. "What's a Teletype machine?"

"It's a message sending machine. I type in the message here," he points to a small keyboard, "and then send it by punching this," his hand moves to a black button. "At the other end, it prints on this tape. He shows us a strip of paper tape, with the Whitehorse weather report on it. We use it for Canadian Government business."

"My boyfriend's on a coast guard ship. Could you send him a message for me?" I ask with a smile, not expecting anything, but Norm says yes.

"I can, but I'll time it, so we don't get in trouble for sending a personal message. Let me work it out for you."

"Super Norm! Thank you." I grab a pencil and paper. I don't want to be personal – I write. *"Surprise from Kathy. Having a great experience. A letter's on the way"* It seems like little to say. I'd better write that letter.

Norm says, “drop by anytime... the place could use some cheering up.” Elke and I walk back to the lodge, both of us silent. Anne is in my mind. She’s always with me, and I’m thankful for her spirit. Did she lead me to the Yukon?

*

The lodge comes into sight, and we see all the stark white sheets billowing in the breeze. The sunshine’s busy making them smell like Mother Nature. Monique and Jane, the ‘creatures’ are lying under the sheets like corpses.

Our group this evening is the Arctic Research Patrol. They’re glacier surveyors; a quiet group compared to the road crew. They could be triplets... all wearing black framed glasses, short military hair and totally dweeby, sand coloured shirt and pant combos complete with a billion flap style pockets. They’re going to fly over the Kluane Glacier and see if they can get an idea of how it’s either shrinking or expanding. After dinner and clean up, Elke and I sit with them.

“Yukon’s a part of Canada, but separated from most of the population, making it seem like it's in its own world.”

Mark says, “the term for leaving the Yukon is ‘going outside.’” I heard one of the road crew use the expression, but I thought it was as it sounds – not actually to leave the territory!

“Do you think you’d like to move to Whitehorse after the summer?” Asks Paul while he sips Johnnie Walker scotch.

“I’m not sure of my plans yet but I’d consider it,” says Elke.

“It sounds like it’d be a fun place to live.” Would I? No... Glen.

“I think you two suit the north... you’re both easy to talk to and smart young women.”

*

At ten o’clock I retreat to the cabin and start the task of writing letters. I’m sitting at the little table with pen and paper, loving the sunlight through the window next to me, sending strong enough rays that I can avoid the dull bulb above me. Playlist tonight is Steely Dan, *Deacon Blues*.

Dear Glen

I’ve been gone a week, and my whole world has changed. I’m in the middle of nowhere on the Alaska Highway. The nearest town is Whitehorse, 200 miles away. The people here are kind and welcoming.

I’ll be truthful with you as I always am. I do miss you, my love. Luckily I’m in a very happy land, which helps our distance become bearable. I’m fine, and the job here is fun.

I decide to throw in some first week observations and explain the other workers. I make Kay out to be the bitch that she is. I do the cliché lipstick kiss on the letter then seal it. It gets sent to a government center and then somehow makes its way to the ship. Glen had said it might take two weeks.

I write home a less gushy letter. I let everyone know I'm having an incredibly fantastic time here. I don't even have to make it up to curb their worries. I go on about the beautiful, endless wilderness, the midnight sun teasing us always, and our urge to be awake much more than usual. I write about the people we've met up to now. In writing, I reflect on how many genuine, real-deal people I've come to know in such a short time.

I don't write I miss Mom and Dad, because I don't. I'm finally out from under their gaze and I feel like an emerging butterfly. I'm on the way to defining my life. For now, I'll keep all these thoughts inside me.

THIRTY-FIVE

We're in the groove now. Elke and I don't always work together. Sometimes there isn't the need to have both of us on at the same time. There doesn't seem to be an urgency to drum up business, and I wonder how they manage, with hardly any customers. It's feast or famine around here. For the past three days there have been the glacier surveyors, but today another bus tour comes in. Shawn won't be the driver this run.

I'm more prepared for this tour. We'll do the same format with dinner and breakfast. It's 3:00 p.m. and we're standing outside to greet them. We wave to welcome our new customers coming down the drive.

The bus driver exits and comes straight over to Elke and me. Eyes following, Leo isn't missing a beat. Our driver has long, thick brown hair to his shoulders, giant black-framed glasses above a thick, neatly trimmed beard. He's all chuckles and hair. "You must be Kathy," he leans in, gives me a tight hug like I'm a long lost relative.

"Yes, that's me... how do you know?" Regaining my position.

"Shawn can talk about nothing else. Kathy, Kathy and Kathy. You've tied his heartstrings in a bow."

"Heh, heh," chuckles Leo, "like bees to the honey." He lopes off. I feel my face burning.

"I'm Ivan... great to meet you two. I know you're Elke. Word gets around!" Elke grabs his big paw, using both her hands and bobs it up and down energetically. "I hear if I bring beer, after shift, you'll drink it with me. I also have other party favours," he offers.

"Sure! We're in for the beer." Elke agrees, and we say we'll go to the cabin when all the work's completed.

Ivan looks back at the bus realizing Karl is halfway done unloading the baggage; he returns to his duties.

The group is elderly, and a few of the ladies have a blue tint in their hair. It must be some old people, trendy, hair-do style. It looks very unnatural. Elke and I welcome all the guests, without hair witticisms.

It's show time!

I'm better this time at the service part, so I joke around and relax a bit. "I'm so pretty and popular that's why I'm in the Yukon, working in the middle of nowhere!" People laugh and seem very interested in how the heck a person gets a job in a place like this. They enjoy hearing of how I went to the Yukon phone book and applied at every lodge. "How adventurous and brave," they all croon, blue hair tossing around, like an ocean in a gale.

"Yes, I used to feel like a terrified adventurer, scared out of my wits for doing this. Now, I think I've made the best decision of my life," I get a cheer from the latest audience.

*

We close up the dining room, all ready for the morning, dreaming about how yummy that beer's going to taste. Ivan knocks on our cabin door shortly after we let ourselves in. Everyone grabs a spot on the couch; I put on Genesis, *Wind and Wuthering*. Ivan lives in Whitehorse, tour bus driving in the summer and driving taxi in the winter. He paints a very appealing picture of living in town and offers us to stay at his apartment if we need a place to crash.

We're part way through our beer; Ivan pulls out a joint. I decide to give it a try since there are no parents to cross. He lights up and passes it to Elke. She takes a puff and passes it to me. I try to imitate her, remembering how Glen did it, trying not to look like I'm new at this. My attempts create a cabin full of laughter. I splutter and gasp all the smoke out, and then for act two, I cough for a long time. When I recover, I confess I'm not a pot smoker. The joint goes around again, and they give me a little more instruction on how to toke properly. I manage all right, except almost immediately, I stop talking. It's like a zipper has gone across my lips. I'm woozy and tired. All of a sudden I'm not very fun. No joking, no chatting or laughing. I sit there like a lump on a log. I don't like this at all.

I listen to Ivan and Elke discuss the north, and I try to talk. Maybe they have sparks flying, but I'm too stoned to figure it out. I tell them, "I'm going to bed."

"Oh, you can't handle it," jokes Ivan, staring at me through bleary, red streaked eyeballs.

"No. I don't think this is for me," I manage to say before crashing into bed.

*

The next morning I'm fine. We feed the tour the same plodding way, and I can't see the morning ever being smooth sailing with the antiquated system. Despite the mediocre service, we do get tips. The cash is difficult to spend around here; I'm saving it all up to supplement the pay cheque.

We all wave the tour bus off on its next leg and turn to get on with the cleanup.

*

Two hours later, we hear a loud rumbling in the distance. The noise is getting closer now; it's above us, making a whapity, whap sounding racket. We run outside to see what it is. A large helicopter hovers and settles down in the open field beside the lodge.

Once the engine's cut and the rotor blades start slowing down, two men get out, duck low, moving quickly from the aircraft. They're dressed for the bush and I'm getting used to this scruffy, messy Yukon uniform. Even *I'm* getting more relaxed with my look. I leave my hair '*au natural*' these days... no need to curl it if it's tied back anyhow. The work uniform's an ugly, shapeless sack of a thing, but comfortable; now, I like it. The northern look is super casual.

"Hi, my name's Alex. This is Stan. We're due to come this evening but popped down for lunch, if the trolley's open. Hope we aren't putting you out," the tall, thin man drawls carefully, his frizzy, gray hair appears as he swoops his sweaty, worn out, bush patina, cowboy hat off his head, pressing it against his chest.

"Not at all," I open my arms, adding a sweeping gesture toward the lodge, "welcome!"

"There's soup on you're going to devour," interjects Elke, not even looking at them. Her eyes seem stuck, by force, onto the helicopter.

Kay's perturbed her morning is been ruffled. "Kathy, was this your smart idea?" She grumbles, like a troll under a trespassed bridge. Elke charms her, saying her cooking's the best and the men came only for her Mulligatawny soup. Kay grumbles, and then, with her head down we see a smile under all that troll. She hastily prepares lake trout salad sandwiches and heats the soup.

The men finish their meals calling out well deserved compliments. "Kudos Kay," Loud approval, and a round of applause, may cause Kay's heart to start beating anytime soon.

They are geophysicists, doing earth studies of some sort. It sounds very academic and scientific. They don't say they're looking for anything in particular. Maybe it's top secret!

"We'll see you tonight," says Alex, grinning, showing a gap in his front teeth, "would you two like to ride in the chopper? We have extra fuel, and a place we want to check out. It's a fly by, over a water system. There was a bear there ... we may get a photo."

"YES," I yip. They laugh; Elke's in too. I cross my fingers for agreeable weather conditions tonight.

*

The evening's clear and the wind calm. Alex and Stan give us a lesson on how to get in and out of the helicopter. We need to duck down and keep our arms down because the rotors rise up and down depending on the revs. Stan's much shorter and stockier than Alex – he barely ducks. I scrunch down extra low so I don't get my head lopped off. We get in: everyone puts a large headset on to hear and talk to each other. The camera's clicking like mad as I try to document every moment.

Taking off is more a vertical lift up off the ground. An invisible giant is picking us up in the palm of his hand. We fly straight up in the air and then swoosh forward as if the giant is gently swinging his arm. "This is the best ever!" I look at the

earth, removing itself from us. We fly along the lakeside, and I see a funny sight.

"What am I looking at down there?" I ask out loud to no one in particular.

That's a native cemetery," says Alex, "Those are miniature houses, 'Spirit Houses' meant for the spirit afterlife. You'll have to visit them." I don't want to wander around the village, but I would go see them. It sounds worth the walk in.

We get lifted up over a range of hills. They're treeless, rocky and covered with moss. We're flying fairly close to the ground. The helicopter finds its way to a stream and we follow it along.

"We'll try landing on that flat area," Stan, the pilot, cocks his head forward, and starts descending. There's a strange dropping sensation. Elke, looks at me, her eyes huge. I feel like we've been thrown off a ledge.

Stan yells, "one o'clock." I look at my watch, and everyone else looks slightly right out the concave windows.

A bear's in the stream showing off a glossy, black coat, whopping frame and, as it looks up at us, a big set of teeth flashes, as it snarls at us. It rears up, standing on two hind legs, a massive animal. Stan aborts the landing to avoid aggravating the bear further.

"Shit, we got too close for his comfort," says Stan as we swing around for our trip back. I manage to snap a few photos of my first Yukon bear sighting.

I enjoy the landing more than the takeoff... the invisible giant gently placing us back onto the ground feels like defying gravity. I remember to duck and exit safely. It's loud and exciting, like a movie scene I would always have loved to be in, except this time it's actually me in the movie. We both thank them for the ride, and we'll see them in the morning.

*

I'm fairly wound up when we get back to the cabin. "My life's way more exciting here," I bubble up.

"I know! You can't get a helicopter ride in Germany like this one. I loved seeing the bear. Europeans don't see much wildlife in our own countries. We have hardly any forests left for them to live in... I bet Germans would be keen to come here as tourists." Elke and I brush our teeth and wash up at the stream. The sky's still a mix of pink, gold and red as the sun makes its way across the horizon displaying the long sunsets only available in a northern summer.

*

After morning duties, Elke and I are instructed to walk to the village and pick up the lodge mail. We ask Enid about walking to the cemetery, and she says it's okay, as long as we're respectful. I grab my camera, and we walk up the wretched road to the dismal situation. I can tell, as we get close to the post office, a rock has been put through a windowpane, and has been patched with some sort of book. I wonder why someone doesn't fix it properly. What a place.

"Hi Betty." She waves while ending a phone call. We collect the mail and tell her we're going to the cemetery.

"Our people have let it get run down. No one wants to look after it." She hands us a bag and asks us to collect garbage if we see any. Of course we'll help. It's a small task compared to what this whole mess will take to fix up. As we turn to go, I see what the hole in the window is patched with. It's a booklet with 'Canadian Passport Application' written on the cover.

Impulsively, I ask if Betty if she has another one.

"Sure. Every post office has them. No one around here ever asks for one because no one goes anywhere, but we have to stock them." Betty passes me the application. There's both a lurch and a tremble in my stomach. "The passport photos can be done by Curtis, in Construction Bay. He'll take the proper photos and send them to Whitehorse for printing."

"Thanks, Betty." What a hassle it would've been to drive two hundred miles for the photos. There must be all sorts of things people can't get here like hospital care, eyeglasses and dental work.

"You'll be free to travel the world," Elke gives me an excited shoulder hug.

"I can't. Recall the boyfriend and a life in Longmore." There's a local coming at us – we veer to the left, avoiding him. He trips past us not even looking up from his booze bottle.

*

We're at the cemetery; Elke stops me from going in the little, paint-peeled gate. "Kathy, you aren't convincing me *at all*! Do you have a fulfilling life in Longmore?"

"I... well... sort of," d*o I*? "Elke, I'm confused about home. I adore my friends, and Glen's all important to me. I guess there's a pull toward them, but I feel a push to drive through Paris with the wind blowing through my hair, like Marianne Faithful's song. Part of me is afraid to go back to my old life and get stuck there. There's no work and not much to do. I don't want to go to school because I can't sit at a desk without fidgeting and spacing out. I promised myself I'd live a life Anne can't have as if I'd live it for both of us. I don't know if I can do that by going back to Longmore. Who would've guessed, in the middle of nowhere north, I'd be exposed to the chance of having a big, giant life? It's all happening so fast for me. I was expecting to be navel gazing, not helicopter flying." It all comes out in a breathless stream of consciousness. Two huge, black birds take flight, startling both of us.

"I get your pull to home, and that you have lifelong friendships. Maybe get your passport and let the summer sort out your plans. Look what's happened so far. There's no telling what may happen the rest of our time here." Is the advice from Elke who has much more life experience than I. Has Anne sent her to me?

We enter the cemetery though the gate we've unhinged from the falling down fence. The spirit houses, built like little playhouses, are placed on top of the grave. Many have curtains on the windows and vases of plastic flowers inside. The houses come up to my shoulders in height, are painted white, with contrasting trim around the windows. The exteriors are in better shape than the human habitations. Wildflowers are creeping in everywhere. It's the one place in this village with redeeming qualities. I enjoy the idea of a spirit returning to a house like this. I tell myself, Anne's a spirit who lives with me. I wish I could articulate my belief about Anne, but I can't because it's a sensation, not an explanation.

The garbage bag fills up quick with beer cans, liquor bottles and other garbage that has found its way here.

We drag the bag to a common bin near the toilet block and toss it in. A few locals wander near us, half pay attention and then go back to ignoring us. I wonder how many go to Father John's church. No one here seems keen on anything except getting drunk.

THIRTY-SIX

I've arranged to have my Passport photos done by Curtis today. Alberta and Marina invited us to the Canada Day dance tonight, so we'll do the photos, look around, and see how 'The Bay' gets down and boogies. Even though it's not far to Construction Bay neither Elke nor I have managed to get there yet.

Fortunately, the lodge is deadsville, so we both get the night off. Enid is going to look after the four random tourists that showed up.

Norm swings by at three o'clock honking the horn. "Is there a band or a DJ for the dance?" I ask putting on my seatbelt.

"Curtis has a DJ system of sorts. He'll be spinning the albums," says Norm.

"Does Curtis do everything?" asks Elke. So far what we've heard he's the man who can run the town, do the photos and be a DJ.

"He's talented... most of what a city manager slash labour force can accomplish, he can do it. I'll drive you to his office first."

*

The Bay is neat and sparse. The houses all look similar with some kind of sheet metal siding, small windows and steeply peaked roofs. Some people are attempting to grow flowers to spruce the place up. A large brightly painted sign, *Welcome to Construction Bay* is just off the highway. Bolton's is a large, modern-looking gas station, attached restaurant, a motel and a small store. It looks like it would blow our lodge over with better everything for tourists. Norm drops us off at the largest building. "This is the main operations building... and the community hall where I'll see you at the dinner and dance."

*

We poke our heads into a nondescript office, "Hello," Elke calls.

"Be right there!" A deep voice responds.

Curtis pops around the corner, big flashy smile and hand extended. Elke takes his hand, eyes clicking on him. She's lost her voice. Now I know what her type is. This guy looks like he walked off the cover of *Cowboy* magazine. Tanned, he's got to be well over six feet. His beige felt cowboy hat adds more height. The snap button chambray shirt, giant silver belt buckle, black jeans and finely stitched cowboy boots make him look like a masculine hunk machine.

"Kathy, let's get your photos looked after... come here ladies." His eyes are fixed on Elke. He gets me to sit in front of a white curtain; I smile, get the photos taken, and then decide to go to Bolton's, leaving Elke and Curtis to sizzle.

"Hi! Are you coming to the dinner dance?" Nurse Colleen is walking toward me, ponytail swinging wildly.

“Yes, but we didn’t bring anything for the potluck... should we bring chips or something?”

“Bring yourselves... not to worry.”

“Thanks. See ya soon!” Bolton’s little store has chips, candy and alcohol. I bought beer for the first time. No one cares about my age.

Well, looks who’s here... it’s the ‘creatures.’ “So ladies, are two bottles of rum and some coke part of the meditation?”

Monique looks like she didn’t understand and Jane looks like she wants to crawl under the counter. “Meditation comes in many forms. We are not attending the dance.”

“Cool, have fun.” I’ll have to thank Elke again for being my cabin and work mate... not the duo from the black lagoon.

*

Well, I’m the fifth wheel now. Curtis and Elke are sitting close, talking non-stop and almost in a lip lock when they realize I’m back. “Just me,” I say to warn them I’m here.

I can hear a clatter of voices. Tables and chairs are scraping along a floor. The hall is a large room within the building. The Canada flag and Yukon Territory flag bookend a framed picture of Queen Elizabeth. People are filing in; the place is humming.

The potluck has enough food to feed the village three times over. I pile my plate with potato salad, coleslaw and beef on a bun. The apple pie wins my vote over Kay’s Blancmange. People are looking at Elke and Curtis with curiosity and approval. I see whispering, nodding and giggles.

I don't know anyone at our table, but everyone's super friendly. Stu's a little too friendly. "Hey Kathy, your smile looks like a Hawaiian beach to me. Where'd you get it... a god? Save me ten dances, and I'll drive you home."

Oh brother. Fend off time. It sounds strange to say I have a boyfriend because people here think that's unfortunate. I smile and go to the washroom.

I'd asked Elke how she deals with unwanted physical advances. She said if a guy's getting too hot and heavy with her and she doesn't want to go all the way, she tells the guy she has a yeast infection! She said it works the best because men don't know what it is and they back off right away. Men think they're going to catch a disease or something, so they stop the fooling around and act all decent and cool. She said it works better than saying you have your period.

I won't be having that conversation with anyone here... I just want to dance!

Curtis plays rock and roll with no slow dances to break up the dance fever. Everyone gets up and dances, no partner needed. It's so much fun not having to dance with one person. Even Constable Davies is grooving along with all the partiers. I danced all night long, with barely a break.

"Need a ride home?" Asks Stu slurring and weaving around.

"No, I have a ride thanks," I beat it over to Curtis and Elke.

"I'm staying with Curtis tonight!" Elke looks like the gold and pink sky behind her.

"We'll run you home first," Says Curtis, his massive arm tucks around Elke.

*

My mind is bouncing as I lay in bed, alone in the cabin. The romance! The dancing! The boozing chambermaids! I should be asleep in two seconds, but I stare at Snoopy and relive the night until my eyes finally close.

*

The lodge is quiet today. Our four guests left after toast and coffee. I'm not very lively after last nights marathon.

Elke and I prepare for a bus tour tomorrow. Shawn will be the tour bus driver. The unconscious opinion in my bowels is one of gut tightening I can't escape. Shawn seems to like me and, yes, I like him. I'm preoccupied with how I'm going to tell him about Glen and that I can't be with him.

*

"You okay?" Enid must see I'm in another world. She puts down her dusting cloth.

"Yah. I'm thinking about my boyfriend at home and how there are distractions here." I start wiping down the salt and pepper shakers.

"Kathy, I've seen many summers here, and I'll tell you it's tough for young women, like you to hold on to a long-distance relationship. There are so many men here. Plenty of ladies have gone through this very predicament every summer I've been here."

"What happens?" Wiping speeds up. Salt. Pepper. Salt. Pepper.

"They break up with the man who's too far away." She picks up a vase and a polishing cloth.

"It seems a betrayal I wouldn't be able to wait three months to be back with him. It's such a short amount of time, I should be able to hang in there," I slump.

"How long have you been together?" The phone jingles in the distance, she looks toward the noise, then back, deciding to ignore it.

"Five and a half months." It doesn't sound like a very long time.

"How many boyfriends have you had?" The phone gives up its attention seeking.

"He's my first boyfriend," my face shrinks up. Don't cry Kathy, *don't.*

"Oh deary," Enid looks at me with either pity or compassion – perhaps both. "Sit down," she says pointing to the chairs. We sit in the gorgeous, light-filled dining room. The geraniums are bursting with red flowers.

Enid continues, "First love is true, pure love. It's pure because you've never been hurt or jaded by loving a man. He's your first love and will remain so for the rest of your life. Everything that has happened between you two has been a first for you. Love's powerful and draws deep emotions. You'll never have a first love ever again. I'm not surprised you don't want to give it up." I look out the window to avoid her gaze. Is Glen my first and only love, or is he my first love?

"Do you want to marry this man?" She asks the question without any judgment in her voice.

"No! I don't want to get married. I want to do what I want to do, even if I don't know what that is right now."

Kathy, you're a smart, young girl," she looks at me, "getting married at your age *is* too young. Go see the world or find something to do that makes you happy for you. Single women, with no children, can do what they want. You live in a generation where women can do much more than I could've done. Women of my generation would've loved the chances you have in today's world."

"I don't want to squander my life... I want to live it with adventure and take opportunities as they come up." I'm *not* going to cry!

"That's why you're here, on your own, way up north in a lodge on the Alaska Highway... you're brave."

"I think I've determined my life will amount to something and I'll make it important every day I wake up." I can't talk about Anne and Rod. Thoughts about them have become highly personal.

"Take a break now and come back for lunch," she suggests as we walk together to the door.

"Thanks for talking to me... helping me think it over. I'll be fine – I need to make some decisions." Enid leans over when I finish talking and gives me a hug.

"Do you know what your cabin's called? The House of a Thousand Funs," she says, and I laugh a giant Kathy laugh. I'm sure it's seen a lot of action in its life.

*

At three o'clock, everyone's in the front of the lodge, ready to greet the tour bus making its dusty way down the drive. Elke barely gets back in time from Curtis's and looks like a sleepwalker with a nutty grin.

Shawn hops out, gives us a wave and his winning smile. My tummy goes flip-flop. I wave hello, and then try to contain racing emotions – if nothing else, to conceal them from Mr. Sarcastic, Leo. Elke gives me a little nudge, and I give her a playful punch in the arm. No one falls over today. So far so good!

Elke and I are comfortable with the routine now; we're a two-woman show out there in the dining room. Out of Kay's earshot in the dining room. Elke and I have perfected saying the line together, "We're so pretty and popular, that's why we're in the middle of nowhere." We prance around like ponies, getting a laugh.

"Y'all are fun gals!" is what we mostly get from these charming United States southerners.

We dance our way through the cleanup, and when we're sure everything's ready for the morning, we shut off the lights.

*

Curtis has pulled up, and Shawn said he'd be along soon. We settle in on our couches, talking about this and that.

Shawn comes in and sits close to me. A buzz of energy shoots through me as I hand him a beer, touching him, making me flutter; a sharp bolt of electricity is more than I expected.

The tape cassette I've decided on is Supertramp, *Crime of the Century*. We're all familiar with the catchy tunes. Shawn's completely at ease, looking relaxed. He tells us funny stories about the old ladies pinching his cheeks and messing up his hair, calling him 'cutie.' He appears to take all this in stride and finds them all delightful. Great for him. If an old man pinched my cheeks and mussed my hair, I'd probably say, 'hands off the merchandise,' but it isn't a big deal for him.

Suddenly Curtis and Elke get up to leave. They're going to Curtis's place for a couple of hours. This means I'll be alone with Shawn. Jeez!

*

"Kathy, I think about you all the time," he says when we're alone, together on the couch. The Kinks scratch along some tune in the background.

"That bored are you?" I bend my head northward in a sorrowful pose. "Poor guy." I shift my sweater together and zip it up, nervous all of a sudden.

"Oh stop. You're easy to think about any time of the day or night," and he, with every confidence, leans in, brushes his lips against mine... I feel my heart flutter. My eyes close as his lips gently pass over my cheeks, forehead, resting just below my ear. I sigh as our bodies press together; he reaches for the sweater zipper, and slowly pulls it down while kissing the swell of my breasts above the t-shirt neckline.

"You're the best..." he lets the words out in one, continuous, shallow breath. We change from sitting to lying down.

Do I stop this? Should I stop this? No. My lips reach his, I arch myself against him, reach around, my arm finds the small of his back. I'm floating, full of his gentle passion. I let the cabin swirl around while it removes me from the man I love for this one I lust.

"I want you bad... I'd better back off." He wiggles away and grabs his beer.

We sit back up on the couch, "Oh, you're a gentleman then?" I whisper, reaching for the now, warm beer.

Yes, I am pretty lady." I get up, rearrange my clothes and flip over the cassette tape while he tells me he loves going to university and hopes to get a degree in communication. Perfect for him. I know nothing about what degrees you could get at university, but communications sounds like it could be fun. I don't reveal how my family has little respect for university. I say I'm not sure where my next step is, and he doesn't question me. He kisses me goodnight and sneaks back to his room

I sure as heck don't bring up Glen. In fact... he barely entered my head tonight and he should have taken over my thoughts... but he didn't...

*

The next morning, after breakfast, Shawn comes to say goodbye. "A girl like you needs some Yukon gold nugget jewelry. I'm going to fix that for you." We manage to sneak in a kiss around the corner. He leaves, and I won't see him for another two weeks.

*

I'm star struck and acting strangely. I put the dishcloth in the fridge and the ice in the cupboard. I catch myself doing these things over the past two days since Shawn left. I need to do something about Glen, but I'm chickening out. I'll wait to get a letter from him first.

*

There are geologists here who want to take us out for an evening of back road driving. Gus is twenty-six and married to a sixteen-year-old woman, with a baby in the bargain. The other one, Brian, is single, not my type, being too short and chubby, but some safe flirtation to hone my skills is in order. Elke and I pile into yet another beat-up truck, and we head to the back of beyond. We all get bounced around on an old dirt road until we arrive at a small lake. Everyone gets out and wanders around enjoying the evening. Gus shushes us and puts his hand up in the air. None of us say a peep. We hear branches breaking in the woods. To our left not thirty feet away, we see bushes moving, something's crashing around, and whatever it is it's heading toward us. A huge brown bear clears the bush and comes at us.

"Grizzly!" Gus screams at the top of his lungs, "Get in the truck," his voice a terrified squeal. We run to the truck; I'm stupid scared. My legs are jelly, I try to run fast, but I'm a wobbly mess – I stumble. Brian gives me a hand up as I gasp for breath.

"Where is it?" Shaking, I'm safe in the cab. Everyone made it in.

"Nine o'clock." We all, including me, look left.

"Shit... it's right there," yells Brian pointing to front of the truck... the Grizzly now a few feet away from the front of the truck. "Let's go before he gets mad and charges." Gus fires up the engine, steps on the gas, slams the truck in reverse and then spins around blasting the bear with loose rock. We watch it bound away. "Close call girls. We wanted to show you an exciting time but didn't plan the bear."

We decide it'd be safer to leave the entire area rather than have the bear possibly show up again. We bounce up another wide path of a road and get out at the top of a hill.

*

Gus hands out beer. Our scare behind us now, we all sit on the hill and stare at the endlessness of the Yukon. There's no sign of human life. No buildings, roads, power lines, or airplane trails in the sky.

"Let's all be quiet and listen," says Brian. We all sit as quietly as we can. There's no sound. No breeze, no birds and no bear. It's the sound of silence I've never heard before. There's absolutely nothing to hear. We sit for a long time before Gus put his beer to his lips, breaking our trance.

We sit awhile longer and then head back to the lodge.

THIRTY-SEVEN

It's mail day! I got a letter from the parents, one from Sandra, and one from Glen!

I run to the cabin and put them in order. Mom and Dad, then Sandra, then to savour and linger, I'll read Glen's.

Dear Kathy,

I hope you're having a nice time. We're seeing our peach tree growing peaches, but our pear tree is not healthy. It rained last week, which helped the front lawn green up. We've been swimming in the lake. Alan hasn't come home, and we're going camping for three weeks. He knows where the house key is hidden. Maybe he'll come back to live at the house. We're both worried about him. Did he ever act strangely around you? Why would he take off like that? I've asked my doctor about him, and he's very concerned there may be something more than him wanting to be independent and a hippie.

Take care, love,

Mom and Dad.

Jeez... what am I going to say? I sure hope Alan's not suffering. I'll have to tell them something. I pick up Sandra's letter and tear it open.

Dear Kathy,

Hi! I hope you're hanging in there living in the center of the vast Canadian wilderness.

I want to tell you about something that happened to me. I've been keeping it a secret up to now.

Last year when Brad and I had the argument on Christmas gift shopping day I wasn't having my period. I was pregnant. I didn't tell you for various reasons. Sorry. I had an abortion over the Christmas holidays.

Kathy, it was awful I couldn't tell you but Brad said not to because he was the one that made me have an abortion.

Then Anne and Rod died, so I pushed the abortion away with pleasure.

Writing is cathartic for me. I feel better when I get it down on paper.

Thanks for listening. Please don't tell anyone what's in this letter.

P.S. Brad misses me so much he might come back early!

Hugs, Sandra

Poor Sandra. Brad's SUCH a dick wad. I'll write her back a nonjudgmental, sympathetic letter in hopes she'll eventually get the picture, and split with idiot face. Her education should be the most important goal, not some jerk head boyfriend.

Finally, the letter to drench my soul.

Dearest Kathy,

I miss you, love. You are in every pore. I keep your picture next to my bed. I love you more than I did when we said goodbye at the airport. I love you more every day we're separated. You keep me going on this ship that is crowded, has had me seasick a few times, and the work's as dull as the ocean is grey.

All I do, all day long, is collect information and type it onto a form, then file the pile at the end of the work day. There are two other women with me. I think they're bored too.

I dream of the moment we're together again. I love you beyond words. When will September be here?

Write me a long loving letter to keep me going.

I love you, I love you, and I love you,

Your love,

Glen

I was expecting a letter full of exciting stories, such as life on the ship, and tales of daring do on high seas. He's bored and unhappy. I hate that he loves me more than I love him. His absence isn't making my heart grow fonder; it's making it forget. I should be flattered to the hilt that this perfect man of my dreams saturated his letter with love for me. All I feel is distance, and I'm going to end it before I make a fool out of him. It isn't fair.

At least there's less guilt and more determination to send the worst ever letter. If I don't want to get married, and don't want a serious boyfriend, I need to get real with myself.

Dear Glen,

I've fallen deeply for the north. A lot has changed. I feel like a brand new person. No parents continually pissing me off. No more childish high school crap. The people I meet here are all adults with careers. I'm working with the most far-out woman, Elke. She's smart and worldly. I'm lucky to have her as part of the summer. I'm starting to learn about what real life's like, and I'm obsessed with every moment I'm alive.

Now for the hard part. I don't want to marry you. I may never get married. I don't know where my life's going, and it's not fair to drag you along. I'm a lousy girlfriend. I love you with every bit of me, but I don't want a boyfriend anymore. There's too much going on up here, and I don't want to be tied down to a relationship.

Sorry, I'm breaking up with you in a letter. I feel like a shit person to hurt you like this.

I hope we can still be friends.

Sorry, Sorry, Sorry

Kathy

I reread the letter and decide it says enough. I don't want to go on and on. I hope keeping it short will be like a paper cut, instead of a knife wound.

In case I chicken out, I zip over to the post office and, without over thinking, drop it in the mailbox.

What have I done? My stomach is lurching around. I have to live with myself while waiting for his reply.

*

"You could use a beer after your breakup letter."

“Thanks... I’m feeling like crap. Beer and friends are the recipe for me,” I say not meaning it, but I can’t mope around either. It was my sole decision... now I have to live with it. Elke and I are out of beer and since we want beer, we’ve gone to the airport to recruit beer helpers.

Simon’s visiting Norm. “Sure gals, I have two times sixty air conditioning, dusty, ripped upholstered seating and nothing left of the shock system. Brace yourselves,” warns Simon.

“Okay,” says Elke, “What’s two times sixty air conditioning?”

“Two windows down – sixty miles an hour,” he looks at us as if we’re dense, and then roars with laughter.

The drive experience is a first. Simon has a CB radio and he says, “breaker one nine,” and “over and out, ten-four.” It’s funny until I start singing the Convoy song and call him ‘Rubber Duckie.’ He’s miffed. Uh Oh! He pulls over to the side of the road and gives me a lesson on CB radios in a grouchy tone. I listen, apologize, and all’s friendly again. Touchy! Simon drops us off in the village. We wave at unfamiliar faces.

We stop in to see Curtis. He says he can run us back to the lodge. We pick up beer paid for by our cash tips we’ve been accumulating. It’s a quick trip in and back. There’s time to get ready, so we go to the laundry and pick up clean uniforms.

*

When we arrive at the laundry, we’re stared down by two cheesed-off women. Marina and Alberta both plunk down their work with a bang. They’re always cheerful and laughing, but there’s nothing cheerful about their faces.

“What’s wrong?” I ask.

"From now on you have to ask our permission if you want a ride anywhere with our husbands," Marina says with slight venom while folding sheets into furious squares.

"Sure. Sorry about that." I'm dumbfounded. Why? What did we do wrong?

Elke apologizes and says, "I understand and sorry to create a problem." She grabs our uniforms off the hooks.

They both perk back up, and Alberta settles down, "no need to speak of this again."

"Okay, I'm sorry too." We start back to the cabin. "What am I missing Elke?"

"It's a really small village. The people we waved to probably called the lodge to report Simon was with us."

"So?" It's starting to rain; we hustle to the door.

"SO, the wives are jealous of us, and think we may sleep with their husbands," says Elke with a smirk.

"EWWWW! That's disgusting. They're old and nothing like what I'm interested in. They aren't even good looking. I can't believe they'd be jealous of their husbands with us. As if we'd go with them," pretending to throw up on the floor.

"Then again, I suppose tongues could wag in such a small place. Maybe the lovely people of the bay are terrible gossips. Not a problem though. We'll ask their permission from now on – if I can keep my face straight," says Elke.

*

Curtis has planned a field trip for us! We have some fishermen staying at the lodge we don't want to hang around with. They're a group called the Donald Bunt Fishing Society.

They want me to think this is a funny club name. "We changed the C to a B," says the largest one sitting down laughing and tapping a beckoning hand on his lap. I hold my face still as the five obese, balding white men laugh while Elke's face burns red.

The fattest says to Elke, "hey sexy, what's up your skirt."

One put his hand on my butt. "Do you like tonsil hockey?" He asks leering at me. I smile to keep the peace and move his hand away.

"I got twelve inches, but I'll do you a favour and only give you ten," says another one of them gesturing to his crotch. Elke's furious we had to put up with these perverts last night. Luckily, they keep to themselves outside of mealtimes.

Curtis picks us up at nine, and we drive to mile 1118. This is our first time going the other way up the highway. He says we're meeting a group of geologists working in the area. There are two women in the group.

Women can be geologists? I should talk to them. The road up the highway is much the same as the other direction. The road surface is packed down gravel, making it solid, except for the clouds of dust and loose rocks. There's an oncoming car, and Curtis tells us to put our hands against the windshield. We do, and as the vehicle drives by, we get splattered with rocks.

"The hands on the windshield absorb the gravel impact. The windshield will pit instead of crack," he explains.

We pull into the Mile 1118 Lodge. It also looks much nicer than Gold Miners Lodge. It's all made of peeled logs and has large windows that must let in all the midnight sun. We grab our beer and go around the back. The road crew's here! Guitars are out, and the guys are loud.

"Hey Gold Miner girls," they all shout and make room for us to sit on logs set in a circle around a toasty fire. We get introduced to the Geologists, Veronica and Marianne, Jos and Patrick. The guys are head to head about an idea to oust Prime Minister Joe Clark. I'm keen to talk to the women, so I settle in beside them. They're both tiny women wearing oversized Khaki coats, matching pants and floppy hats with a bug veil, 'northern accessory' pulled behind the brim. I ask how their summer's going.

"Mosquitoes and sweat mostly! Worth it though. We're in third year U. of Ottawa. The project we're on is the Kluane Glacier, where the ice has retreated... we're collecting samples," says Marianne.

"Smoke?" Veronica holds out a package of Players.

"No thanks, I quit after candy cigarettes got boring."

"You may want to start... it keeps the mosquitoes out of your face."

"You two are brave women to work in the wilds." I ask them about working with men all the time and they both say it's fine.

"A thick skin for the kidding around is part of the job requirement," Marianne jokes. Veronica agrees with a tip of her head as she chugs down half a beer in one go.

“I think it’s cool you chose an education men usually do. I thought the only education choices women get is to become a teacher, nurse, social worker, secretary, or like my friend with writing.”

“What are you taking in University?” asks Marianne.

“I don’t know what I’m going to do... maybe Geology!” I doubt it though.

Wade and another guy pick up guitars. “Play something,” Frank says, and then he and Curtis continue bantering about how shitty the Toronto Maple Leafs are compared to the Edmonton Oilers.

“Your Bob Seger is damn good,” Veronica waves an empty beer in the air. Ray rushes to replace it.

“Lard tundering jasus, we gotta keep the ladies happy,” he passes us Labatt’s Blue.

*

It’s almost 4:00 a.m. when Curtis drops us off. He lets us off at the top of the drive so we can sneak down to the cabin, so no one knows how late we got in. The sun’s breaking over the horizon even though it just went down not long ago. Through streaky clouds, pink and fired oranges light the sky,

“Look!” Elke grabs my arm and stops me. We see Father John leave Kay’s room. He looks in both directions, tugs up his pants and sneaks away.

“Holy hell, and he’s a Catholic Priest! He’s having it on with Kay?” Elke’s face is drawn up into a contorted ball of horrification.

"He's fat and ugly... shouldn't priests be celibate?" There's no right reason for them to be together.

Elke's upper lip curls, "my brain can't get those two being together. Gross!" She mimes barfing the way I did earlier today. "He's going against his religion, with Kay. He's a *wichser scheisse,"* spitting out German swear words I've learned to be 'wanker' and 'shit.'

"Sour puss and the Father. We could send hints like we know what they're up to. Could be fun," I say in a devilish tone, rubbing my hands together; the thought of messing around with their heads makes me happy.

"She's all yours... maybe you can get back at her for being such a bitch to you," Elke's still shaking her head. It's hardly worth going to sleep, but we catch a few before the alarm goes off.

*

The last two days have been brutal. Staying up super late, then working isn't a smart idea. Tomorrow, July 18th, I mark the arrival of Shawn!! I promise myself a full night's sleep; I need to be my full-on, perky self when the bus rolls up.

*

I received the passport photos! I've filled out the application. I need a guarantor – someone professional that can vouch that I am who I say I am. I'm able to ask Constable Davies, who's glad to fill out the form. It's ready to send to Ottawa! I'm having it mailed home when it's completed. I package it all up and walk, by myself, to the post office.

I run into a villager, Lena Enoch, whom I was once introduced to in the post office by Betty. She's a tiny old lady, wearing a huge, heavy, filthy, yellow coat, and a scarf around her neck, despite the warm weather. She says hello and bares her two remaining teeth in a big grin. I ask to take her photo, and she poses for me. I want to have some record of the people who live here. No one down south will believe how desperate it is here.

Another piece of life-changing mail gets sent into the system. Betty's pleased at my decision to at least plan for travel, even if there are no plans yet. The rest of the day I walk, and dream.

THIRTY-EIGHT

Elke went to Curtis's after work so Shawn and I can be alone in the cabin. He's poured wine into juice glasses. We have all the time we want and no one to bother us. Having our own place for the night is heavenly. Tonight's the night!

The fire's crackling in the stove, the one candle is lit, and Neil Young is in the cassette deck.

'You're making me horny," Shawn slides in beside me on the couch.

"I'm just lying here," I smile teasing him by hiking up the hem of the yellow daisy summer dress I'd put on after work.

"It's the way you're lying there." I can feel what he means as he pushes against me.

"Black lace under there?" He touches my ear with his tongue.

"White cotton... sorry!"

"Hm... we'll have matching underwear,"

"You're a nutcase," I pull his shirt off over his head, and start on the jeans.

"Are you a real redhead?" His eyes sparkle; his mouth is full of desire.

"I guess you're about to find out." I get up off the couch, take his hand and lead him to the bedroom.

"Holy fuck..." I hear him whisper.

"Here..." he says. As I lay face up on the bed... he places my hands on the iron bedstead headboard rails. He puts his own hands over top. "Don't move..."

The way he moves over my body makes me want to scream... the soft touching, knowing where to put his mouth. My eyes are closed, shifting only a touch from his touch. Hmm... I could go on forever.

And then he falls off the bed. "Shit, bugger damn!" The landing's loud, the dresser he just hit is wobbling.

"Your head is bleeding." I leap up and get a towel, "The blood's dripping all over the floor," pressing it on his forehead. I rifle through a box of miscellaneous and pull out a bandage.

"Sorry Kathy... not so smooth. I think my manhood skills are more wounded than my forehead."

"Hard to be smooth in a saggy single bed Shawn. No biggie! You were showing some fine talent there... maybe another time?"

"Ya, but where's the black lace bra and panties?"

"There's no black lace anywhere... I'm going to cuff you," and I do.

*

What the heck? How could I have this much bad luck when it comes to trying to lose my virginity? Twice I've tried, and with different men! I must be some sort of unlucky freak. Maybe I should give up trying to lose my virginity... except Shawn returns in two weeks and I want him again.

*

The next few days are spent turning over thoughts and plans. I walk over to the airport for company because Elke's on shift looking after a group of tourists who somehow found us.

Norm's working and hands over a thin strip of paper. "It's a Teletype message that came in this morning," He passes it to me and then walks away.

The message reads, "*I'm a joke. No letter to follow. Glen*"

I burst out crying – Norm returns, sitting quietly across from me. "I broke up with him in a letter. He obviously got it... I'm a horrible person. I've hurt him... he doesn't deserve it,"

"He should've known it would be hard to keep hold of a vivacious woman like yourself."

"I don't know if he saw me that way. I've changed since I've been here. I was in high school and overcame a tragedy. He saved me when I needed saving, and now I dumped him. He must hate me."

“I’ll tell you a secret about men,” Norm doesn’t ask about the tragedy, “When a man falls for a woman he falls long, deep and hard. We make out that we’re all tough, but inside we’re marshmallows when it comes to women. This’ll hurt him for awhile, and then he *will* get over it.” He continues. “Big relationship hint – don’t ask him to be ‘just friends.’”

“I did in the letter! I may as well have stuck in the knife *and* turned it.”

“Men aren’t looking for more friends Kathy, they’re looking for girlfriends.” He breathes into his cup.

“What do I know? He was my first boyfriend.” I crush a snotty tissue into my hand.

Norm laughs and tells me I’ll have many men. “Men don’t completely grow up until they’re around thirty years old. We guys are pretty immature until we sort out a few stupid acts. In the meantime, shore up your own life goals and have fun along the way. When you’re looking for a man, I’ll quote Winston Churchill, ‘be kind, but fierce.”

“Thanks... and thanks for putting up with me freaking out.”

*

I think I should write Glen right away. I get pen on paper and spill my guts.

Dear Glen

I received the Teletype message. I don't think you're a joke. What happened between us was pure love I'll have for the rest of my life. No one will ever take your place. I'm sorry we didn't 'do it,' but so what? You came to me when I was shattered. You glued me back together. I'm grateful for you being there for me. I should've said more in the last letter.

I'm very young here. Everyone's older than me and living their lives. I see freedom of movement, thought and lifestyle here. It's not in the direction of relationships, but a choice to singly wander the country or the world. People live and work with passion and happiness. They care about themselves, what they're doing, and their lives. I see that as something I want, even though I don't know what that is right now. I don't know if I'll come back to Longmore. I'm your crummy ex-girlfriend.

I know you must detest me.

Sorry,

Kathy

I seal it without a kiss and mail it before I rip it apart.

*

It's August 3rd, and there's a letter from Sandra! I run to the cabin to read it in peace.

Dear Kathy,

I have exciting news! Brad missed me so much he came back from Alberta! Brad and I are engaged! He loves me enough to marry me, and I'm overjoyed. When I'm married, I'll have a companion to share my life with. I want to share my life with Brad so everything I do won't be a passing experience unobserved. I'll stay in school, not get pregnant and get my university degree. He's promised not to ever hit me or shove me again. For my part, I've promised not to provoke him into anger. I'm sure I've changed him into the man I hope him to be.

How's the north? It sounds like you're having fun. You're such a fun person Kathy. You could have fun in a swamp.

Let me know when you're coming home. I can't wait to catch up. You have to see my engagement ring. I have almost everything I want. I feel whole and ecstatic!

Feeling loved,

Sandra

Crushed, I put the letter down. After the big talk with Norm about men and marriage, I'm disappointed, even angry. What an idiot! What's the big rush? What's wrong with her? Why Brad? He's such an asshole. Couldn't she witness her own life without having Brad there too? Is he going to stop being violent?

*

Elke comes running in the door. "Want to fly over the Kluane Glacier? We have to go now. There are two seats, and the geologists said we could sit in for a fun flyover. We have time to go and come back."

I drop the letter and grab my camera. We all cram in the truck, and head to the float dock. I decide to forget about Sandra for now. Hell, I'm going to fly over a glacier while jerk face is probably yelling at her for writing.

*

We pile into the back of a Piper aircraft. "Blake!! Blake Grey!"

"Hey you! How's the summer going?"

"Couldn't be better... Dan was right... I'm super happy!"

"Well, let's make it even better!"

The Kluane Glacier is enormous. It looks like ribbons laid across the valley floor. The undulating pattern of white and brown ice curves gently around the base of the mountains. It's difficult to figure out where it begins. We fly close to the surface and see the very deep crevasses as if knives have plunged the surface in methodical never-ending cuts. We cross over the face seeing chunks of ice crash into the milky blue water. I'm told the colour is due to glacial silt – a fine powder that stays suspended in the water, causing it to look otherworldly.

I'm clicking the camera and knowing I'm not anywhere near a swamp! "Thank you for inviting us along... this is incredible." We fly back to the lodge; the sun's blazing, and the glacier disappears from the lens.

*

There's a newsflash for us. We find out the lodge has been for sale for a year. A couple, running a fly-in fishing camp, will be coming here to check out the place. They want to add to their business, with this property. I hope they both know how to fix stuff!

Wendy and Tony Coulter arrive two days later in a Cessna 182 floatplane. It's a sleek-looking aircraft, all shiny and brightly painted white and blue. '*Wakes Lake Lodge*' is highlighted on the side. I'd heard about this place. It's fly-in, only for rich fishing enthusiasts.

They look way younger than Leo and Enid. Wendy has a warm smile, a Wakes Lake ball cap on her head covering brown hair. Tony is a short guy... the same height as Wendy. With his matching ball cap and hair colour, they look more like twins than Alan and I ever have. They both laugh easily... I immediately relax around them.

We all exchange greetings while making our way to the lodge. We've been able to keep the place 'ship shape and Bristol fashion' because there hasn't been much business in the last few days. Hopefully, they have big imaginations as to what the place could be with a renovation or ten.

They all go off on a tour of the lodge. I get a solid feeling from the prospective buyers. As much as I can overhear, they ask plenty of questions. "We have children 20, 19 and 16. The youngest is working at the camp for the summer season. They could all chip in here!"

Kay puts on a dinner extraordinaire to impress them. "Nice dinner Kay... wouldn't your secret lover enjoy," I say to her in a whisper.

"Get back to work," she sputters and then drops a frying pan, and I run off silently feeling unbridled glee.

The couple leaves after dinner, with not a word said to Elke or me on how it went. We do get an exciting offer though. Enid asks if one of us would like to fly to Wakes Lake Camp to help out next weekend. She graciously says we can talk it over and decide who wants to go, or she'll flip a coin if there's a conflict.

Back at the cabin, Elke says, "You go. I never camped as a child. I don't know all those skills like you do. I can't build a fire if you hadn't already noticed. I don't know how to set up a tent, or how to survive in a camp."

I get to go! I camped plenty growing up. That's going to come in handy at the fishing lodge.

*

Shawn's coming tomorrow and my period showed up. Bad timing. No third time for the first time this week. I've heard women can have sex during their periods, but that sounds gross to me.

He never knew about Glen, and now Glen's history. I still get a sick grinding in my stomach when I think of what I did to him. I understand all those gushy songs on the radio now. 'Love Hurts' is in my head. I hope to get a letter from him soon. I need to face the music – the sooner, the better. I'm prepared for a soul-devastating letter of vile hatred from him. I deserve it.

THIRTY-NINE

The bus arrives; a tour group from Texas. They're a fun group of loud, festive oldies. I'm getting used to the blue, or violet, tinted hair. Shawn has them all wrapped around his finger. The dinner's finished; we're serving the weird, white dessert when a tall, greying gentleman gets up and yells, "Who's Shawn's gal?" Everyone in the room takes a breath and screams as loudly as possible, "Kathy!"

My mouth opens up like a cavern, and the laugh comes barreling out. They all start cheering, "Kiss, kiss, kiss." I'm like a fake bride, as Shawn takes me in his arms and gives me a peck on the cheek.

Everyone claps for us. I'm embarrassed but touched Shawn would set up this gag for me. As the folks make their way to their rooms, they all say what fun they had getting this party going, at the expense of me. They also comment on how sweet Shawn is. Yes, he's 100%, pure sweetheart.

*

We have the cabin to ourselves, and after some hot necking, Shawn presents me with a velvet box that says 'Murdoch's Jewelry' in gold lettering. I stare at it, backing, away from him.

"It's a present for you. I said I'd buy you something." He passes the box to me.

"Oh... Shawn." I open the box and inside there's a single, gold nugget necklace and earrings of two small nuggets suspended by delicate chains. It's way more than I should receive from a man I barely know.

"Thank you. It's gorgeous, and very Yukon... you're spoiling me!" I remove the necklace from the box, and he puts it around my neck. I attach the earrings and look in the little mirror hanging on the wall. I know this is special jewelry because nuggets are rare and expensive. "Are you sure about this Shawn? It's very generous and too much."

"You look even more beautiful with those nuggets gracing that sexy body." I stop him talking his embarrassing talk by kissing him a wet thank you. The thank you gets heated, and I push his hand away.

"What's wrong?" Shawn says.

"Ummm..." moving his hand to my waistline.

"Tell me," he crawls off me and sits on the edge of the couch.

I close my eyes and whisper, "I have my period."

"Oh, honeybunchyness... we can stay above the bellybutton. I want to hold you tight." He piles back on top of me, pushing his nose against mine.

I start giggling uncontrollably. "Okay! Stop squishing me!" He unpins me slightly, moving his hands above the belly button to a position that makes me tingle.

*

The Cessna flies in at 3:00 p.m. I strap myself into the co-pilot seat. It's only three days, but I'll miss Elke. Tony gets us off the lake and on our way. It's a bumpy ride, and I'm told the drill if I want to throw up: I open a large, green, garbage bag, put my entire head into it, up to the shoulders, and try to be quiet and tidy. I'm a bit woozy, but I don't think I'll throw up.

There's more turbulence than I've ever experienced on a plane. I'm getting nauseous, so I close my eyes. "I think I may need the garbage bag." I gag – sweat's starting to form on my face.

"Get your head in quick!" Tony yells and passes me the bag. "Don't puke all over the plane!!" He has both hands tight on the wheel and is concentrating on controlling the plane as it lurches and bounces all over the sky.

It's the long, sideways swooping that takes me over the edge. I get the bag over my head, just in time, and everything comes out. My head's trapped in the bag and the smell makes me lose everything again. I'm spinning out of control and want to be on terra firma ASAP.

"The camp isn't far away," says Tony as we descend into calmer territory. I pull my head out of the bag. "See that box?" Tony points, letting go of the wheel for a second, "get a beer out and drink it right now."

"A freaking beer? How's that going to help me?" My stomach's aching; my mouth is gluey and gross.

"It's a Yukon remedy. Trust me... it'll work." Tony nods at the beer, I crack it and start drinking. After two, giant, very unladylike burps, I immediately start feeling better. No more dizziness, my stomach settles... it's a miracle cure!

The lake is long and narrow, with the mountains hemming it into a tight watery landing strip. It must take some skill to land in such a constricted spot. I hold my breath as we approach the mirrored surface. It looks like we're going to fly into the mountain – the reflection is perfect. It's scary and astounding to hit the water, break the surface – spoiling the scene, but I enjoy the soft, safe landing. We glide to the dock – Tony, with his new employee, who smells of beer and barf.

*

I think I've landed in a photograph. The lodge is constructed with peeled logs. There's a large, wrap-around deck leading to double doors. Lounge chairs are set amongst shrubs and lupines. We walk up and into the building. A fireplace made of rough rocks reaches two stories up the main lobby. There are taxidermy deer and sheep, proudly staring at each other. The air's tinged with the smell of campfire.

"Hi Kathy," greets Wendy. "Would you like a tour?" First I quickly wash up and rinse the acrid taste out of my mouth.

"It's a paradise," I choke up a bit with emotion. "It's the flawless ideal of the log cabin in the woods. I thought it was going to be tents!"

"We have tents to sleep in... the lodge is used for dining and relaxing." We walk into the dining area, already set for dinner. The lodge isn't big. I see where I'll be working. There's a wood stove, door set open, cleaned out and reset with wood for a fire later. I'll be helping in the dining room, kitchen and tent duties. The kitchen's small, but well-equipped, with a propane stove and large fridge/freezer. No one else is here right now.

The lounge area is equipped with a small bar. I'll write down what people drink.

The ten tents, set to the right side of the lodge, are glamorous. Canvas walled, wood floors, queen-size beds, covered with fluffy duvets and plenty of pillows. There's a couch, chairs and a wood stove in each. Wendy and Tony's son Richie tends the fires and wood. There's tea and coffee in each tent. They've made each tent unique, and thoroughly comfortable.

I'll be sleeping in a bunkroom at the rear of the lodge. We get to work preparing for the guest's arrival. There are hot towels and a reception cocktail to greet them when they disembark.

*

Eventually, I hear the drone of aircraft. Wendy and I will look after the reception, and then we'll dash to the kitchen.

Two Beaver floatplanes come in. It seems eight men are our guests. The reason I'm here, I understand, is because they're some sort of VIP group filming a TV special on fishing in the north. Tony and Wendy want the guests well looked after; I'm here to help make their stay a memorable experience.

Everyone's joking and laughing as they hop off the plane. Obviously, they had a smoother flight than I did. There are older men and a few younger guys. I stand with my back straight and the bar tray ready for them to be handed a scotch whiskey.

Holy shit! My knees buckle and I turn to liquid. That guy looks exactly like David Cassidy. He has the same dreamy feathered hair, perfect complexion, and those lips look moist and ready for action! He's spectacular, and I'm a quivering blob. Maybe it is David Cassidy! We get introduced, and indeed he's *not*, but I'm still a mess staring at his scrumptious looks.

"Hi, I'm Buck. I didn't think there'd be a beautiful woman here," he says to me, in the silkiest voice, "I'm sure I'll see you around." He looks at me with those amber eyes, like I'm the only one in the Yukon. I hand him his drink and can't speak, which these days is pretty amazing. I've become fast on my feet with the comments, but this perfect specimen has me fogged in.

I smile politely, mutely, and turn to the kitchen, with the empty bar tray dangling loosely off my nervous hand.

*

I race up to the kitchen. Dinner smells inviting. There's a ton to do. I place freshly baked Parker House rolls and butter pats out along the hefty length of timber beautifully wrought into a long table. There's water to pour into glasses and wine to open. The prime rib roast is out of the oven, and gravy's being made. Our cook is a real chef unlike Kay, who cooks through experience and grumbling. I like the way her short black hair is kept in place with a large black hairband. I watch her efficiently stir the gravy while adding flour. She seems to put extra pizazz into the meal. I see her using different herbs and spices, not found in Kay's pantry. "Hi! I'm Greta," she says with a smile.

I go to introduce myself and instead am greeted by a guest at the kitchen door.

“Hi! I’m Eric... I have a favour to ask.”

“Hi, I’m Wendy, this is Kathy. I’m sure we can grant your favour!”

“It’s Tibbs birthday today. He’s the other cameraman. Could we have a little fun at his expense?”

“Sounds deliciously evil...” I say.

“What do you have in mind?” Wendy asks.

“When dinner’s over I was wondering if I could get you to sing Happy Birthday, and give him this crown and sceptre.” He unfolds a shiny, gold metallic crown that says “King Badass Birthday Boy” in black marker. The sceptre is a gold, spray painted toilet plunger.

“I’ll do it... is it okay to improv a bit?” I ask

“Keep it clean Kathy!” Wendy says.

“Clean’s my normal.”

“Good luck, a cake was made for dessert. I’ll put ‘Happy Birthday’ on it... Kathy, you finish here.”

“Thanks ladies... should be fun.” Eric leaves us.

*

I’m definitely nervous about this. I want it to be fun, but not embarrassing for Wendy and Tony. Here goes.

After we’ve cleared the main meal plates, I walk back into the dining area, hands raised to call everyone’s attention. “Who’s got a birthday today?”

“Oh no...” says Tibbs smiling, head down shaking his head.

“Tibbs,” everyone cheers.

“I can’t hear you!” David Cassidy is checking me out!

“TIBBS!” At the top of their lungs.

“We’ve got a new name for the birthday boy... come on up!” He’s hesitating, I continue, “come on... it’ll be like ripping a Band-Aid off!”

He has no choice. The crew is cheering and goading him. “Come on big boy... it’s payback time,” says Eric.

Wendy’s on one side, I’m on the other. “Here is your scepter... what’s your name?” Wendy asks.

I hold up the crown so he can’t see what it says. Everyone chants out “King Badass Birthday Boy!” I crown him, and everyone sings Happy Birthday.

When everyone quiets down, I add, “you have to wear it all night, or I’ll spank you and NOT the way you like it!”

I look at Wendy, scared I stepped over the line, but she’s laughing just as hard as everyone else.

I back off to clear and clean dishes. The men hang out for a while. “We’ll see you in the bar Kathy?” Eric asks.

“See you there!”

“I think you made some memories for these guys... almost too many, but no worries... they loved your enthusiasm.”

“Thanks Wendy... I was afraid I overdid it.”

“I think you gave them what they wanted. I’ll finish up the rest... you go over to the bar.”

The whole crew is there using the honour system. I sit on a high stool behind the peeled-log bar and copy into a notebook what everyone has in their hands, plus empties. Most of them are playing cards. David Cassidy looks over his hand of cards at me... he winks.

"Hey Kathy, what do you think of this?" Asks Tibbs. He's holding up an impressive bottle of wine. Black glass, cylindrical in shape, with a label done in old fashioned script, "Black Tower."

"I'm more of a beer drinker. I've never seen this before."

"Have a bit." He pours a bit into a glass.

"This is good and sweet... I like it!"

"Another splash?"

"What's the size of a splash?" Eric asks.

"Look in your pants," Says Tibbs.

Big Kathy laugh comes out, making them look at me and laugh along.

*

Tomorrow is a long day for these guys, so they start filtering out. I tidy the room and then wander outside.

The sky's darker here because the high mountains block any light. I see a sky filled with stars, reaching down, reflecting off the lake surface. I'm filled with awe at the beauty handed to me on this dazzling evening. I'm tired from the long day and find a spot on the shoreline to rest my feet. It's the sound of silence that calms me. I'm tired of being full of enthusiasm and energy. All the guests have my full attention every minute I'm with them. I've come to understand, a *huge* part of the tourist enjoyment is us, the staff. Guests are incredibly delighted to engage. They adore our passion for the north. *I* adore my passion for the north.

"Hi there," it's Buck. My whole body is charging up. I'm electrified, merely by the sound of his voice.

"Sit down. Isn't the lake beautiful?" I say, quietly and evenly.

"You're beautiful," I can see his David Cassidy face: mottled, amber eyes, smooth, tanned skin, and a face to stop any control. I say nothing. He sits so close to me there's no cold air to separate us. His lean, sexiness is next to me. I shiver and silently demand my body to behave.

"You're cold. Let me warm you up," His arm slides gently around my back. I don't refuse. I say nothing.

"Cat got your tongue?" He presses closer; his heat's warming me. He could be a famous actor one day, and here he is, interested in me. I giggle like a two-year-old and look into his perfect face.

"Humm," he mutters and starts to kiss me. His lips are soft, wet and warm. I respond back, my head tilting toward him in consent. I'm not hurting anyone. It's just a kiss, right?

He caresses me: eager arms around my waist, across my shoulders, hands through my hair. His soft hair brushes against my face. I lean into him, forgetting who I am, and not caring.

He tightens his grip around my waist and eases me onto the lakeshore. It's not comfortable. There are round and sharp stones under me. There are twigs and branches prodding my back. He's pressing his lips against mine and sliding his hand where I slap it away. He's climbing on top of me - his hardness grinding into me; hands are everywhere.

"No," I grunt under his weight, "stop it."

"Are you kidding me, baby? I can't stop now."

"No, I'm not... I have my period." David Cassidy look-alike, or not, I don't want to do this on a rocky beach, with my period. This is not romantic and not what I want. "No," I repeat, trying to push him off me.

"I don't care... I want you now." I can feel him pulling down his jeans, and then pulling at my clothes.

"I have a yeast infection... you could get it," I speak into his ear, through shiny, brown, feathered hair.

"Fuck." He moves off me, zips up his jeans and retreats into a seated position. "Goodnight." He gets up and walks away into the darkness.

I sent the wrong signals. I shouldn't have been easy. I led him on... I wanted his attention, not sex. Stupid! I fix myself up the best I can. There are bits of tree in my hair. I smooth my clothes and hair, slowly get up, and walk to the bunkhouse room. I'm shaking with fear and cold. My back hurts from him smashing me into the shoreline. It's all my fault.

*

The next morning, I show up for work and act like I don't have a thing on my mind other than to look after our VIP guests. Buck comes in for coffee and muffins. We exchange a glance. I smile and greet him. I learned to smile growing up at home, where smiling and getting along were important tools. I act like last night never happened. I'm a superb host: smiling and joking with the camera crew. I was having fun, and now I've clouded the weekend with my bad judgment.

But my sweet girl personality is in top form as we see them out to the planes for a day of fishing. Cameras and equipment are added to the cargo area, along with picnic lunches I made for them.

"I don't like the way pretty boy looks at you," says Wendy looking at me, and then back at the plane.

"I don't either. No sweat... he doesn't get near this," I wave my hands over my body.

She nods and places her hands on my shoulders. "Great for you Kathy. You aren't easily bowled over."

If she knew what happened last night, I'd never get over it. She's together and cool... I want her approval. I'll never tell anyone about what happened. I'll try to forget it happened. Why did I put Shawn out of my mind like that?

*

Thankfully, the rest of the weekend is without incident. It's far-out spending time with Wendy and Tony. I get an invite I can't resist. They're taking the plane across Kluane Lake next week. Elke and I are invited to come along for a hike, where a friend of theirs died, crashing his helicopter. They want to place a cairn in honour of him. I immediately say yes for both of us. Wendy will talk to Enid and find out what day works best.

FORTY

When I return to our cabin, Elke grabs me in a huge hug and says, “Let’s go to New Zealand!”

I don’t even quite know where that is. She’s talking fast, saying Curtis is going to Australia in January, she’s going to meet up with him there, but we should first go to New Zealand. It’s inexpensive to get a flight, and she’s bubbling over that we’ve made plenty of money this summer. It’s a rad idea.

“Umm... no I couldn’t,” I say.

“Are you caring for a sick parent, or giving birth to a child anytime soon, and what else are you going to do?”

"Okay... give me a moment!." I don't need parental permission. There's nothing at home to go back to. I have money and a passport. "Yes... I'll go... it'll be another adventure! Best of all, I have you to travel with!"

I whip a letter home to tell them about my plans.

*

We wait at the float dock under cloudy, but clearing skies. The mountain to climb looms across the lake. My shoes aren't the best for such a difficult hike, but they'll do. My daypack is full of snacks, water and the all-important mosquito repellent, commonly known as 'bug dope,' around here.

The familiar drumming of the plane is heard before we see it rounding the bay: it lands in front of the dock, Karl ties up, and we hop on for probably the last big outing before closing for the season. The leaves are starting to turn yellow already, and it's only August 17th!

It's a short hop to the other side of the lake. We exit the plane and start up what's left of an old bush road.

The helicopter crash story is awfully sad. The pilot, Randall, was a cousin of Tony's. "We spent every summer together at Clear Lake, Manitoba. He always had a passion for flying... probably from watching military training in the province. He was proud to get his license. The north is a good way to get your hours up, so he never hesitated to work in the Yukon. He had ten years in... you'd think he'd be unbeatable. A bad storm showed up... he couldn't gain control of the helicopter, couldn't gain enough elevation to get over the mountain, crashed into the top, not quite making it over the peak."

"I..." I know what loss of this type is like, yet I can't say anything about my friends dying. I listen with empathy – they don't know how real this is for me.

*

The hike is well, hard. What's left of this road is grown over with weeds. It's steep and uncompromising. It's full of large rocks and holes. The bug dope's working its stinky charm, but we still swat mosquitoes away from our faces. I'm sweating under the hot sun, climbing steadily. Everyone walks at their own pace, developing into a string of humans along the path.

I'm okay. I'm better than okay. We rise above the water's edge; I can see the lodge in the distance. I'm getting a second wind. My breath and pace sound even, strong. Despite the demanding ascent, I'm enjoying myself. I guess I like to hike. Who knew? I never bothered at home going anywhere to climb a hill or mountain. All the walking this summer between the job and wandering has made me fit. I can see the summit – I increase the pace to meet up with Wendy and Tony. Elke's not far behind.

The view is spectacular. I think we can see the Yukon in its entirety; the vast lake and endless forest of the funny, stumpy trees I've learned to appreciate. With such a short growing season here, it's a wonder anything grows.

We search for rocks of any size to try and build the cairn. It looks feeble, but there's tenderness when we place a stone atop another. We take turns having our photo taken with the finished memorial.

I sit in front of the cairn; the wind blows through my hair. My smile for the camera will say it all. Here I am, far away from everything I've ever known, and feeling the closest to myself. I think I'll remember this moment of pure joy forever. I have clarity and vision for the person I want to be. If I'm brave and have a force of will, there's nothing I can't tackle.

I know every footprint I make on this earth, will be made with Anne. She's with me always in my heart and spirit. I'll go everywhere in life with her beautiful presence moving me forward, and through whatever may happen. Anne's around me, and I'm grateful knowing my life has profound meaning because we'll walk in life together, taking whatever comes along. I'm whole, knowing her spirit's here.

*

I've been with my own thoughts for the entire walk back to the plane. We fly back the 'long way around' as Tony puts it, passing over a small lake they're considering getting the fishing rights for, to further expand their business. It's a perfectly round pothole. We see streams entering and exiting the lake.

"Perfect for grayling," Tony declares, waving his hand down to the lake. "They're a pretty fish."

I decline comment–I don't think fish are pretty.

*

Back at the lodge, we find out there's a road crew in for a week, and Shawn's last bus tour will come through. After that, we'll start packing up the lodge for the close of the season.

"You sure look happy," Wendy says, as we unload at the dock after our long day.

“I’m like the luckiest girl to have met you and Tony. You really are the coolest most laid-back couple.” I feel my grin gaining strength.

“Well if you ever need a job you can come work for us. I mean it. You’re great with the guests and know how to get work done.

Okay! Next summer?”

“Yes! I’ll give you our address and you can write to let me know how you’re doing. We’ll let you know what date we open.”

“Far-out!!” I already have next year partly planned! “I’ll be here for you.” I stop hopping and start hugging.

*

A lot needs to get done. Shawn’s returning to university; we’re going to spend a night together before he goes. I’m going to Whitehorse with Elke to get the plane tickets, and see the town. I’ll go home to see friends, pack for New Zealand, and then meet Elke in Vancouver for the flight overseas. The worst item on my mental list is to see Glen.

I haven’t heard from him. There’s been no other correspondence. Not from Teletype or mail. I’d asked the airport guys how the Arctic ships get mail, and they figure there’d be no way to send or receive mail once they left the last Canadian port of call. I don’t know if Glen got my last letter or not! I need to see him and explain myself better than in a letter.

*

It's past nine o'clock when we finally tuck the dining room into bed and head up to the cabin. Shawn and I say goodnight to Elke and Curtis as they take off for his place.

Shawn tucks me into bed. We start out slowly. He knows how to get me going... strong-arming me against the bed... making me lay still while he plays with me in long sensuous strokes. I writhe as he toys with every part of my body... slowly... painfully wanting more.

"Sniff this," he produces a tiny brown bottle from the dresser I didn't see him place there.

"What is it?"

"Poppers... it'll make you feel everything a hundred times more," He loosens the cap and we both sniff the sharp smelling aroma.

I feel my whole body heat up and lift off the bed. My skin is pulsing, sweating, throbbing. Shawn draws me under him. I'm heaving, grabbing his back... I lift my hips and grab his hair with both fists and pull him in.

This isn't making love... it's *fucking*. I put my fist in my mouth and scream in a stupor of drugs and sex. We're colliding over and over... I don't want it to stop. The room is hot, the bed's crashing against the wall. I'm attacking him with vicious strength, like a crazed animal.

Shawn bears down, shuddering and then collapses on me, as I let out a final scream.

Recovering from the effects of the drug, I lay there in a woozy, drippy state of happiness. "Woah... that was real?"

"Hm... I felt it too. Better than Saturday Night Bingo anytime," he hands me a pile of tissues.

"You really are a nutcase." We lay there until the sweat dries, cooling us off. I grab the quilt and cover us.

"I love you, Kathy," Shawn chokes out, softly touching the nape of my neck.

"Love? No... don't love me. No." I urge.

"I can love you if I want and there's nothing you can do about it!" He laughs, shaking his head. If he only knew about the Buck incident, I'm sure he wouldn't be too excited about loving me. I won't tell him though. No point.

"OKAY! I think you're swell," I tease him. I don't say I love him, though I loved the sex!

Somehow love has been reserved for a future date. When I said it to Glen, I meant it, but with Shawn, I won't say it. He doesn't seem to get that I don't reciprocate.

"You're the best. I'll miss you..." his wet eyes overflow.

"I'll never forget you, the man who makes me feel like a princess." I touch my necklace and go on, "I'm sure no one will ever shower me with such gifts ever again."

"I hope you get all you want out of life, and even more jewelry," he cradles my head in his hands. "Hey... what's that flash?" He leaps up, looks out the window and cries, "northern lights!"

We put on warm clothes, grab blankets, pillows and then scramble up the ladder to the cabin roof while gaping at the night sky. The heavens are lit up by bands of green and yellow coloured ribbons. They're undulating, waving, soaring across the sky. A break causes them to search for other paths; the world has become a non-stop light show. We lie on the roof, warm under the blankets, silent. The movement's steady, fast and incredibly bright. It's the perfect ending to our summer romance.

*

It's time to go; I watch Shawn walk down to the lodge. It's five thirty and I haven't slept all night; breakfast service is now. I put on my uniform and Elke breezes in the door. I give her a thumbs up, and she slaps me on the back. "I finally got laid," I say pumping my fist in the air.

"About time Kathy!"

The entire summer has gone by, and I'm still fascinated by the coffee makers. We get to work.

Shawn and I hide in the pantry... Elke covers for us. "Shawn... my best friend died and I'll never see her again... I never told you because it hurts too much to have to say goodbye to you too... I have a problem saying goodbye. But I could see you again... one day... couldn't I? I can't say goodbye forever... I can't."

"Kathy... I'm sorry... I wished you told me. There'll be no goodbyes. Write me love letters... I'll write them back... I'll see you again one day." Our last kiss is sadness and lust.

*

The rest of the week is hard work. We clean everything down to the corners. The 'creatures' gather up the flowers and speak in whispers to each bloom, wishing them a safe winter. They wave a crystal shard over each flower before giving them to Kay, for safe tending.

There are last visits to Construction Bay. "Enjoy New Zealand ladies... they'd better be prepared!" Constable Davies says.

Colleen strides up, "I'm happy for you girls... take on the world!"

"He's a good one to hang onto," says Elke crooking her head at the policeman.

"You knew?"

"Oh please... you're *almost* worse than Curtis and this one," I say, turning to Elke.

"I'll take your advice... glad to hear I'm on the right track!" Colleen jokes.

*

One last trip to the airport is hard for me. "I learned a lot about life from you and Simon in this little room," I say to Norm. "Thanks for listening and all your advice." I hug them both like they're the dads I wish I had.

I feel myself choke up thinking about leaving this magic part of the Yukon. I remember to visit the post office to see Betty. She's off to university right after we leave.

Soon, it seems, our bags are packed, and we're saying goodbye to Leo and Enid. I hug them hard and tell them, "you've been my parents for the summer. Parents without a lot of rules! I'll see you next year when I work at Wakes Lake... I'll miss you terribly," Leo huffs, and Enid puffs with parental pride.

*

Curtis is driving us into town. I haven't seen a building over two stories high, a streetlight, or pavement, for almost three months. He thinks we must be 'bushed,' a term used for those who've been in the wilderness too long. I feel a bit that way.

We load into his truck, and he does a slow drive by the front of the lodge. Leo and Enid wave us off; I crane my neck back and don't take my eyes off them until they're out of view. The three of us watch the Yukon speed by, all of us quiet. The lake goes on and on until we finally leave its rocky shores behind for mildly sloping, scruffy landscapes. There's hardly anyone living around here, checking the emptiness, one last time.

Listening to Genesis, 'Follow You, Follow Me' has me singing along, and now the lyrics mean something. I hum along to the comforting song, thinking of Anne.

*

We pull into the Fourth Avenue Residence, booking rooms for two nights. I'm keen to go see downtown and go to a bar!

FORTY-ONE

Frank and Ray have had a few by the time we get to the Golden Nugget.

We settle into a horseshoe shaped table, up against a wall covered in pictures of gold miners panning in a river.

“Bruce, get over here,” Ray says to a man in a coat made of fur from some mangy animal. Bruce extends a gold nugget laden hand. Large raw nuggets are set on a ring for every finger. He’s wearing a nugget clustered watch and a huge piece around his neck suspended off a thick gold chain.

“Did you pan all that yourself?” I ask.

“Sure did... way past Sixty Mile. Got lucky is all.” His grin shows off at least three gold teeth.

“Not luck wit ya,” says Frank. The bar lady, dressed in a satiny, feathery get-up of a dress comes over to take Bruce’s order.

“Six pack us Gloria,” he says expansively.

“What’s a six pack order?” I ask Gloria.

“Honey, that’s six drinks each, all at once.”

“Hm... I can’t drink that many beer... I’ll come up to the bar and see my choices.”

Elke joins me at the bar counter.

“Ya want a tip on drinking with the likes of Bruce?” Gloria leans over the bar conspiratorially, “do ya like white wine?”

“Sure... Black Tower?”

“Good choice. I’ll pour them into old-fashioned glasses with some ice... you should be fine. I’ll bring water if you need it. The rest of them I’ll ‘SS.’

“What’s ‘SS’?” asks Elke.

“Short shots... they’ll never notice and won’t get so effing loaded.”

*

We weave off to Foxy’s nightclub. After six wines, I’m pretty *shlammered.*

No one IDs me... we sit down in the large room already half full at eight o’clock. Comox introduces themselves as the house band. “We’ll be doing a few covers.”

Elke and I are up on the floor. ‘Hot Blooded,’ ‘Hollywood Nights,’ the hits keep coming. I take a break to drink my cider then I’m back on the floor.

*

Jeez, I'm hung over... last night was fun! Even though I'm very fuzzy, we're going to pick up our New Zealand plane tickets, and I need to confirm the flight to Victoria. Whitehorse is groovy! We're on the main street lined with stores. I see Murdoch's where Shawn bought my jewelry. We step in and see lots of gold nugget jewelry.

"Should I get this?" I show Elke what I'm thinking of. She's looking through watches.

"Yes... you deserve it!" She holds up a watch with delicate gold nuggets set in a gold band.

I treat myself to a pinkie ring coated with small nuggets. It cost $50.00, and I can afford it! Elke puts the watch down and goes for a set of nugget stud earrings. "I'll mail them home, so they won't get lost in my travels."

*

Elke says we should go to the Taku for the best breakfast. Everyone's there apparently. We walk a few blocks to the breakfast epicentre. It's crowded and loud. There's cigarette smoke in blue layers, floating around, lit up by sunshine pouring in. The interior says tacky lumberjack. Fake wood walls and creepy faded-brown checked carpet under our feet. Sort of a dump, but heck, here we are.

"Kathy!" I hear my name shouted, but no one knows me here, so I ignore it. "Kathy from Longmore!" shouts the loud voice. Who knows me here? I look where the booming sound is coming from.

"Dan! Dan the Mountain Man!" I run over yelling and laughing. He motions Elke and me to sit in the booth with him and another man. Good luck for us – the place is packed. I introduce Elke and Dan introduces Jack, his breakfast partner.

"Well missy, how was your summer?" Dan asks, hunching his shoulders forward.

"It was the best time I've ever had in my whole life. It was everything you said it would be, and more!" I'm lit up like a firecracker.

"Glad to hear... now you won't tell me off! You gals had fun, and some jewelry too I see," he points to my earrings and necklace.

"I did okay on that score too!" I fiddle with the earrings to show them off.

We order breakfast - whole-wheat toast with butter, which we haven't had the entire time at the lodge; only cold, dry, white toast and cranberry jam was on the lodge menu! Slabs of hot, thick toast, dripping with butter, are placed in front of us. Packages of peanut butter and jam sit in a rack – as many as we want.

We fill Dan in on our summer. I'm trying to chew and talk with some politeness. Between bites, I tell him about our next adventure. "We're going to New Zealand!" I get out, without spitting food. The men look at me kind of funny. "What?"

"Jack lives there now. He designs sunglasses in Auckland." Dan says introducing him all over again.

Jack holds his hands up, "guilty as charged mate," putting on what I'm guessing is a New Zealand accent.

“No way! Right on... you can help us figure out the first bit of travel!”

“You’re going to be awed by New Zealand. It’s a bit of heaven, sort of like the Yukon. It’s outdoorsy, without the bears and cougars. It’s very rural... easy to get around and the people are the nicest you’ll ever meet. Wear hiking boots... bring a backpack... try an overnight hike to a hut. For the fun of it, get some work there.” We’re all ears. “It’s a little more old-fashioned and a bit backwards there... keep an open mind.”

“Well, we survived an ancient lodge all summer. I guess we’ve had some training,” says Elke enjoying our fate. I think working in New Zealand could be superbulous.

Turns out, Jack is Dan’s cousin and is here visiting family. “We’ll be phoning you for sure!” We finish up breakfast and head out.

*

We find the travel agent and pick up the tickets. It’s real now!

“Kathy, Elke!” We turn around; it’s tour bus driver Ivan! “Hey, I said you could stay with me if you’re in town!”

“Oh thanks, but we thought with all that we have to do while we’re here... it wasn’t fair to crash at your place and never see you,” I explain. “But we’re going to New Zealand! Here’s our tickets!” I hold them up in the air flapping them around.

"Hey! I knew you'd have a plan and not go home! Good for you two. You can tell me all about your adventures over a drink. Let's go to the T&M!" We haven't gone one block, and it's time to socialize again! How does anyone get anything done around here?

We get seated in the bar, beautifully carpeted, dark wood tables and chairs, make it look like we've stepped into a living room. A waitress in a 'Sound of Music' red and white Edelweiss' dress swans over and takes our order. I thought our lodge uniforms were bad.

After drinks, Ivan escorts us on his very own Whitehorse tour. He takes us up to the Kopper King Pub for sweet and sour pork–the house specialty, and to watch the model train go around its track at ceiling height.

And then we hit the Capitol... one of the older bars in town. The place looks like it could survive the apocalypse. Heavy-duty white tiled walls, a thick wood bar and everything held together with large brass fittings.

It's all over town that the bartender is seventeen years old but she needed the job, and no one cares. Two husky dogs trot through the place getting pats from customers. The character following the dogs looks like he walked out of an 1800's gold panning advertisement. He's wearing a nondescript filthy hat, has long scraggly hair, and a beard that could house a flock of geese. Ivan explains, "that's O.D., a Whitehorse feature. He doesn't have to look like that... he has money to dress better and get to a barber, but he likes the attention from tourists." says Ivan. "There's even a postcard made of him."

We finish up the night at Foxy's. One of the guitar-playing road crew is there. He joins our table swerving and mumbling. "I'd like to dive for your muff burger."

I'm pretty sure he's laying out the worst pick up line in town. "No thanks, I'm fine." He drags me up for a few dances and doesn't try anything else except stumble when we do 'a little bit softer now... a little bit louder now," dance moves. I'm on the floor dancing until I can't move anymore.

I'm not drunk when we land into 4th Ave... I need to fly home without a hangover.

FORTY-TWO

Is there any chance I could land home without a zit breakout? No way. Two huge ones are on my chin. I want to look like a new woman, but I guess not. I cover them up the best I can. I'm wearing all the gold nugget jewelry so they can see it as I burst out the Victoria arrival doors.

Mom and Dad give me huge hugs and Mom starts to cry! "I missed you!" She burbles. "Now you're leaving again so soon."

"I want to Mom. I have a new life. Be happy for me." I try to be my best smiling self for the parents. Dad nods his sage nod, and we retrieve my bags. "You can look after the gold nuggets," I joke, trying to ignore mom's tears.

I fill them in on all the parts I choose to tell them about. They don't know all of my life, and I'm super glad about that. I'm me, and you parents don't get in where I don't want you to be.

Alan's still living in the forest, camping. People see him, but he hasn't come home. Everyone who sees him says he's happy about living in the woods, and apparently, he looks healthy. I need to see him before I go.

*

At Taffy's Tea Joint, Sandra and I hug extra long and squish tears on each other's faces. She tells me about her summer of writing, and how blissful she is with Brad. Her engagement ring is small like Brad's brain.

"We're going to move into a little apartment together! I'm searching the second-hand stores for kitchen items, a bed, and I'm just dying to get one of those matching bathroom rug sets. You know the one with the toilet seat cover, a little mat for the front of the toilet and a bath mat? I'm thinking baby blue."

"That sounds very nice Sandra. Maybe I can find some bamboo chimes to add to the décor."

"Oh no, Brad's not into wind chimes. I think making a home for us is going to be great for our relationship. I picked up the snazziest little apron, and I've started cooking meals out of "Everyday Great Meals For Your Man." It's from the 1950s, but still has some relevant, good old home cooking. Brad's *mega* happy about coming home to a hot meal."

"I'm going to New Zealand," I manage to fit in during the only breath Sandra has taken.

"Oh... that's nice. Anyway, we're thinking of moving closer to the university so travel time won't be too long. Plus, it's cheaper out there. What do you think – a three-floor walk up or a suite in a house?"

"Umm... suite in a house," I mumble. Did she just completely ignore *my* big news? I stir my tea, clanking the spoon around and around the porcelain edge.

"Yes... me too! That's why we're best friends... we think alike! I'm meeting Brad... want to come along?"

"No, I need to find out if Glen's back in town. I'm going to talk to him." I stare at the half-finished drink, leaving it. There's a lump in my throat beginning to build. Maybe I'll choke.

"As far as I've heard, he's not back yet," Sandra chirps. "Now, did you hear Chloe got a part in a movie? It's called 'Fame.' Acting and ballet together!"

"Cool... I knew she'd leave and make it big!"

We hug good-bye, and off she goes into the arms of her undeserving boyfriend. She didn't even ask me how I'm doing.

I go back home and sleep in my bed for the first time in months. Snoopy is back in position, on his shelf.

*

After breakfast, I'm determined to figure out where Glen is. There's no one at his house; I hop on the bus into town to Glen's mom's shop. I want to ask her what she thinks. Is Glen hurting badly, and did I mess with his brain? I want to tell her how guilty I feel, and how wrong it was to break up with him in a letter.

Holy crap... there's Alan. The bus is trundling along... I bang on the window with both hands, "Alan... Alan," I'm yelling, making a racket. "Stop the bus!"

“Stop banging, and I’ll stop at the next stop.” It seems forever for the bus to get there. I run back. He looked clean-shaven and clean clothes. Maybe he’s okay...

I can’t find him. I run into every store... he’s nowhere! It’s like that horrible Ray Bradbury story, *All Summer In a Day*, about the girl getting locked in the closet when the only sunshine in seven years happens, missing it entirely. I missed Alan! I’m out of breath when I finally give up the search and get back on the bus.

*

I turn the corner in Harbour Mall and see Julie’s shop. Glen’s standing there talking to his mom. Before I can duck out, he sees me.

I choke down the nausea, walk forward in slow motion – will he yell at me, or tell me to disappear?

“Hi.” I weep, stopping short of hugging him.

“Hi,” Glen’s eyes are downcast. His hair I loved, [*love*?] is waving over his forehead. He stands still as a plank; there’s no movement toward me.

“You two go talk. It’s meant to be, you both showing up here at the same time... go and be kind to each other. You’re both mature enough to face each other without collapsing,” Glen’s mom says to both of us.

We toddle off like scolded children, make our way to the seating area in the courtyard, and take a table.

“Do you hate me?” I can barely look up at the face I adored [*adore*?] I hold my breath, waiting for the onslaught.

"No Kathy. I was pissed at first... most of the crew I was working with heard how we broke up, but I'm okay now. I got your last letter this week... it explained more about what was going on in your life." He smiles, and I breathe before passing out.

"I'm sorry Glen. You're my VIP, and I treated you like crap. A letter wasn't a decent way to break up," I stammer, pulling at my gold nugget pinkie ring.

"Look... how were you going to break up with me? In the end, I was happy you didn't lead me on all summer and then break up with me now. You did the honest thing Miss K... I'm sorry about the Teletype... I was angry." He looks into my emotionally hammered, burning face.

"Forgiven, if you forgive me?" I venture. The ring spins off my finger and across the tile flooring. I leap up to retrieve it ten feet away. *Okay Kathy, it's okay*. I yoga breathe to calm down.

Glen offers peace, "Of course. You know, I had plenty of time to think about '*us*.' We got together during a real bummer of an experience, and before you knew it, we were pulled apart by circumstances neither one of us could have known."

"You were there for me..." I know he knows this, but I make double, triple sure.

"We saved each other Miss K. I'll never forget you. You came into my life when it was crashing down around me. There was no job, the parents angry with me... the directionless floating around I was doing wasn't working. You helped make me feel loved and wanted."

"Are we going to be okay?" I stop fiddling with the ring, draw up my guts, and look at him. He's *so* gorgeous.

“There’s one more thing,” he shuffles his feet under the little table. “It’s about that big romantic night that turned into a turn-off.” His eyes drop, he picks at a divot in the table.

“It wasn’t... honestly.” I want to know–*or do I*– maybe he’s a homo?

“Let me just say it. I think I was wound up about trying to make it special and then got a case of stage fright... then the cassette and the album. Shit... it was such a big deal for you... I ended up a nervous wreck.” He moves his hand painfully near mine.

“I’m sorry.” I don’t know what else to say. How could he be *that* nervous?

“Don’t be,” he renews picking at the divot with his non-homo finger.

“I’m going to New Zealand for a few months.” He stops picking and smiles.

“No kidding? You’re *really* leaving Longmore!”

“Yes, I’m leaving Longmore,” thumping my fist on the table. “I’m going with Elke, my friend from the lodge.”

“Righteous! I’m going to continue working on the project until it wraps up. One big smack I got from you, Anne and Rod is to get out there and live. Shit... how many times did we listen to Pink Floyd, ‘Time’ and I’m finally listening to the lyrics. I’m not waiting ten years to find out I missed the starting gun.” He’s so close to my face... I want to kiss him.

“Cool... what are you thinking of?” I could jump him right now... better not.

“Music... work with a band, learn an instrument, write lyrics... not sure yet.

“That’s decent... you’ll figure it out. Could we be just...”

“DON’T SAY IT, MISS K!” He laughs at my beet red face.

“Different kind of ‘F’ word I guess.”

We get up from our chairs and hug close... say goodbye, and I walk away. The guilt washes away from me; I’m light as a breeze.

*

It may be the most joyful music I’ve heard all summer. As I near our house I hear Jethro Tull, *Aqualung* playing at Alan’s favourite volume – ten. I rush down to the basement where he’s lying on his couch looking tanned, but as thin as ever.

“Alan... you’re back! I was *so* worried about you... everyone was.” I crash on the other couch.

“I said it’d be just for the summer... what’s the trip? I’m fine... it was good... I missed the stereo though. What about you?” We hung out all night. I wish he’d stop tapping that pen on his knee... he’s been doing it methodically for over an hour. If he goes weird around the parents I won’t be here to cover for him. I can’t stay here anymore even though he may need protecting. I’m only seeing him for a few hours before I leave again. I want to believe he’s fine... I’m full of hope, because that’s all I have to hang onto for him.

*

I leave Snoopy to guard my room while I'm in New Zealand. He's been my friend and comfort all these years. I prop him up on the bed, his ears all neatly draped on his front paws, his worn out face looks at me. Bye Snoopy. I walk out of my bedroom, without looking back.

Anne's Gift Acknowledgements

Many people helped with the final product, Anne's Gift. Thank you to my husband John who was a terrific support throughout. My editor Lorna Lynch who guided me through the seriousness of the content and how to convey Anne's Gift as a thought-provoking read. If not for Lorna, there would not have been a finished book.

My readers, Michele, Veronica, John M., Donna, Wendy, Carley, Heather C. Anne, Christine, Cindy, Wendy [also my proofreader], Anne Marie, Susan D., and Sue Y. Thank-you for your input and feedback.

Additionally, Heather Fox who wittingly or unwittingly mentored me through some of my teen years and Colleen J who knew I wanted to tell this courageous story.

More About the Author

Heather Kingston suffers from CADD [Career Attention Deficit Disorder!] In her early twenties she worked in mining as a Concentrator Operator, a job usually done by men, but found the door open to her. Thanks to all the women in the 1970's who came before her, paving the way for women's rights and choices.

She worked for airline companies, ran her own successful businesses, became a mom to two fabulous children. After selling one of her business's she went back to school earning an International Sommelier designation. Teaching and writing led her to have the courage to write Anne's Gift.

Writing may be her last career…but who knows.